Partners

D. M. McGowan

Strategic Book Publishing
New York, New York

Strategic Book Publishing
An imprint of Writers Literary & Publishing Services, Inc.
845 Third Avenue, 6th Floor – 6016
New York, NY 10022
www.strategicbookpublishing.com

ISBN: 978-1-934925-81-2/SKU 1-934925-81-0

Printed in the United States of America

Book Design by Stacie Tingen

The following is a work of fiction. The characters depicted and the events described including those with some historical support, are all figments of the author's imagination. Any suggestion that these characters represent real people, either living or dead, would be highly flattering and completely without foundation.

Contents

Chapter 1

He wasn't sure, but he believed it had been two months. It had been June 1 when he left Pembina in Dakota Territory and a week later he had been struck down by fever. He laid in his tent for either two or three days, but he thought it was two. If it had indeed been two days, then it was June 29, 1866, two months to the day since he had ridden away from his land, his home, and his life near Kingston.

Swinging around in the saddle to check the loads on his two pack-horses, he thought of that other life. Not only had he ridden away from a hundred acres of farmland that he owned free and clear, but he had also left a steady and rewarding job teaching his neighbor's children. He had turned his back on thirty-five years of life, and all the things he had worked toward during that time.

"Turning my back on that life was nothing," Tom said aloud, something he found himself doing more and more as the long days of sun, wind, and rippling grass ran one in to the other. "I turned my back on a way of life to make that one, and perhaps this new one will last longer."

Tom Brash had once been a husband and father. When he rode away to the west he left behind the graves of his wife and two sons.

"We should be close to those lakes," he said, attempting to turn his mind away from painful thoughts of the past. He turned again to look at the gaunt horses knowing that his mount looked no better. Except for the days he had lain in the grip of a splitting headache they had traveled every day, and the pace was taking its toll on the fine animals. "When we find those lakes we'll rest for a few days. I'm sure you'll appreciate it," he assured them.

In his saddlebags he carried maps of the country through which he rode. Some of these he had made from information to be found at Queens University. Most notable were copies of the Palliser maps. Some of the information he had collected had proven to be inaccurate, but not to the point that it had caused him great difficulty. He had discovered most of the discrepancies by talking with men who knew the land, but at this point had not found anything on the ground that varied from his charts.

Two days' ride west of Pembina a Métis man had confirmed the existence of what he called "Old Woman Lake" near the eastern edge of the Cypress Hills. However, the existence of both the hills and the lake had been touched on earlier by a mountain man he met in Fargo.

"Yer maps is all which-a-way," the old trapper had declared. His finger touched a point far to the west near the mountains. "Them two rivers don' meet. One takes of south 'bout here," he touched a curve in the river as shown on the map. "Turns in t' the Milk an' then in t' the Missouri. This un here turns and goes in t' what they call the Saskatchewan." He appeared ready to say more when something farther east on the map caught his attention. "This here shows some swamp or marsh. That there's Cypress Hills country. I ain't never bin there, but that's 'bout where the Old Woman Lakes should be."

He had then thrust the paper at Tom. "You be sure t' take that with yuh when yuh head out, 'cause if yuh depend on it, you're gonna die; an' if it disappears with yuh, we won't have to worry 'bout it leadin' somebody else off the track." Though his face showed no expression the twinkle in the old trapper's eye took the coldness from his statement.

Tom's last contact with his fellow man had been at the Métis camp. Two days from Fort Garry on their first big hunt of the new season, these people had little to offer but hospitality, but of that they gave in plenty. In return Tom gave them coffee and flour, sure that he had more than enough on his two packhorses.

Turning once again to glance at the horses, Tom thought about the supplies that remained. He swung his eyes around, taking in the vast land through which he rode. "Perhaps I was somewhat hasty in estimating my requirements," he said aloud and thought he might have been hasty in estimating what he would need.

Gently he halted his mount and swung down. Pouring water into a large handkerchief, he wiped dust from each of his horses' noses. After a short drink he removed the bandana from around his neck, poured some water into it, and wiped his face and neck. Hanging the canteen from the saddle he began to walk, leading the horses.

At five feet, ten inches, he was taller than average. Even though his legs were slightly longer than his torso, many overestimated his weight for he was as thick through as he was wide. He wore military-style, knee-high riding boots, heavy cotton pants and shirt, and a leather vest. His long moustache was streaked with grey, and the long sideburns under his flat-crowned, flat-brimmed felt hat were almost white. On June 29, 1866, he would turn thirty-six.

He was well into the Cypress Hills now and climbing on foot, leading his horses behind him. Despite the heat and tired horses he altered his course and angled up the hill. From up on top he might be able to see something that would indicate the location of the lakes. Perhaps he would cross the trail of some animal going to water. Seeing a grove of trees might also help, for many trees could not grow without some water.

Pausing for a moment, he turned and looked southeast. Although he had been in this wide-open land for more than a month, he still was not used to the vastness. Distance seemed to contract, and what appeared to be a hundred yards would prove to be five hundred.

The climb was much steeper and longer than he had anticipated, but he finally approached the top of the hill. Before he crested the ridge however, he heard a murmur of what he thought might be human voices.

His mount stopped when he dropped the reins. He stepped back beside the animal and drew a Colt revolving shotgun from the scabbard that hung down from the cantle. Holding the scattergun at the ready, he continued up the slope, cautiously scanning the country as he moved forward. He knew he might meet full-blood Indians who would not be as friendly as the Métis with whom he had camped. The Assiniboine, Cree, and Blackfoot all claimed these Cypress Hills as their own. None of them looked kindly on those who might trespass, but those who met the Blackfoot seldom complained about poor treatment. If they did object it was only to their captors just before they died.

The voices grew more distinguishable as he advanced, though he could still not make out any words.

A shot rang out so close that Brash dropped to his knees thinking for an instant that it had been aimed at him. A scream was cut short by the sound of a blow. He dropped to his stomach and crawled to the top of the ridge where he could look into the hollow beyond.

A lake lay before him, perhaps the very one he sought, one arm of it disappearing to the left. Directly below him, on the shore of that lake, were the remains of a camp, now destroyed. A small teepee lay torn and scattered through the remains of a cooking fire and utensils. The body of an Indian man lay tied to what was left of a travois frame, there was a hole near the center of his bare chest and blood stained the earth beneath him. Another form, from which Brash thought he could hear moans lay near the bound corpse. From the clothing, he guessed this was a woman. The camp was bordered by the lake and the hill, and by thick stands of aspen and willow, which gave way near the water to wide strips of cracked and drying mud.

Two men stood in the clearing. Each of them wore full, dark brown beards and buckskins, their clothing showed as much grease and was almost as dark as their facial hair. One wore a battered felt hat, his leggings tucked into high-topped riding boots. The other wore a fur cap, the ear lugs tied together on top, his feet in moccasins, which extended to just below his knee. The one with the felt hat held a rifle in his left hand, and a coil of rope in his right. Fur Hat had just finished loading his rifle and was removing the ramrod.

"Well, I reckon we isn't gonna have any more fun with the Injun," Felt Hat commented.

Fur Hat cursed. "Wasn't much fun in 'im, Seth. Got more out o' watchin' his chest blow up."

Seth poked the moaning bundle with the toe of his mule-ear adorned boots. "Well, mayhap Mrs. Injun'll be more entertainin'."

"No!" a new voice announced.

Both men spun to see a slight figure step from the trees. From his perch high above, Brash saw a boy of perhaps fifteen in cloths that were little more than rags. He wore no hat and his hair was a long, snarled mess. A piece of rope was tied around his waist to hold his pants up, but just under it was a gun belt. The right side of his too-large coat was hooked behind the butt of a large holstered revolver. In his hands he held a rifle, thumb on the hammer and finger on the trigger.

"What's yer prob'em, boy?" Seth asked.

The boy nodded at the moaning bundle. "No more hittin'," he announced.

Fur Hat grinned. "Well, she ain't no use then, is she?" He cocked his rifle and swung the muzzle.

The boy cocked his rifle and swung it toward Fur Hat.

"Look out, Hank," Seth called.

Before Brash could even realize that what he had thought was a rope was actually a bullwhip, Seth flicked it toward the boy. The very end of the braided rawhide snapped around the barrel of the boy's rifle. Seth jerked and the rifle landed in the dirt.

Hank laughed. Seth grinned and brought the whip back, swinging it over his head for another strike at the boy. A shot rang out and the whip flew from his hand.

The boy stood with a smoking pistol in his hands.

Brash knew his eyes had been on Seth and the whip, but the appearance of the weapon was a shock. Apparently it was also a shock for Seth and Hank. Seth was doubled over holding his ringing right hand between his legs, eyes large and round, and fixed on the smoking muzzle. Hank's eyes were similarly fixed, his thumb still holding the hammer of his rifle at half cock.

"Hammer down," the boy instructed.

Hank gently released the hammer.

Seth took his hand from between his thighs and shook it violently. "He ain't fast enough to shoot us both," he concluded. He still held his rifle in his left hand.

On the ridge above, Brash realized that at least twenty feet separated Seth and Hank. Even for someone as fast and accurate as the boy appeared to be, it would be difficult to stop both men before being hit by someone's return fire. Brash also suspected that there was a great deal of luck involved in the shot that took the whip from Seth's hand.

"You first," the boy announced, his revolver pointed at Seth.

Hank smiled. "Then you second," he said swinging the muzzle around toward the boy.

"I believe you may be second." Brash did not know what made him call out. One of the things that had forced him from his home was well-meaning people who, after the death of his family, constantly demanded that he communicate with them, and here he was getting involved with people he didn't even know. What he had just witnessed, however, was brutal, and the boy needed help. He shoved the muzzle of his shotgun over the hill and into view.

In the clearing, Hank had stopped the swing of his rifle. Seth had started to raise his own weapon and the weight of it against his left wrist was starting to make his arm tremble.

"Put 'em down," the boy said.

Seth and Hank leaned over and carefully placed their weapons on the ground.

"Short guns an' knives," the boy said.

Two large bowie knives, a Colt, and a Smith & Wesson revolver hit the ground.

The boy pointed with his chin. "Over by the Injun," he commanded.

Both men walked backward until they stood near the corpse.

Still holding his pistol, the boy retrieved the weapons. The knives he left on the ground. One pistol he put in his own holster, the other behind his rope belt. The rifles he picked up with one finger looped through their trigger guards. His eyes never leaving the two men, he returned to the edge of the clearing, leaning the rifles against a tree.

The pistol at his waist was a Smith & Wesson. He broke it open, dumped the cartridges on the ground, and then threw it to land near the knives. "Stand," he ordered, then exchanged his own weapon for the one that had been in his holster. It, too, was a Colt, so he used the tool from his gun belt to pull the caps from the nipples, then threw the weapon to land by the Smith.

Still facing Hank and Seth so he could keep an eye on them while he worked, the boy turned to work on the rifles. The first was a Springfield .58 muzzleloader, so he simply pointed it over the lake, cocked the hammer, and pulled the trigger. Throwing the empty weapon to land near the pistols and knives, he raised the other rifle. It was a Spencer, similar to his own, so he opened the loading tube in the stock and dumped the rimfire cartridges on the ground, then worked the action to eject the one in the chamber. He threw the Spencer to land by the Springfield.

With his chin, the boy indicated the pile of weapons, then the horses. "Mount up," he advised. The heel of his hand rested on his holstered Colt.

Hank and Seth looked at each other then slowly and carefully picked up their weapons.

As he picked up the Smith & Wesson, Seth eyed the cartridges that lay on the ground at the boy's feet. "Them car' ridges is hard t' get," he complained.

"Rough," the boy replied

Keeping an eye on the boy, the two men moved quickly toward their horses. In turn, the boy didn't fall too far behind them, watching to ensure they took only their own mounts and packhorse.

On the ridge above, Tom Brash rose and returned to his own animals. With reins in hand he led his mount over the hill and down into the campsite, the pack animals following readily.

Having just watched the two men ride away, the boy returned to the campsite, but didn't acknowledge Brash's existence. Instead he went to the Indian woman and rolled her over on her back. Her left eye flew open and her arm came up over her face.

The boy squeezed her shoulder gently. "Won't hurt yuh," the boy said.

Tom could see a bad cut on the right side of her forehead that was already causing that eye to swell and close. The left side of her mouth and left cheek were also swollen and discolored.

"I have some medical supplies," Brash announced.

The boy looked up at him and nodded.

Tom removed his bandanna and held it out to the boy. "Perhaps you could take this to the lake and get it wet? We will need to wash her off before we bandage her."

The boy nodded again, took the bandanna, and rose. Tom turned to his horses to retrieve bandages.

As he reached into the pack, a scream came from behind him that made the horse jump. He turned to see the woman sitting up and looking at the dead man, her hands over her mouth. The boy was running back from the shore.

The woman jerked sideways and fell over the body of the man just before Brash heard the sound of a shot. Both he and the boy looked to Seth and Hank, who were in the relatively open area along the lake perhaps two hundred yards away. Hank held his Springfield over the limb of a tree, smoke still rising from the barrel. In the silence following the shot they could hear the two men laugh.

The boy cursed, threw the wet bandana on the ground, and picked up his Spencer. Hank and Seth sprinted for their horses.

Tom put his hand on the boy's shoulder. "Does there need to be more killing? You will become an animal like them."

The moment was gone. The two men disappeared behind the finger of hill that pushed out toward the lake. The boy lowered his weapon.

Pointing with his chin toward the dust cloud that remained, the boy said, "Hunt us now. Should a shot 'em."

"You think they'll come back?" Tom asked.

The boy nodded, and then indicated Tom's horses.

"For my horses?" He was aware his horses would be highly valued. They were not yet used to the food or climate, and had been worked hard, but they were both taller and heavier than the local mounts.

The boy nodded again and added, "An' packs."

"Well, I would think your shooting skill would be enough to keep them away unless they are completely stupid," Tom observed.

The boy shrugged. "Ambush."

Ambush was not new to Brash. His early training had been full of the honor of addressing an adversary in a gentlemanly manner, but his experience had included attacks from cover. Those attacks, however, had come from people of a different culture on the other side of the world, and not from white men with Christian backgrounds.

"I suppose it takes all kinds," Tom said. "And one's proclivity for fast and accurate marksmanship is certainly curtailed when one is dead."

The boy indicated the shotgun in Tom's hand. "Only weapon?" he asked.

"I have a rifle." Tom responded.

"Best get it," the boy responded, almost sneering at the shotgun.

Tom felt his anger rising. "This is the finest of shotguns. It is a Colt ten-gauge revolver. I have four shots available and another cylinder in my saddle bags."

The boy turned and looked at the dead woman, then at the trees from where Hank had fired. "Two hundred yards?" he asked.

Tom's irritation increased another notch, for the boy was right. Loaded with heavy ball the shotgun might be good for half that distance but not with him shooting it.

He also realized that annoyance was rapidly becoming the strongest of his feelings. As he stowed his shotgun in the scabbard and removed his Colt revolving rifle from its place in one of the packs he considered the source of this irritation. In a country in which he had come to expect no fellow humans, he had suddenly found five, two of them torturing and killing two others. He had just witnessed acts of barbarism of a type that he thought only happened at the end of a long battle. In an earlier life he had heard of such actions, but had never actually witnessed them. The sudden appearance of the fifth person—that one a boy—and the subsequent confrontation had been an additional shock.

He had also been a teacher. He was used to acceptance and obedience from his pupils, not ridicule and orders. True, now that he was closer he could see the boy was older than his original estimate, but he was still young.

Behind Tom, the boy cursed, then asked, "That a rifle?"

"A Colt revolving carbine, actually," Tom replied, his pride in the weapon obvious. "Six shots, forty-four caliber."

The boy shook his head and cursed again. Tom marked another reason for irritation—the young man's constant foul language.

"Better go with yuh," the boy concluded, pointing with a thumb over his shoulder toward where Hank and Seth had disappeared. "Yuh got no range, an' them boys'll kill yuh."

"I've handled things quite well up to this point," Tom protested. He had no wish to be accompanied by this foul-mouthed youth. He had been enjoying his solitary travel.

"More 'n likely ain't had to face up to nothin' like them two," the boy pointed out. He nodded at Tom's pack animals. "Them two's carryin' light. Double up the load. I'll ride the other un."

"My horses need rest," Tom protested, "not a greater load." He waved his hand toward the three Indian ponies. "What is wrong with those animals?"

The boy cursed. "Nothin' 'sept they's Blackfoot." He indicated the two bodies. "They'll have folks. Any young buck's got three horses an' all this truck layin' around is pretty well off. Young buck that's well off's gonna have friends. Them folks find yuh with them horses, you'll be wishin' yuh got shot by Hank an' Seth."

Again Tom fought down his anger, forcing himself to admit that, in this land in which he was a newcomer, the boy might be right. He had certainly heard stories of the Blackfoot and their dislike of white men. There was also no doubt that the youngster had managed to handle the two killers. True, the Indians were dead, but he and the boy still drew breath. He began to loosen the packs for redistribution.

"Perhaps we should bury these unfortunate victims?" he asked.

The boy cursed, shrugged, then added, "Don't know as they dig holes fer the dead. Might put 'em up on platforms. Best just leave 'em lie."

Having set one of the pack bundles on the ground, Tom turned and looked at the two bodies. As he did so he realized he had been avoiding looking at them. "Perhaps we could take a moment to lay them out in a more, uhm, seemly position?"

The boy turned, looked at the bodies for a moment, shrugged, and then cursed. "Reckon."

When Tom had loaded all the freight on one pack saddle he led the animals into the remains of the camp. The boy had rolled the bodies around until they lay side by side, one right hand clasping the left hand of the other. Seeing the arrangement, Brash found it suddenly difficult to swallow. He had to clear his throat before he spoke.

"I do believe we should be moving on," Tom noted. "We still must find a suitable spot and make camp. The day is quickly disappearing."

The boy was down on one knee and resting his forearm on the other, his gaze on the bodies. He turned his head to look at Tom, who was surprised by the complete lack of expression on the boy's face. His deep blue eyes where neither cold nor hot, not full of love or hate, but as blank as a deep pool.

There was a pause while the boy came back to the present, then he responded. "Reckon," he nodded. He pointed with his chin toward the east. "We'll light a shuck that a way."

"But that's east," Tom protested.

The boy cursed. "Yuh don't say?" He pointed with his thumb toward the west. "Them two went west." He stood, rifle in one hand, and walked to the edge of the trees where he picked up a small bundle. Returning to the now unburdened packhorse he grasped the forward sawbuck and swung astride. "We'll go 'round the east end o' the lakes and turn back 'long the north side. It'll keep them away from us fer a few days." He jammed the small pack down in front of himself and against the forward sawbuck. The rifle he carried in his right hand.

Tom realized that once again the boy was right. "That would seem to be prudent," he agreed and mounted his own animal.

"Be a spell 'fore we camp," the boy added. "Tomorrow 'fore them two realize we ain't on their trail. Get a lead while we got the chance."

They rode in silence for some time while Tom thought about the blank expression he had seen on the boys face when he turned from the bodies. It dawned on him that he knew nothing about this boy except that he was particularly adept with a firearm, had attempted to protect a stranger, and had an especially wild appearance. True, much of this appearance could be attributed to the rags he wore, but his long, slightly bent nose also added to the perception of uncaring coldness.

"I'm afraid I have been severely remiss in not observing the normal social graces," Tom observed. Leaning over in the saddle he extended his hand toward the boy. "Thomas Brash, late of Kingston, Canada West, and now of where you see me."

The boy looked at the extended hand for a moment, then took his Spencer in his rein hand and grasped Tom's. "Frank Clement," he responded.

Tom noted there was no mention of his origin.

Chapter 2

On the east end of Old Woman Lake were several acres of swamp and deadfall. At some time in the past the land had been dry enough for aspen and willow to take root, some of the trees reaching six inches in diameter. In subsequent years, the water had risen to cover the roots and drown those trees. Nature's natural cycle brought back the dry years, the lake level dropped, and wind pushed the trees over into an impenetrable mesh that hung over the thick water and soggy soil.

The two men and three horses had to travel some distance east to circle the swamp. There was much open grassland in the surrounding hills enabling them to make good time despite the approaching darkness. When the lake became only a phantom in the darkness to their left, the sloping land and the stars in the clear sky helped point the way. The night was well along when they finally found a good place to spend the night.

Frank halted the packhorse he rode, and then swung down on the banks of a small stream that flowed into the north side of the lake. There was water, trees to supply fuel, and protection from the wind. The banks that rose above the stream would help hide their fire.

Tom swung down and leaned on the saddle while circulation returned to his legs. He looked over to see the boy dropping down on the edge of the creek for a drink and suddenly found his irritation returning. He had been riding in a good saddle and felt as if he had been beaten. The boy had been riding a packsaddle, but rose from the creek with the smooth grace of a dancer. More to take his mind off the difference in age than anything else, he looked to the north for Ursa Minor around Polaris, their position telling him it was after midnight.

"We should stay here for a few days," Tom announced. "My horses need rest."

"You don't?" Frank asked in return, and then followed it with the brief flash of a smile before continuing. "Ain't a good spot. 'Spect them boys can sneak up an' shoot down on us from the hills."

"I believe you suggested that we could get ahead of them by going this way."

Frank nodded. "She'll do t'night. Find us a high spot t'morrer."

Tom didn't really believe that he and the boy were very important to the two killers. At that moment he expected the two men to be laughing about their encounter with the boy and the dude with the three horses. However, he was also aware that he knew almost nothing about the country or its people. Avoiding a confrontation was the safest course of action.

They stripped the saddles, and Tom started to hobble the packhorses.

"Best stake 'em out, if'n yuh got the rope an' they can handle it," Frank advised.

Why is it that the younger one is, the more one knows? Tom asked himself. He knew he had been guilty of the same wisdom at that age, as had his students. What he said out loud was, "They need grass."

"Get the chance fer lots o grass, them two killers show up," Frank responded. "Funny how gunshots can make a horse forget his feet is tied."

Tom forced himself to admit the boy was right. He straightened and moved toward the pack to retrieve coils of rope. "Good thinking. I certainly have no desire to be afoot."

"Mighty long ways 'tween water holes when you're walkin'."

As he tied the rope to the halter ring, Tom thought about the boy's last statement. Somehow, perhaps because of the exciting circumstances of their meeting he had not considered how Frank had come to be at the Indian camp. The boy had no canteen, or any other parts of an outfit, other than the small bundle he carried. True, he had two excellent weapons, but he didn't even have a hat.

"You mean you walked to that camp?"

Frank cursed. "Bin ridin' your horse, ain't I?"

"I hadn't thought about it, probably due to the confrontation I witnessed. And the deaths. I suppose I thought you had lost your horse somewhere along the trail."

"Could a had one a time 'r two," Frank responded, "but I ain't no hoss thief."

"From your reaction to the treatment we saw today, I expect you were given strict teachings against theft," Tom prompted.

Frank cursed. "Surely was. Maw learned me better. 'Sides steal a hoss an' yuh make a trail."

Tom asked himself why a boy would have to worry about someone following him. He claimed an aversion to theft, but was he averse to other crimes against society?

Having finished staking the horses out, Tom returned to the pack and removed his blankets. He also took one of the pack covers and dropped it next to Frank along with a blanket he separated from his own kit. "You must have been very thirsty and hungry on occasion," Tom observed. "Not to mention all the walking. It was a long, dry trail for me."

The boy looked at Tom for a moment. "Don' recollect sayin' I'd come a fur piece."

"You must have," Tom noted as he lay out his bed. "It's quite some distance to any community."

"Maybe I come from some wagon train got wiped out by Injuns."

"Perhaps, but it has been some time since I saw wagon tracks, and the usual trails taken to the west from Independence are several days ride to the south."

The boy was silent for a moment then turned to the task of preparing his bed. Finally he returned to Tom's earlier observation. "Ain't bin all that bad. Mostly follered rivers an' streams an' the like. One of 'em peters out, go over a few ridges an' there's another. I ain't sure how long I bin travelin', but since I started out on May 16 there's on'y bin a couple a days. . . ." Frank stopped and cursed, this time making it into a whole phrase. He shook the tarpaulin out and lay the blanket out on it, then rolled up in the arrangement with his rifle close at hand.

Several moments passed and Tom was beginning to doze. The murders, the unknown quantity of the boy, and the strange land had made him tense, but fatigue was beating it down. He felt he could reach out and touch the silence. "Is there a problem, Frank?"

The silence continued for several minutes before Frank broke it with another curse. "Ain't p'lite to ask where a fellers from. He maybe wants to make a fresh start, an' don' need his past hangin' over him. Folks judge a feller by how much they can depend on 'im, an' not what he done yesterday. Maybe you bein' from back east some place yuh don' know that."

Having considered this for a few moments, Tom responded. "I suppose that would be prudent when one considers the lifestyle, and the many people one may find himself looking to for assistance," he agreed. "However, that still doesn't tell me why you are upset."

Frank cursed. "You was pumpin' me. Wouldn't a bin long an' I'd a bin tellin' you my whole life story."

There was another silence while Tom considered how to answer. "Now that I look back on it, I suppose I was trying to get information from you, but that was not my primary intention at the time. I was simply making conversation. I was concerned and curious, of course. I don't know how you could travel across open wilderness without horse or supplies."

Much later, Frank asked, "What is it worries yuh?" but Tom had been asleep for some time, and did not respond.

The following morning they moved their camp to the top of a knoll where they could see much of the surrounding country. They picketed the horses on the south slope so that they could lead them to water with a minimum of exposure. Once they were in position they lay in the sun and took turns scanning the prairie.

"My full name is Thomas Eastman Simcoe Brash. Eastman was my matern... my mother's maiden name. Simcoe was a governor whom my father admired. My father was a major in the Grenadier Guards, and later a colonel in the Colonial Guard."

When he paused for breath, Frank cursed and asked, "What the hell you doin'?"

"I wouldn't want you to think I was trying to 'pump' you, as you put it, without giving at least as much in return," Tom responded.

"Don't know's I wanna hear all that stuff. 'Sides, I hadn' planned on doin' no more talkin'."

"Well, that does not mean we should avoid conversation altogether," Tom observed. "You have not been the greatest of companions this morning."

Frank shrugged. "Used t' bein' alone," he responded.

"During the past year, I, too, have learned to accept my own company, but that has not forced me to become surly and uncommunicative."

"Don't know as I can talk t' yuh anyway," Frank said. "Most o' the time I got no idea what yer sayin'."

"Oh, but you do get the idea, regardless of what words I use," Tom responded. "Perhaps constructive conversation will give you an opportunity to improve your communication abilities."

Frank looked at him for a moment. "What?" he asked.

"You could learn to speak English."

As usual, Frank cursed. "I talk fine. 'Sides, I'm 'Merican."

"You start most sentences with an expletive," Tom observed, and then added at Frank's blank look. "You curse continually. I find it extremely disconcerting....it bothers me. And you are not in the United States now."

"Well, maybe it ain't a State, but it's still part o' the country."

Tom looked at him for several moments, and then put his attention toward leveling the coals in the fire. He poured water from a canteen into the coffee pot, placed it on the coals, then turned back to Frank. "Where do you think you are?"

Frank shrugged. "Montana Territory."

Tom nodded as he placed a few coffee beans on a rock and began grinding them with another. As he continued grinding, he said, "You are several miles north of the forty ninth parallel."

Not receiving a response, Tom looked up to see a puzzled expression on the boy's face. "The United States border," he explained. "Perhaps as much as eighty miles north of it." In the boys eyes he could see uncertainty, perhaps disbelief, perhaps shock.

To give Frank time to recover, Tom expounded on the information. "This is Rupert's Land," he said, waving his hand toward the distant horizon, "granted to the Hudson Bay Company in 1670 by King Charles the Second. It is bounded on the west by the Rocky Mountains, on the north by the Arctic Ocean, and Upper Canada is to the east. Technically, I suppose the western terminus would be the border with the British colony of New Caledonia. I believe the original grant actually states that it includes all land drained by rivers that flow into Hudson Bay, but that has already been subject to several changes."

During the long pause that followed, the water came to a boil. Tom dropped the ground coffee into it.

"Fer a fella got as much trouble as you do, yuh seem t' know an awful lot 'bout where yer lost," Frank observed.

Tom looked at him in stunned silence. "Whatever gave you the idea I was lost? Or that I'm in trouble, for that matter."

"Yuh got big trouble, Mister. Wasn't fer me yuh wouldn't be here."

Tom was still puzzled, but responded. "True, I would probably be over on the south side of this lake and would have had two days rest instead of one."

"Nope, you'd be dead. Seth an' Hank would o' had yer outfit all split up by now. What ya think I saddled myself with yuh for?"

Tom chuckled. "You are saddled with me? You, who have no proper clothing, no horse, and no food?"

"Bin doin' fine fer more 'n a month," Frank protested. He slapped the breach of his rifle. "Had me lots o' meat from the Spencer, caught me some fish, an' there's plants all over a body can eat."

"You have been lucky, then," Tom advised. "People have started across this land with far more than I have, and have not been heard from again. You have not run into country suffering from drought, or a land stripped bare of game by an overpopulation of predators. Both those circumstances could yet come to pass, for it has been very dry."

Frank cursed, and then looked away. He made a show of scanning the horses, but did not return his eyes to Tom or the fire. "Well, I ain't the on'y one's bin lucky. You ain't run intuh the likes o' Hank an' Seth. Shotgun's a might handy rig fer the likes o' them, but yuh gotta be up close. An' yuh gotta be ready t' shoot 'em when yuh get the chance, even if they ain't lookin'."

"You would ambush them?" Tom asked. "Shoot them in the back?"

Frank nodded. "Sure would, now I know their sign. They'll be tryin' t' do it to us, 'less we can lose 'em." He looked up at the clear sky. "An' chances o' losin' 'em are 'bout the same as snow fallin' out 'o that sky. Course, snow 'd cover our trail."

The coffee had come to a boil again. Tom moved it back from the coals as he thought about the young man and his comments. He was more than a little perturbed that this illiterate, backwoods boy would have the audacity to think that he had helped Tom at a difficult time when it was Tom who had offered the boy transportation and food. However, when he considered the actions of Hank and Seth, and the boy's shooting, perhaps there were mutual advantages to their present arrangement.

"What do you mean by 'knowing their sign'?" Tom asked as he poured two cups of coffee. "Are you referring to recognizing the tracks they leave?" He wondered if the boy had ideas about finding their trail and eliminating them. If so, he wanted nothing to do with such an action.

Frank chuckled as he leaned forward and picked up the cup Tom had left for him. "I ain't much of a tracker, but I reckon I'd know their tracks again ifen I seen enough of 'em. What I meant was, we know what kinda folks they is an' I think I heard 'bout that Seth. Could be Seth Nation. Least that's what he calls 'imself. There's folks back home figure he killed a homesteader's wife. He ain't nice folks, an' anybody'd travel with 'im 'll be just as bad."

Tom blew against the rim of the tin cup then took a small sip of coffee. To harm a white woman was something that was completely unthinkable for most men of the day. It was something that Tom couldn't understand so he had to ask, "Was there any indication that she may have been, uh, bothered?"

Frank cursed again. "Was wonderin' how a toney feller like you was gonna get 'round that. Yeah, there was. Pro'ly why he killed her."

Chapter 3

"So how come yer so damn sure 'bout this bein' English?" Frank asked.

"I assume you are referring to the country within which we now take our leisure," Tom responded. He set his cup on a rock, rose, and walked over to where his saddle lay. "As to its being English, it has been some time since I have heard it spoken, and certainly not in the immediate area. If you mean to inquire if it is British, there are certain questions about that. During the past one hundred and five years the Hudson Bay Company has turned this land into their own kingdom with their own laws." He removed the composite map from his saddlebag and returned to his seat near Frank. "During my journey I avoided Fort Garry for precisely that reason. They may not be pleased to have someone they can't control wandering around in their domain. They have been less than understanding of free trappers who do not trade their furs with the Company.

"A further consideration is what is happening in the east. A confederation of eastern colonies is presently in progress, and by now, may even have been accomplished. If Rupert's Land is not presently part of the new country, I'm sure it soon will be. Those who have been comfortable with their responsibility, answering only to their superiors within the Bay, are more than slightly concerned. They may well lose some of their power and prestige."

Kneeling down with his back to the fire Brash unfolded the map, turning it so that it was oriented to the terrain. "I made this from reports and maps I collected over the years. There are gaps in it since most of the material I used as a reference also had gaps." He pointed to the low marshy area around which he had sketched the rough circle of a lake. "This area, for instance, was shown on the Palliser maps as a marsh. It was not until I spoke to a man in Fargo that I suspected it might be a lake, and then some Métis hunters confirmed it."

"Supposed t' be this lake?" Frank asked, jerking his thumb to the south.

Brash nodded. "I just sketched a circle in the area. I really have no idea of the actual shape."

"An' yuh really don' know where yuh are," Frank objected. "Map's just a bunch 'o old stories."

Brash slowly folded the map while doing his best to control his temper. Outwardly he was completely calm as he returned the map to his saddlebags, dumped the cold coffee from his cup, and replaced it with fresh. It was only then that he trusted himself to speak.

"Approximately ninety years ago your homeland declared itself an independent nation. Your founding fathers signed the Declaration of Independence." He sipped his coffee then looked across the cup at Frank.

"So?" Frank asked.

"Have you seen the Declaration?"

"No."

"And since you are not a hundred years old, I suspect you didn't see the document signed," Brash added. "Therefore, from your viewpoint at least, the whole thing is just a bunch o' old stories."

Frank's sun-darkened face seemed to become even darker before he said, "You sayin' that map's important as the Dec'aration o' In'ependence?" Brash noted that he did not swear.

"Certainly not! I suspect that I will never accomplish something as massive as was done by those fifty-six men, singularly as well as collectively. I am saying that I used historical, proven information as the basis for the map. I added information that I do not believe has been collected in any other document. True, some of it is questionable, but the vast majority of it has proven to be true as I have moved across this land."

Frank shook the coffee grounds from his cup. "You got you a river showin' on that map a ways north o' here. Where's it go?"

"It is called the Saskatchewan. Indian name, I suppose. Eventually it flows into Hudson Bay; perhaps a thousand miles to the north and east."

Frank cursed. "Ain't plannin' on goin' east, an' I damn well gone far 'nough north."

"Upriver it leads almost due west for perhaps two hundred miles then turns south. The Red Deer River joins it at that point."

"How 'bout folks?"

"I assume you mean white communities?" Brash asked. Frank nodded and Tom continued. "To the north there are several. Near the headwaters of both the Red Deer and the North Saskatchewan there is Rocky Mountain House. East of there and further north on the Saskatchewan is Fort Edmonton. They are fur trading posts."

"An' south, on this other fork?"

Brash shrugged. "I was unable to collect much information on the area. Some whiskey traders and some very dry country." Knowing that Frank was asking about the south because he wanted to return to his own country, Tom added, "Of course, further south one finds himself in Montana Territory."

"Sounds like the way fer us," Frank suggested.

"Montana Territory?" Brash asked with feigned astonishment.

"Better 'n anythin' else we got," Frank replied with a shrug.

Brash shook his head. "Going southwest," he said "I believe Fort Benton is the closest supply point. The only information I have on the country between here and there is from Captain Palliser's notes, and I have already found reason to question them. It should be less than four hundred miles, but I've been lead to believe it's quite dry.

"On the other hand, toward the northwest we have Fort Edmonton. It should be about four hundred miles. We could follow the South Saskatchewan, then head up the Red Deer. Where that river comes from the west, we would continue on north to the Fort. No more than two days' ride, I'm sure. That way we will have water for ourselves and the horses.

"That is to say," he concluded, "we may have some difficulty carrying enough water for a trip to Fort Benton, but no difficulty with the route to Fort Edmonton." He didn't mention that his supplies were quite low and Fort Edmonton was the most likely place to find what he needed.

Frank shrugged. "Reckon you got the horses." He stood and looked toward the horses. "An' we best move 'em an' us into the trees for a few hours. Gettin' mighty warm."

When they had the animals moved into the shade, Frank returned to the earlier subject. "Yuh got some need t' go t' this Fort Edm'nt'n."

Tom sat down under a poplar and leaned back against the trunk before replying. "Provisions are low, but there is more. You seem to think we will have trouble with Seth and Hank. I really don't believe they will go north, but, if they should, I would prefer to have witnesses for such an encounter."

"They'll be after yuh," Frank assured him.

Tom shrugged. "Perhaps. I don't think they will go to the trouble for what we have to offer, but there is the possibility."

"They gone t' lots more trouble fer lots less."

Tom nodded, and then continued. "As to going south, I believe that is where they will be. I have been told it is an area full of whiskey traders. All the legitimate traders, the Hudson Bay people, and a few independents operate in the northern country where the furs are better. The whiskey traders operate in the dryer country to the south and lure the trappers to them with the whiskey. If this is indeed the case, I believe we would be going toward Seth and Hank, rather than away from them. I would also not expect the presence of their partners in crime to cause even the slightest hesitation in their attempts to murder and rob us."

Frank cursed and pointed with his chin toward the northwest. "Them Hudson Bay folks up t' other way won't do much more 'n slow 'em down. They'll just wait."

"So your suggestion is that we go southwest," Tom concluded, "where they won't hesitate. They will simply kill us."

"Ain't killin' me."

"Yes, I'm sure," Tom responded, managing not to convey what he thought of the boy's chances against two killers, despite his obvious ability with firearms. "However, Hudson Bay people tend to frown on people who interfere with their trade. Their presence will supply us with a small measure of protection."

"Maybe," Frank responded, doubtfully. "On'y if they take time t' look while they're countin' furs."

"Yes, there is that," Tom said, but putting very little importance on the boy's complaint. "We can spend some time at Edmonton. We can go south once we are sure that these two killers have left the area. There will be a trail southwest to Rocky Mountain House, and many others leading into Montana Territory. We will be traveling an area where there are streams coming out of the mountains, and avoiding the dry country which, at that point, will be on our left."

"Don't look like you're in no hurry to get some place," Frank noted.

"I'm not going anywhere," Tom said. Extending his arms he turned slowly, his eyes on the hills, the trees, and the lake. "I came to see the country, and it doesn't matter to me where it ends."

"Right now it looks like it'll be where Seth an' Hank find yuh," Frank said.

Chapter 4

Three days later, Tom almost changed his mind. They were back on the flatland again, traveling northwest toward the Saskatchewan River when Frank saw the tracks. He stopped and leaned over in the makeshift stirrups they had created. He studied the trail for a moment before Brash noticed and turned back.

"What is it?" Brash asked.

"Looks like Hank an' Seth 'r goin' north," Frank informed him, trying with little success to hide his satisfaction.

"Going north? Why?"

Frank knew that Tom didn't really expect an answer, but he was taking great pleasure in having some support for his predictions. "Lookin' t' cut us off I reckon," he replied.

Brash could not understand why the two traders had chosen to follow them, but also trusted the boy's ability to read tracks. Why *had* the two men chosen to follow? Other than general support for such actions, the killing of two Blackfoot would create little comment in most white communities, so there was no need for them to try and hide that event. And the few goods Tom carried were important to him, but not worth the effort Hank and Seth would have to expend to steal them. True, his three horses were of considerable value, but worth enough to draw the two men from their usual business?

The two killers would probably go north to the Saskatchewan River, which, if his maps could be believed, took a sharp turn north of their present position. Should that actually be true, he and Frank should reach the river before Hank and Seth by traveling west of north. Once Hank and his partner realized they had missed their quarry, they would probably not be long in catching up, but the bend in the river should give Tom and Frank two or three days' lead.

Brash looked off toward the unknown southwest. "We can't go south. We run too great a risk of running into more whiskey traders by going that way, perhaps friends of Hank and Seth."

"They maybe know some folks, but won't many of 'em be friends," Frank observed.

Tom nodded. "I can certainly understand how being a friend to those two would be difficult to manage."

Brash looked off to the northwest and continued his deliberations. "The Saskatchewan is a highly traveled route. If we continue on in that direction, we have an excellent chance of meeting traveling companions. With a group of Hudson Bay trappers or boatmen, we would be much safer than we would be by ourselves."

Frank cursed, and then said, "Reckon we could shoot ourselves."

"I beg your pardon?"

"Maybe talk yerself into this, but it ain't doin' a damn thing fer me. Man needs t' look fer help in this country, he ain't got no business startin' out. Ain't nobody gonna get his self in a pickle t' help us. Save a lot o' time if we just blow our brains out."

Tom smiled. "As you so correctly noted two days ago, you are helping me, and I am helping you. Two complete strangers offering assistance to a fellow traveler."

Frank shrugged. "Way things worked out. We wound up havin' the same two fellers wantin' t' shoot us. Ain't right t' ask some trapper t' put his partners in danger by helpin' us."

Tom nodded. "There is certainly something in that, but we won't need to ask. Simply having others in the area will help to turn Seth and Hank away from what you say is their intention.

"As to the subject of helping those along the way, I noticed you stepping in to help an Indian woman avoid rape and murder. Perhaps you had known her a long time?"

Frank studied him a moment, nothing to be read in his stony face. Slowly he shook his head and said, "your horses."

Tom started his mount toward the northwest. "We'll continue to travel slowly to save the horses, fifteen or twenty miles a day. Hank and Seth probably think that we went around the end of Old Woman Lake and then straight north. When they reach the river they will turn down stream expecting to meet us coming up. They will soon realize what has happened and turn back to find our trail. Since the river runs on an angle to the north, we should reach it before they do, following our present route. Therefore, we will be on the river at least two days, perhaps three, before they catch up to us."

"One of us ain't gonna have no trouble tellin' when they do," Frank said, but not loud enough for Tom to hear. "Other un won't care."

Turning in the saddle, Tom said, "I still find it hard to understand. Why would they go to all this trouble? They did not appear to have any whiskey with them when we saw them earlier. Therefore, they can not do any trading unless they make some, or return to Montana and buy some. It seems to me, they are interrupting their method of income for very little."

The men traveled in silence for several minutes before Frank responded. "Yuh got three horses an' a new saddle, even if yuh gotta sit on it, stead o' in it."

Tom grasped the steel hoop that stood up before him. "This is a very fine saddle. It has a steel frame that will not rot or warp. One of the latest and finest military saddles available."

"Well, ain't no doubt it's better 'n the one I got," Frank admitted, dropping the palm of his hand on the sawbuck that stood up before him. "Point is yuh got things folks don't see after a few years out here. Yuh got that fancy spy glass I seen yuh lookin' through. Yuh got real pots, and them steel plates we was eatin' out o'. Why, yuh even got a real, honest t' God coffee pot, an' coffee t' put in it."

"But surely they wouldn't kill a person, two people, for such paltry items," Tom objected. "I could understand if it was to hide the murder they committed, but there are few white people will give anything but support to those who kill Blackfoot."

"Nope, it ain't t' get yer goods. Them's just a little extra. An' they ain't wantin' t' kill yuh 'cause yuh seen 'em kill them Injuns. Ain't nobody but Injuns cares about that. Part of it's 'cause we made 'em look the fools. Kid an' a greenhorn made 'em take water. But more 'n anythin' it's somethin' t' do of an afternoon."

He patted his mount's neck. "Not that they won't like t' have these here hosses. They's gaunted up some, but there ain't many got mounts half as good as these. Ain't never seen the like."

"They are a breed developed in Lower Canada from French stock," Tom said, turning sideways in the saddle to look at Frank. For several moments he rode that way, and then said, "You seem to have an understanding of these men."

"Damn well should. Lived with a man just like 'em fer most o' my life. Matter o' fact, reason I knew the name. When that Seth Nation was down t' Fort Union, he spent time with the man married my momma when I was fourteen. Never come 'round our place, mind, so I ain't never seen 'im, but he was 'bout the fort."

Chapter 5

Four days of riding through the long grass brought them to the banks of the South Saskatchewan. By Tom's calculations it was the late afternoon of July 5. They stopped on the hill overlooking the river and he dismounted with his telescope.

On one knee, his elbow resting on the other, Tom scanned the vast area they could see from their vantage point.

"Fancy eye piece," Frank commented.

"I inherited it from my grandfather," Tom said, his eye to the scope. "He was a British naval officer, captain on men-o-war."

"Well, I c'n see a river bend," Frank said. "Maybe five, six miles west an' the same north. Upriver on the far bank is two deer. What more d' yuh need t' see?"

"Jump down and have a look," Tom invited.

Frank swung down in one of the loops of rope he was using as stirrups and took the glass from Tom. Putting it to his eye he trained it on the river below.

"Mighty blurry. Can't make out much o' anythin'."

"Kneel down as I did and rest your forward elbow on one knee."

"Ain't heavy."

"Perhaps not, although it will become quite cumbersome if you have held it for a few moments. However, that is not the problem. What is happening is that, along with magnifying light it also magnifies movement. Each of those movements causes the blurring of which you speak."

Frank knelt as instructed and put the eyepiece in place once more. "Wow! That's somethin'. Bet I c'n see fish in the water."

"Train it on those deer," Tom suggested.

Frank studied the hills on the north side of the river for a moment. "Three deer. There's an old doe up higher an' a little this way. She's a might hard t' see 'cause she's got some trees behind her. First two I seen 'r a doe an' maybe last years fawn."

Tom watched his face, studying intently the changes of expression not hidden by the telescope.

Frank cursed. "Coyote comin' over the hill t' the west," he said. "Headed fer a little grove o' brush. Bet there's a new fawn in it."

Frank cursed again and took the glass from his eye. He stretched out prone on the hill, his left elbow out ahead in the dirt. With the barrel of the scope cradled in his left hand, he held the eyepiece with his right. "See what yuh mean 'bout 'er gettin' heavy."

When he had studied the deer for a moment, he cursed and said, "Yup! Coyote's goin into them willows." He swung the scope slightly to the right, and then back left. "An' here comes the ol' doe. An' there goes Mr. Coyote. Reckon he'd like a good big meal, but he ain't stupid."

Frank took the telescope from his eye. During their time together Tom had only seen cynicism on the boy's face those few times that it didn't look like a mask of stone. Now he saw a look of delight.

Seeing the smile on Tom's face and the sparkle in his eye, Frank's expression returned abruptly to one of indifference. "See a lot with 'er," he said, returning the telescope.

Brash suddenly found it necessary to concentrate on the simple task of compressing the scope. Having managed to both close the telescope and stop his grin from turning into a chuckle or a laugh, Tom cleared his throat and said, "There appears to be a well used camp site below us on the river bend. I expect several travelers have used it over the years. An excellent place for us to rest for a few days."

Frank cursed. "Lot o' high ground."

As he put the telescope in his saddlebag, Tom thought about what the boy was alluding too. Finally he said, "We rode over their tracks four days ago. They must know we have gone to the river, for it is the only thing in this direction. However, as you can see, the river turns north here. They will have to go some distance before they hit the river and turn to follow it upstream to us. They know about the river, but since they are traveling by dead-reckoning, without the assistance of maps such as we have, they have miscalculated and it will take them some time to catch us."

"Maybe not that much," Frank said, after beginning with his usual curse. "They ain't got no maps, but they'll know the country."

"How well? I understand that most whiskey traders work much farther south."

"Closer t' the whiskey, an' a place t' sell the furs," Frank admitted.

"So they probably don't know the area that well," Tom concluded absently as he studied the slopes below. "We should have three or four days before they find us. More than enough time to make use of the water and grass."

Tom pointed along the slope. "A great deal of open ground on the steep slopes. We only have trees right down on the riverbank. When Hank and Seth arrive, if indeed they do, we should be able to see them long before they are within range."

"Depends on who's range yer talkin'," Frank responded. "Yuh seen Seth make a shot o' more 'n two hunnerd yards with his Springfield. Bet he c'n do seven 'r eight hunnerd. An' more 'n likely Hank c'n do the same with his Spencer."

With his hand on the horn of his saddle, Tom looked at the butt of his Colt revolving rifle. He thought he would be doing well to hit a target at two hundred yards. Turning his gaze to the boy, he asked, "Can you shoot that far with your Spencer?"

Frank shrugged. "I reckon."

Tom smiled and swung into the saddle. "Then, I suppose I will have to load for you," he said and started his horse down the slope.

Chapter 6

Travelers throughout the ages have discovered the same thing. They might ride for days and meet no one, but each night would find a camp that had been used quite recently, if not that very morning. The reason for this is simple. Most people want the same things in a camp: water, protection from the elements and attack, and firewood. Perhaps soft sand on which to lay one's bedding, or material to make a mattress. If it has all or most of the requirements, a good spot may have been used for hundreds of years.

The camp they found on the banks of the Saskatchewan River was excellent. In a land not noted for its timber, a semicircle of logs had been set back from the river; time and moisture already turning some of them to soil. Toward the river lay a band of gravel laid down over the ages by the rushing waters, and on the other three sides were stands of willow and aspen, none of them older than the last flood, but full of dry wood for a fire. Despite Frank's objections, they would be able to see the approach of an enemy for some time, regardless of the direction chosen. Not only had the spot been popular for many years, but, judging by the ashes of cooking fires and the marks made by boats and rafts pulled into the bank, the site had been used a few times that spring.

For two full days and nights, Frank was nervous. The only thing he liked about the camp was the large logs. They would provide some measure of cover when the whiskey traders found them. Several times each day he took his Spencer and scouted the hills, looking for some sign of the two killers, and becoming familiar with each tree, brush, and fold in the hills.

Tom found more than a little humor in the young man's nervousness. He still didn't expect to be hunted down and shot by two men he had only met briefly, and to whom he had done nothing.

On the second evening they saw a boat coming down river toward them. Tom smiled. Frank scanned the hills.

By the time the York boat was a few hundred yards away, Tom had a full pot of water boiling. The York men extended oars and back rowed to slow the heavy vessel while the tiller man stood and studied the two men on shore.

"I have water boiling," Tom called to them. "Would you care for tea or coffee?"

"'Ow many are you?" the tiller man called, his English heavy with the inflections unique to those who's first language is French. "'Oo are you?"

"Thomas Eastwood Simco Brash, late of Kingston, Upper Canada." He turned and gestured toward Frank who stood by the fire, hands on his hips. "Frank Clement, late of Fort Union, Dakota Territory."

There was a short discussion between the York men that Tom could not hear. Finally, the tiller man called, "Tea is magnifique," and the oarsmen levered the boat to shore.

Before leaving Kingston Tom had read much about Rupert's Land and the Hudson Bay Company, and so knew of the York boats, and the loads of furs they carried to York Factory, the post for which they were named on the shores of Hudson Bay. They would return with loads of supplies and trade goods almost as heavy, poling and hauling with ropes in late summer and fall. He estimated the vessel before him would be approximately twenty-five feet in length. It appeared to hold two or three tons of fur, a stove, and personal supplies. He found it hard to believe five men could bring it back against the current.

His doubt was somewhat tempered as he watched the men pull the boat up to the shore and tie her down. All of the traders were at least five inches shorter than Tom's five foot ten inches, but none appeared to be lighter than his one hundred and eighty pounds. They seemed to be swinging the York boat around with little conscious effort.

They were all Métis', descendants of French-Cree stock. All spoke a form of English, but the tiller man, Jean, was the only one who was readily understandable. Tom was pleased to have the opportunity to speak French, though he wondered if they would be insulted if he showed a preference to use their mother tongue. In the end he decided against using French, primarily because it would have cut Frank out of the conversation.

Jean introduced his companions as they approached the fire. Jean, Rene', and James carried the conversation while the other two remained relatively silent. With no communication, Tom quickly forgot their names.

When each man had filled his cup with tea, Tom set the pot down and gestured toward the fire. "Help yourself to the fire when you are ready," he invited. "We have eaten, and had we known you would be coming, we could have prepared enough for all."

"Merci, non," Jean replied. Holding his cup in one hand he gestured toward the tethered boat with the other. "We 'ave the food."

"I am surprised to find you here," Tom said. "I understood all the furs leave Fort Edmonton as soon as the river is clear of ice."

In the act of sipping his tea, Frank stopped his cup halfway to his mouth to stare at Tom. If what Brash had just said was true, why had he insisted they come to the river in search of help, or, at the very least, witnesses?

Jean shook his head and pointed at the water. "Dis is da sout' river. We 'ave come from Rocky Mountain 'Ouse." Once again Jean swung his free hand to indicate the York boat. "We 'ave many plew dis time. We make up da new boat an' come down. After we 'ave mad de boat, she is late."

"Can you return before winter?" Tom asked.

Jean shook his head. "Non. I will go to my 'ome at Fort Garry. It 'as been five year since I see la mere'."

Frank shook the dregs from his cup and set the cup down near their packs.

"Plan to have another look?" Tom asked.

Frank's only answer was a nod of his head as he picked up his rifle and stepped over the surrounding logs. The boat men looked to the retreating youngster and then to Tom, their faces puzzled.

"We had an encounter," Tom explained. "Two men, whiskey traders, I believe. They tormented an Indian brave and his wife and then murdered them."

The traders retained their puzzled expressions. Finally, Jean said, "It 'as 'appen many time."

"Perhaps, but not when someone else was watching," Tom responded. "It was murder."

Jean shrugged. "Day is on'y Indian."

The other men expressed agreement.

Tom worked hard to hide his astonishment. He was surprised to hear such sentiment from men who all carried Indian blood in their veins.

"At what place did you see dis?" Jean asked.

"On the shores of Old Woman Lake."

"Dey was da Cree, den," Jean surmised.

Tom shook his head. "The boy said he thought they were Blackfoot."

"Ah! Da fewer da better!" Jean exclaimed. "Blackfoot 'ave no place in dat lan'."

"Well, no matter," Tom responded, attempting to regain his composure. "The two men have been following us. Frank has gone out to see if they are in the area."

Jean turned to his partners and said in rapid French, "These two are being followed by whiskey traders. For sure they are after their horses and packs. And to kill them."

Rene' looked to the York boat, and said, also in French, "We must care for the load. If there is a loss, our families will pay."

Jean shrugged, and then smiled. "We will eat. If there is firing we will cut lose and float away." Turning to Tom, he said in English, "We agree. It is good the boy watches."

Tom nodded, leaned forward for the pot, and poured himself more tea. He was more comfortable now, no longer concerned about not speaking to these men in their own language. Had they known he spoke fluent French they would never have told him of their intentions. He also had an idea of the kind of support he and Frank would get in Fort Edmonton, or any other trading center.

Chapter 7

There was still plenty of light when Frank returned, although the sun had dropped behind the hills above the river. The York men had finished their meal, and Tom was asking Rene' and Jean about the country upriver when Frank slipped silently to the edge of camp. Conversation stopped at the young man's sudden appearance.

"See anything?" Tom asked.

Frank looked quickly to the others, and then said, "Nope. Not much. Wondered if I could get a hand t' move the horses."

"Sure," Tom responded immediately, folding his map. "I have been going over my maps with these men. I should have moved the horses some time ago." The map safely stowed in his saddlebags he rose and stepped over the log.

When they neared the horses, Tom said in a low voice, "What did you see?"

"Campfire maybe five miles down river," Frank said.

"You believe it to be Hank and Seth?" Tom asked.

"Yup, 'spect so."

"They should be here in the morning, then."

"Maybe," Frank said, nodding.

"I have most everything packed," Tom said. "We can leave at first light. I left out only what we will need for breakfast."

"Them Hudson Bay men gonna be any help?"

"They are not with the company," Tom replied. "They're free trappers hoping to make a big return on their efforts by dispensing with a few of the middle men. And no, I don't believe they will be assisting us."

Frank did not curse but looked around at the hills. "Well, this sure ain't no place t' bushwhack them two, so we'd best pull out first thing." He turned to the horses.

With one picket rope coiled in his hand, Frank asked, "I hear yuh talkin' with them 'bout this bein' late fer them comin' down river. If there ain't no travel, how is it we come up here?"

"Primarily an attempt to lose Hank and Seth if they were following us, which appears now to be the case," Tom responded. "Also, as I said, we need provisions, despite the deer you shot, and there are posts up here. As for travelers, I hoped there would be someone coming upriver that we could travel with. I hadn't counted on anyone coming down river this late in the year."

Frank grunted and led off toward the camp.

When the horses were tied closer to the fire, Frank stepped over the log and walked to his bedroll, nodding at the trappers as he passed. He rolled the tarp and blanket out near one of the large logs surrounding the camp, lay down, and closed his eyes.

"Da boy is right," Rene' observed. "Id is time for us all."

Tom voiced his agreement, wished them a good night and went to his own blankets. He was careful to listen to the whispered conversation in French as he turned in.

Several hours later, Frank shook Tom awake. "Boat's gone."

"Yes, they talked about leaving as you and I lay down."

"Yuh talk that lingo?"

Tom sat up and rubbed his eyes. "Quite fluently. I learned the rudiments as I grew up, and later I went to school in Montreal. I also spent a year in Paris."

"Speak French in them places, do they?"

Tom looked at the boy who knelt beside him. Without thinking he had made the boy feel foolish about a subject outside of his understanding. He had once again hurt the boy's feelings.

With some effort he pulled his gaze from the boy and looked out across the river at the northern sky. The stars told him it was well on toward morning.

"Our horses are rested and we can be on the trail in twenty minutes," Tom said. "We can stop later for coffee and food." He pushed himself up onto his knees and began rolling his blankets. As he did so, he said, "I must apologize, Frank."

Frank stood and went to pack his own bed. He cursed, then asked, "Fer what?"

"For wasting time in coming up here. We didn't lose them, and we didn't get help." Tom rose from stowing the remainder of their goods. "Having spoken with the boat men, I can see we are on our own. I'm willing to go southwest as you originally suggested." He stepped over the logs and toward their horses.

Frank cursed. "Didn' lose nothin'. Horses got some rest; an we got some deer meat." He scratched his unruly mop of hair. "Can't say as I'm all fer headin' south," he admitted. "You said there was more people up this way."

Pulling the picket pin, Tom stood and faced the younger man. "We can't possibly make it to a settlement or post before they are upon us. We have to face them, and we will have to do it at a place of our choosing."

Frank did not say I told you so but only nodded and walked to one of the other horses.

"West of us, perhaps a good hard day's ride, there is a river that comes in from the south," Tom said, then swung his saddle in place. "Swift River, I believe it's called. We can follow it south. Not only will it supply water, but perhaps we can lose our tracks in that same water."

Frank cursed, and continued to cinch his own makeshift saddle. "Them boy's is trackers. Maybe slow 'em down by ridin' in the water, but it don't mean they ain't gonna find us."

"Then we will settle for slowing them down," Tom responded, bringing up the packhorse. "If we follow that river for two or three days, we should be back in the Cypress Hills, although far west of where we left them. From there we should be able to see them coming across the prairie."

Frank cursed, put his foot into the rope stirrup, and climbed aboard the patient mare. "I figure she's a lot more natural t' just let death come an' get yuh by su'prise. Don't know as we should go t' all this trouble just so's we can see it comin'."

With the horses all saddled, Tom swung onto his own mount. "As I have noted before, there really is very little reason for these men to be following us. Should they kill us, they will be doing so for no reason. I'm sure that if they are aware we are prepared for them, in a position to make the small reward even more costly for them, they will quickly go on their way." He turned his horse and led the way up river.

"Seems like all the edeycation yuh got's a dangerous thing," Frank said. He hadn't thought he had said it loud enough to be heard, but Tom surprised him by responding.

"Why do you say that, Frank?"

"Seems like the more edeycation yuh got the harder it is t' see what's right in front of yuh. Maybe all that readin' ruins yer eyes."

Tom smiled, shook his head, and urged his horse up hill and onto the prairie.

Chapter 8

For two days they rode south and west. During those two days they saw no sign of pursuit, though Tom scanned their back trail from any place that even offered a suggestion of height. Tension diminished, as did his need to keep looking through the glass.

"You're sure it was Hank and Seth at that camp?" Tom asked.

Frank shrugged. "Didn' see them, but it was the same hosses."

They did what they could to make their trail difficult to follow. It wasn't practical to try and hide the tracks of three horses crossing fertile ground, but they did their best to mask them. Each morning they picked out a spot and rode to that point by separate routes, the packhorse following wherever it chose. On the third day they turned south and up Swift Creek, riding in the water whenever possible. Their efforts wouldn't stop any determined follower, but it would slow him down.

Tom longed for the sight of buffalo. He had heard stories of men seeing the humped backs of these animals reaching to the horizon, the dust of their passage blocking out the sun. Even a much smaller heard would wipe out the tracks of three horses, but they saw only the occasional deer, and those from some distance. Perhaps it was the lack of rain.

Four days after leaving the Saskatchewan River they saw the first indication that the killers were still on their trail. Tom took the telescope from his eye and compressed it against his thigh. "Something out there now. I can't see them, for they are several hours behind us, but I see dust."

The only surprise for Frank was that they had taken so long to show themselves, but he made no comment.

Tom turned and looked to the hills that broke the horizon to the south. Extending the glass he surveyed the south and their chosen trail. Their horses stood under them, heads down in the hot sun.

"We need rain," Tom said from behind the glass. "Even a shower would help the country, but we need a good long, drenching rain."

"Wash out 'r trail," Frank agreed. "Been mighty dry." He looked off toward the Cypress Hills where Tom had his glass trained. "Seems t' me it was greener in them hills when we left 'em than it is down here."

Tom compressed the glass and put it away. "They are still showing some green. Perhaps they've had some rain, or perhaps I'm seeing what I want to see. We should be in them by tomorrow afternoon."

Frank cursed. "If the horses don't drop."

Tom patted his mount's neck. He felt a special attachment for this horse he had known from its first day on earth, but was worried about all of them. Perhaps he should have sold the animals and left them to the life they had known. He could have bought animals used to this open land instead of hauling them on the railroad. "They'll make it," he said, more to calm himself than to assure Frank. "They're good animals."

Frank cursed again. "Yup, but they ain't been raised on prairie grass like them that's behind us."

Tom knew what the boy said was true but made no acknowledgement. He urged his mount to continue south.

It was the middle of the next afternoon when Tom chose their camping place in the Cypress Hills. It would not have been Frank's first choice.

"Best t' be up top," Frank objected, nodding at the knob that rose above them. "Ain't no way fer them t' get at us up there. Clear shootin' down each side."

"I thought you wanted to ambush them?" Tom asked. He kept his eyes on the north looking for a dust cloud. He didn't look at the hill, for he had already studied it.

"Well, uh, yeah. I reckon that... Well, how d' we know they's gonna come by where we's set up?" Frank asked.

Tom turned his gaze on the younger man and smiled. "It's much easier to talk about shooting a man in the back than it is to actually do it. As a matter of fact, you want to give a great deal of thought about shooting at any man, front or back. After you've thought about it, don't do it."

Tom gestured toward the hill that rose south of them. "Impossible for two of us to cover all slopes at once," he pointed out. "Besides, there isn't any shade, and it won't take them long to realize that we will be getting hot and dry. They will just wait for us to ride down here for water." He gestured at the spot he had chosen and the small stream. The small terrace they stood on sloped down and back from the front edge making it impossible to see into from downhill. "Down on this shelf we have shade, and water isn't far away. It would be much better if the water ran through where the best protection is, but we still might be able to get to it while under fire. It's not perfect, but quite serviceable."

He turned and gestured to the brush-covered slope behind them. Under the brush was a thick blanket of old, dead branches and leaves. "We can only see the very top of the slope, but we shouldn't need to watch that side, only listen. I doubt there is anyone that can make it through that mess without making some noise."

He gestured downhill. "There are several trees and hillocks behind which they can take cover, but we have a slight height advantage, plus a foot of protection from the shape of the shelf."

Frank cursed. "Back on the Saskatchewan I said yuh wasn't learnin' nothin', an' yuh still ain't. They bin follerin' us nigh on two weeks. They ain't gonna quit now."

Tom smile was grim. "I don't expect they will."

"Yuh ain't figurin' they'll see how we're laid out an' turn tail?"

"No I don't think they will. True, we have certain advantages with this location, but many of them will not be immediately seen by the casual observer. They have shown a remarkable tenacity in their quest, and I don't expect them to stop now, although I still wish it. This is not such a superior position as to chase them away, but it will give us the advantage."

"Yuh mean yuh want them t' fight?" Frank asked. "After runnin' all over the damn country, we're gonna shoot?"

Tom began hauling dead trees up to the edge of the shelf to form a breastwork. "The reason I was so insistent about going to Fort Edmonton is that we don't have any food," he repeated. "I really didn't see any reason for them to continue this stupidity, and thought to go on and buy supplies. But now they have pushed us to the point where we can not continue. Our horses need to stop and eat, and we need to hunt. The few days on the river were certainly a help, but we need more time. We can fight, or we can run and starve."

Frank cursed and turned to picking up dead branches for a fire. Dropping them in a bundle, he said, "All yuh had t' do was say so. I bin gettin kind o partial t' yer cookin', an' I always bin partial t' eatin'. 'Sides, it's what I bin tellin' yuh we had t' do, anyway."

"This will not be easy," Tom said. "We have our stock and equipment to protect, and now this camp. It puts us at a disadvantage. It is always better to be the attacker instead of the defender."

The young man knelt down, pulled his knife and began slicing shavings to start a fire. "Guess I shoulda figured it anyways. 'Bout the grub, I mean. Ain't much weight in that pack."

The boy wasn't prepared to listen to any tactical wisdom from a tenderfoot. Tom threw up his hands and went to unsaddle the horses. When he returned, Frank had coffee started and was adding logs and limbs to the pile on the front edge of the shelf.

"We need to make this good enough to offer protection, but not large enough that it scares them off," Tom advised. "If they perceive it to be an impregnable defense they will just wait for us to come out of our hole. We need to stop this now."

Frank was silent for several moments before he responded. "They been follerin' us fer a long time an' we didn't do nothin'. On'y reason they ain't shot us is we ain't slowed down long enough fer 'em t' bushwhack us. Take a fair bit t' give 'em the idea we're dangerous. Truth t' tell, we ain't."

"I think they will be surprised by what we have to offer," Tom said. "Perhaps that surprise will give us some advantage."

They had used all the material close at hand to build up some protection, but Frank continued to find smaller pieces to fill any holes. Tom walked downslope to look up at their handy work and found that the casual observer could easily mistake it for a natural deadfall.

Returning to their camp, Tom went to the packs, removed much of their remaining food, and carried it to the fire. He took their single pot down to the stream for more water.

Tom's problem was that he didn't completely disagree with Frank. It appeared to him that Hank and Seth were comfortable and experienced at killing. He suspected they had done this sort of thing before, and were therefore better prepared for what was about to happen. True, he had several years of experience that would help them here, but that was a different time, a different place, and there were far more men involved. Frank's shooting ability might help, but his accuracy would certainly drop during the action. No, Frank had been right, they were not very dangerous.

There was something else that upset their chances. Although he had caught only glimpses through his glass, he thought there might be three men after them instead of two. That being the case, he and Frank would be outnumbered, outgunned, and could be easily outmaneuvered.

Thomas Brash had done battle before, but that had been another life. He had seen brutality and death, and the stupidity of man. However, nothing in his past had prepared him for what he had witnessed on the shores of Old Woman Lake. Nor was he prepared for the idea that two men would stay on the trail two weeks for little more than the chance to kill. Perhaps the only way to deal with such people was in ways they understood. He still found it hard to accept that the two whiskey traders had followed them for close to two weeks. But the country, the weather, the lifestyle, and the men involved—including young Frank—were not part of his experience.

Tom returned to the fire, pulled the coffee back from the flames, and placed the pot of water on the coals. He dropped a few more sticks on the fire, away from the pot, and then went to get the fry pan.

While he waited for the water to boil, Tom took his telescope and scanned the country to the north. There was no dust.

"I can't find them," he announced.

Frank dropped another stick on the breastwork before he responded. "Be there some place."

"Do you suppose they have already come up on us and are moving in?"

"Ain't had the time," Frank responded. "Horses they got is tough cusses, but they'll be gettin' tuckered. They rode further'n us while we was settin' on the banks o' the river." He looked out over the plain for a moment, and then shrugged. "Maybe they gotta do themselves some huntin' 'fore they set in t' round us up."

"Perhaps they are like most other bullies" Tom said, although he didn't really believe it. "Faced with actual resistance, they have chosen to abandon the field."

What might have been a smile flickered across Frank's lips. "You keep tellin' yerself that, it makes yuh feel better. Maybe yuh won't even hear the shot that kills yuh."

Tom smiled. "Allow me my dreams. They give me comfort." He sobered and added, "Yes, they are probably waiting for dark."

Frank nodded. "More 'n likely. Big stretch o' hills, an' lots o little places fer 'em t' lay up. They know we can see 'em comin', if we're up in here. Get themselves a spot t'night an' take a look fer us in the mornin'."

"Well, that being the case, perhaps we should eat."

"Yup, an' dry the rest o' that deer meat," Frank advised. "Won't get a much better chance, an' them boys pin us down I don't reckon they'll take a break 'cause we wanna do some cookin'. 'Sides, we don't dry it she'll be goin bad soon."

"That will require smoking it," Tom said, protesting. "It will only make it that much easier for them to find us."

Frank cursed. "Gonna find us anyway. They do, least we'll have somethin' t' eat. 'Sides, we don't need smoke. Cut it thin an' hang it in the sun. Got maybe six hours o' sun left." He slid the long knife from the sheath at his side and walked toward a group of young saplings.

"I wouldn't have thought sun drying would be that effective," Tom said following him.

"Ain't as good as smoke, 'r salt, fer that matter," Frank said, as he began to cut pieces for the frame of a drying rack, "but it don't matter. Last a couple a weeks an' we ain't got that much meat."

With a few long, thin willows cut, Frank pulled them from the stand and piled them out of the way. He turned and pointed the knife at Tom's waist. "Take yer skinnin' knife an' cut some long strips from a couple a them big cotton woods. There's some stuff on the inside we c'n use t' tie this rig t'gether."

Tom nodded and drew his knife. "The inner bark."

Frank cursed. "Yeah. Sure." He turned back to cutting willows.

Chapter 9

Thin strips of meat hung on the racks arranged around their camp. Twice Tom had moved the horses, and twice Frank had circled the camp at a distance of a thousand yards or more. The sun would soon fall behind the faint line of mountains far off to the west. Tom was once again scanning the country to the north through his telescope.

"Be out there some place," Frank said from near the fire where he sat with a cup of tea. "They been tryin' t' catch us fer two weeks. On'y time they ain't been on our trail is when they missed us up on the river."

Tom compressed the glass, rose from the ground, and put the leather lens caps back in place as he walked to the fire. Did Seth and Hank manage to sneak into the hills while they were cutting and hanging the meat? If they did, it must have been at some distance, since Frank had been checking the area for signs. He set the glass down and picked up his cup, then scanned the lower land. To both east and west there were groves of trees that would offer cover for the killers once they were close enough, but it was impossible to approach from the north without being seen.

Squatting down by the fire, Tom poured himself a cup of tea as he said, "Yesterday afternoon we saw their dust. Since then we have seen no indication of their presence. They must have realized then that they could not catch us before we made it into these hills." He stood and took a seat across the fire from Frank.

"Seems likely," Frank agreed.

"When they realized we would make it to a defensible position, perhaps they chose to end the chase."

Frank muttered what Tom was sure would be another curse, then said, "Follered us hard fer two weeks, then jus' up an' quit." He nodded vigorously. "Yup, makes sense t' me."

Tom grinned and looked out across the plains turning gold in the setting sun. "Well, there goes that dream I was building." He sipped his tea again.

"We should be getting into the country where these men usually operate," Tom noted. "There are probably other whiskey traders in the area. Could it be possible they went looking for help when they realized we would make it into the hills?" He didn't mention that he thought they had already been joined by one other man.

Frank's tilted head and pursed lips expressed his doubt. "Maybe. But they do that they gotta split yer stuff. Like yuh said before, ain't enough stuff fer two men t' split."

"For some time now the Hudson Bay Company has been urging the Colonial government to stop the lawlessness here in the west. For a variety of reasons I expect it will be some time before anything comes of it, but there is still talk of stopping the American whiskey traders. Perhaps these two men think it's important to ensure news of their murder does not reach the east? Perhaps the possibility of having their trade interrupted is more important to them than stealing my goods?"

With his mouth full of tea, Frank shook his head, rose, and reached for the pot. "Them boys laugh at their own gov'ment. Sojers is just young fellers in blue they play tricks on. Can't see them givin' much of a damn 'bout yer Canadian gov'ment."

Tom drank tea for several moments, his eyes still on the north. Finally he said, "Then where did they go?"

"They gotta know we'll be keepin' a watch," Frank suggested. "Maybe camped along the creek so's they don't make no dust. Move in after dark."

"You suggested that earlier, but is that a particularly bright move?" Tom asked. "They will be moving against an established position in the dark."

Frank cursed. "Them boys is good shots, meaner 'n wild boars, sneaky, an' dirty. None o' that makes 'em smart. 'Sides, they don't gotta move in an' find us in the dark. All they gotta do is get into these hills an' set up camp in a grove o' trees. Comes daylight they can start lookin' aroun' fer sign."

As he took another drink, Frank gestured toward the horses with his free hand. "They know what them horses is like. They know we ain't goin' no place fer maybe a week. They got lots o time."

"Then we should continue to look for their trail as you did today," Tom concluded. "Perhaps one of us could circle east and the other west."

Frank shook his head. "Fer a tenderfoot you move along mighty quiet in the brush, but we gotta leave somebody t' make sure there's a camp t' come back to. 'Sides, I ain't much fer cookin', an' after a day o' crawlin' round these hills I'll be wantin' t' put on the feed bag."

Frank took a drink of tea, and then gestured toward Tom's shotgun and rifle leaning against a tree. "Don't have much use fer them weapons, but up close they'll be fine."

He gestured to the hill that rose up behind the brush south of the camp. "Makes yuh feel better, take yer glass up on top an' have a look t' the south 'fore the light's all gone. I'm gonna crawl into the hay here directly. All this tea I been drinkin', I'll be up long ahead o' first light. Time yuh have mornin' coffee brewed, I'll come back an' tell yuh where they's camped."

Tom dumped the remainder of his tea and set the cup near the fire. Picking up his telescope and rifle he started up the hill, stopped, and turned. "I'll keep my ears open as long as I can. Until after midnight, at least. I'll have coffee ready when you get back."

Tom opened his eyes to a golden sunrise. He had intended to be up by first light, but had been asleep for less than four hours. Worry that Hank and Seth would creep into their camp during the night had kept him awake and on watch far longer than he had planned.

As he rolled to his knees, each muscle complained. He stood up, stretched, and walked to the remains of the fire. Once he had teased the coals to life he took the coffee pot down to the stream, filled it, and washed his face and hands. Once he had the water on the new fire he took the horses to water then staked them out on fresh grass.

When Frank stepped back into camp the air was full of the smell of coffee. Tom lay behind the breastworks with his glass scanning the prairie.

As Frank poured himself a cup of coffee, he asked, "Any dust?"

Tom dropped the glass and grabbed his rifle. In the act of swinging toward Frank he stopped, set the half-cocked hammer back down on the cylinder, and lay the rifle down. With both hands he rubbed his face.

"Didn' mean t' make yuh jump," Frank said. "Thought yuh heard me come in." He blew on the cup rim then took a sip.

"Well, I didn't," Tom replied, his voice harsh. He sighed, and then said, in a more normal tone. "No, I still don't see any dust."

"Maybe have a bite t' eat an' then catch some shut eye. Have a look fer 'em 'round noon."

"They should be here by now," Tom said mildly as he stood.

"We got water, an' meat, an' ain't nobody shootin' at us," Frank observed.

Tom poured coffee for himself. "Quite true. We should enjoy what we have while we have it. I take it you didn't see anything during your morning stroll."

Frank's coffee was much cooler so he took a good sized drink. "Seen lots. Deer, grouse, bunch o' ducks, an' a whole family o' beaver."

Tom nodded. "This stream appears to start at a beaver pond on the other side of this hill. Watched them through the glass last night while I was up on top."

"Yup, but I didn't see no two-legged critters. Seen the tracks o' some Injuns maybe a mile east. Ten 'r twelve. Think they had some old folks with 'em. Wind already blowed some o' the sign away. Two, three days old."

Chapter 10

They began sleeping in shifts that morning. After a breakfast of jerked deer meat and three eggs Frank had found, the younger man lay down and slept for most of three hours.

Tom built a makeshift corral for the horses. He used fallen trees, or dead ones he could push over to form the bars, setting them in the willow clumps to form a rough but strong enclosure. While there was someone to watch over them, the animals could be staked out on grass, but secure in the corral at other times.

When Frank awoke, Tom turned in. They had lunch together and then the day was too hot for either one of them to sleep.

They sat in the shade of the trees up hill from the camp, each of them leaning against the trunk of a large poplar. The horses had also been moved into the shade.

"An iced tea would be most welcome," Tom observed.

Several moments were filled with the buzzing of flies. One of the horses stamped a foot.

"Ain't never had some," Frank said.

The heat filled several more moments before Tom responded. "Perhaps I'll make a pot before supper tonight. I can put it in the Dutch oven to cool. After dinner I'll place it in the stream for the night. The nights are quite cool, so by this time tomorrow we should have a refreshing beverage. Not iced, certainly, but suitable to the occasion."

"Can't see as it'll be worth all that," Frank observed.

"It won't be a great deal of work."

"Wasn't talkin' 'bout the work," Frank responded, then paused. "Was talkin' 'bout all the talkin' yuh just did in the heat t' explain it."

Tom smiled.

Later in the afternoon, Tom woke to find himself covered in sweat. He had slipped from the bole of the tree and lay in the blanket of leaves. Sitting up he looked around to find Frank was gone, perhaps on another scouting mission.

Rising to his feet he looked off to the north. Still no dust. He turned to care for the horses.

With the animals on fresh grass, Tom built the fire up, and then carried water from the stream. When the water was boiling he used some to make tea and carried the rest back to the stream where he removed his shirt, bathed, and shaved. When he was finished he felt better than he had in several weeks.

He had started a stew that was already filling the camp with its rich aroma when Frank returned. This time he saw the boy coming up hill from the east.

"Clean shirt an' a shave," Frank observed when he stepped into camp. "'Spectin' callers?"

"Well, I'm still hoping there won't be any," Tom responded. "However, you have assured me we will be having guests. As for the freshening, I am much improved. I'm sure similar efforts would improve you as well. Despite your youth you could also benefit from the loan of my razor."

Frank cupped his face in his hand and rubbed his soft whiskers. "Ain't got no more clothes," he said.

Tom removed the lid from the stew pot and stirred the mixture. "My trousers would be somewhat large but could serve to maintain modesty while yours dry." Replacing the pot lid he gestured toward the stream. "I dropped a small bundle of soap weed down by the water." Going to the packs he removed a pair of pants and his shaving kit. Handing them to Frank, he said, "By the time you've cleaned, dinner will be served."

"Smells mighty good. Whatcha fixin'?"

"Venison stew. I found arrowhead and cattail over by the beaver pond. There's also nut grass and lamb's quarter in it."

Frank was skeptical of such a mixture of weeds, but he sniffed the air with appreciation and turned to the stream.

After supper they sat back from the fire, each with a cup of tea.

"Ate too much," Frank proclaimed.

"As did I," Tom agreed. "However, it's the first full meal we have had in more than two weeks. I suspect it's been even longer for you."

Frank broke several moments of silence by saying, "Ain't never ate that good."

Tom smiled as he scanned the north. "Still no dust."

Frank shrugged, then rose and went to the fire for more tea. "Be here in the mornin'."

Tom nodded. "I expect you're right. They've been gone some time. Although, they may not see the need for any great haste. As you observed, they know the condition of our horses, and that we will not want to move for several days."

"Maybe," Frank said. "But they'll be worryin' on it, same as we are, what with not bein' able to see us an' all."

"Well, get some sleep," Tom advised. "I'll wake you around two."

Chapter 11

The eastern sky was just showing a hint of light when Frank shook Tom awake. It was warm, promising another hot day.

"They's here," Frank said his voice low.

Tom looked to the North Star, and guessed the time to be about four. "Won't they hear you?" he asked in a whisper.

"Ain't likely," Frank responded, holding his voice low, but still not whispering. "Maybe a mile east in that grove o' trees just past where the hill sticks a finger out t' the north. Come in the dark like we figured an' makin' camp right now. They's picked up a couple o' partners. Find us in maybe an hour an' move in by sunup."

"There are four of them?"

"Uh-hu. Don't know who the other two are. Didn't get much of a look at 'em in the dark."

So now it was two to one and the larger party was the aggressor. Tom rolled to his knees and stood. "Well, if they're bound to find us anyway, we might as well have some breakfast. I'll start coffee and heat some of the stew."

"They get a smell o' what we been eatin', it'll make 'em mad."

Tom smiled into the dark. "Perhaps you could ensure all containers are full of water and the horses secure in their enclosure."

The sun was high in the sky and there had been no sign of the whiskey traders. Off to the north-west they could see several black dots; a small herd of buffalo moving slowly south. They lay behind the breastworks and watched each grove of trees and clump of grass.

Frank broke an hour-long silence. "Takin' their damn time," he said.

"They must surely know our location by now," Tom observed. "It is also reasonable to assume that they believe we know of them and their location. Therefore, they are letting us consume our water and letting the heat take its toll. Allowing our tension to build."

Frank cursed. "One of 'em'll be watchin' fer us t' go t' the creek."

Tom took some jerked venison from his pocket, worried a piece loose with his teeth, and then replaced the remainder. "They can't get a clear shot from behind us and up hill so they will be down there in front of you and off to your left. Pick out the best spots for someone to make a stand, and keep an eye on those places. They may try to make us believe the main attack will be from my right. Once they have our attention focused, those over on your side will attempt to flank us along the creek. That way, if they fail they may still be in a position to cut us off from the water."

"Seems reas'nable," Frank agreed.

Tom turned and looked to his partner. "Reasonable? My, my! It appears my steady influence is beginning to make some impression."

"Wore me down, more like," Frank responded, gazing off to the North West. "Them buffalo, now. We ain't seen them 'till now, an' this here's buffalo country."

"We could have used a herd of them to wipe out our tracks," Tom noted, then asked, "What would be the import of this observation?"

"Musta been a whole passel o' Injuns over west o' here. They been huntin' buffalo an' run 'em out o the country 'r we woulda seen more. Injuns ain't been east o' here or we'd a seen tracks."

"You saw tracks two days ago."

Frank grunted. "Weren't more 'n a dozen. Maybe four huntin' age men in the bunch." He paused a moment, then added. "Maybe they was goin' t' meet the bunch that's been on the hunt."

"Perhaps white men have been hunting buffalo?" Tom suggested.

Frank shook his head. "Must be gettin' mighty close t' Blackfoot country, ifn we ain't in it. They's a few white men trade whiskey t' the Blackfoot. Ain't many stupid enough t' kill their buffalo."

"You said the people Hank and Seth killed were Blackfoot."

"Don't know Injuns all that well, but I reckon so."

"Then Hank and Seth won't want to meet the main party."

Frank shrugged. "Long run it might not make no difference. Them two been dealin' whiskey to Blackfoot afore this. An' there ain't no way them Injuns c'n know what happened over t' Old Woman Lake. Maybe even figure you an' me killed them two."

"So, what does this have to do with our present situation?"

"Maybe make them killers nervous," Frank suggested. "They can't watch the country fer Injuns an keep an eye on us, too. Blackfoot ain't noted as bein' real friendly folks. They won't treat us any better 'n they'll treat them whiskey traders, but it might give them two killers somethin' else t' think about."

Following several moments of silence, Tom said, "I don't really believe Hank and Seth are capable of enough thought that it could be interrupted, but I suppose every little bit helps." Privately he thought that Frank was looking for any glimmerings of hope in the face of hopeless odds.

Frank rolled up on one elbow and yelled across the hills, "Hey, Seth, yuh see them Blackfoot yet?"

There was no answering call and Tom could detect no movement. He kept his eye on the ground below and to his right, the barrel of the Colt revolving rifle behind the logs, but ready to be thrust through a convenient hole.

"Better keep an eye peeled, boys," Frank called, his attention trained on the ground below and left. "Them Blackfoot don't give much warnin'."

"Traded with them Injuns," a voice called back. "Spent more 'n one night with 'em."

"All night?" Frank asked. "And was it a village 'r just a camp o' young bucks gettin' drunk on yer rot gut?"

There was a few moments of silence broken by Tom's call. "I don't think any of you have the guts to face a village of Indian families."

"Listen t' the pilgrim talkin' 'bout guts," the voice from bellow responded. "Feller that hides behind a hill back t' the Old Woman Lake."

"Now that is an interesting story," Tom conceded. "Did you tell your new partners how you backed down from a fifteen-year-old boy and a greenhorn?"

Rock fragments flew from the breastworks in front of Tom. Smoke and sound came from the trees below. Tom thrust his rifle forward, fired, then again to left and right. As he pulled the center pin and shook out the half empty cylinder he could hear shots from Frank's side. He forced himself not to look at his partner, but alternated his attention between changing cylinders and the source of the first shot. He had the fully loaded cylinder mounted and was priming the three fired chambers of the other when the firing stopped.

"How are you doing?" Tom asked, just loud enough to be heard over the ringing in his ears. He could hear Frank slide the magazine tube from the butt-stock of his Spencer just before he answered.

"Doin' better 'n them boys, I reckon. An' I ain't no fifteen, neither."

Tom heard the magazine tube being pushed back in place as the boy finished talking. He had just finished loading, and tamping, three chambers that still required priming in the time it took the boy to replace four rimfire cartridges. That did not take into account the time it took to change cylinders. He knew his Colt would have some advantage over the Springfield muzzleloader, but the enemy also had a Spencer similar to Frank's. What other weapons did they face?

"I thought you might be a few years older than that, but it was my intention to make them fire. Apparently, something I said was effective."

Tom saw movement in the trees below him. Slightly to the right another shadow flitted from tree to tree.

"They're getting ready," Tom said. Just as he spoke the man on the left broke from cover. Tom swung his rifle muzzle but the man dropped. The man on the right broke from cover. Tom kept his muzzle trained on his last sight of the first man. When the second man hit the ground, the first man rose. Tom fired.

The man had risen from his face down position to lunge forward. The .44 caliber ball drove him over backward where he disappeared in the grass.

Tom swung his muzzle to the right. He had only seen the second man move out of the corner of his eye. He was not sure where his target lay.

Frank fired, levered the Spencer and fired again. At least three shots were fired in return. Frank fired again.

Below his own position, Tom saw the grass move. The second man was working his way over to his wounded partner. Tom followed the grass movement but held his fire.

"Still here?" Frank asked.

The man crawling through the grass stopped near where the first man had gone down.

"Yes, I'm still here," Tom responded. He moved several feet to the right, bringing the shotgun and extra rifle cylinder. He heard Frank replacing fired rounds, but made no move to reload his own weapon. He still had five shots. "I had given serious consideration to perhaps stepping over to the neighbors for tea, but decided against it."

As he answered, Frank also moved. "Had enough tea, have yuh?"

"Actually, I could use a spot. I just thought the weather was a bit warm for a long walk."

The grass in front of Tom was moving again, but this time to the left of where he had shot the first attacker. He had expected them to move back to the trees, but perhaps the man had not been hit very hard.

"Watch it! They're going to try again."

Tom's warning was hardly out of his mouth when Frank began to take fire and return it. The wounded man began to fire at the spot Tom had just left. The second man made a rush. Tom saw his shot hit the center of the lunging man's chest. He swung his rifle back to the first man and fired twice.

The wounded man began to crawl back toward the trees. Tom watched for several moments, and then quickly changed cylinders in his rifle.

"They appear to be pulling back," Tom observed. "One wounded and one dead over here. I expect they have found it somewhat expensive."

When there was no reply, Tom swung his gaze to the left. Frank lay near the fire, his head bloody.

Chapter 12

The left side of the boy's face, from cheekbone to ear and up into the hair was filled with small pieces of stone. Tom could find no bullet holes. It appeared that one of the stones in the breastwork had taken a direct hit, exploding into fragments that hit the boy.

Tom tried to remove all the stone chips he could find and washed the wounds. It was difficult task while still trying to keep watch for another attack. He placed a pot of water near the remains of the fire, and then tried to run his fingers lightly across the wounds on the chance that he might feel more fragments. When the water was hot he used some for tea and washed the wounds again. He covered the side of the boy's head with one of his shirts, tying it in place with the sleeves.

The Ojibwa Indians near his old home had taught him a great deal about the plants that grew in the wild, and he had seen some of those same plants in this land. There were herbs that would have helped the healing process, but he couldn't leave camp to get them. There was every possibility that one of the many stone fragments had penetrated the skull and might eventually kill. All he could do was hope the boy would wake up.

Having done all he could for the boy's wound the next step was to do his best to stop the next attack. He had no doubts now that there would be another one. How that attack would be attempted would depend a great deal on how many attackers were still functioning. He knew he had killed one and wounded another, but he had no idea how many the boy had accounted for.

He collected Frank's rifle and pistol and placed them near the center of the breastworks along with his own rifle and extra cylinder. Carrying his shotgun he returned to the tea and poured a cup then crawled up beside his arsenal.

"Well, Frank, I wish you could tell me if you hit anyone. Considering your shooting ability, I expect you did, but it would be nice to know how many and how well."

Perhaps thirty minuets after the gunfire had stopped the birds began to sing. As the day wore on and heat mounted, those songs were silenced. Tom kept himself well supplied with water as the sweat poured out of him, knowing that his vision and hearing would suffer if he became dehydrated. He would need all his senses if he was to stay alive. Occasionally he heard a bee buzz by or the sound of a raven overhead.

It was late afternoon when a voice called from down the hill. "Hey, tenderfoot! How be we make a deal?"

Through a gap in the stones Tom could see someone standing near a poplar on the edge of the woods. He scanned the left and right, wary that they might try to flank him while the speaker offered distraction.

"And what, pray tell, might you have to offer in this trade?" Tom called back.

"Yer life! Seems t' me that might be somethin' you'd be interested in."

Tom looked across the fire at Frank whose shallow breathing and steady heartbeat were the only signs of life. He turned and scanned the low ground as he responded. "And what must I offer in exchange for this marvelous gift?"

"Why, all yuh got t do is load up yer packhorse and send her out here. An' that gelding you been ridin'. We'll let yuh keep the other mare."

Tom looked over to the teapot thinking he would like another cup. "Of course, we would keep all our weapons."

"Well, I don't know as that's such a good idea. I think we should have that youngster's rifle an' pistol. He's a might too quick on the shoot, that boy."

And he might shoot a little too far, Tom thought, but said, "I really don't think you have anything to bargain with. By the way, is this Hank?"

There was a pause before he asked, "Where'd yuh get that name?"

"I heard you and Seth talking back when you murdered that man and his wife at Old Wives Lake. Besides, Frank knew you."

"Killin' a couple o' Blackfoot ain't murder," Hank responded, then asked, "Frank who?"

"My young partner. As I was saying, I don't believe you have anything to bargain with. The only individuals who seem to have a problem maintaining life are the attackers. That's you."

"An' where's yer partner? This Frank kid?"

"Well, Hank, I would like to think he's returning from your camp. Perhaps having already stampeded your horses."

There was a course of curses and the crash of brush as Hank and another man retreated.

"You lied t' them boys," Frank said, his voice gravely.

Tom turned, a smile still on his lips that became broader at the boy's voice and the sight of his open eyes. "How do you feel?"

"Like muh head's way too small fer all the poundin' that's goin' on in it."

Tom knelt beside the boy and untied the shirt sleeves. "Let us have a look at this.

"I didn't actually lie," he continued as he looked at the boys wounds. "I said I would like to think you had raided their camp. I didn't actually say that was what you were doing, although it would have been preferable to your actual situation."

Tom rose and walked back toward the horses. From a bunch of willows near their corral he cut several strips of bark and returned to the fire. "The bleeding seems to have stopped so we'll leave your wound uncovered. I'm going to boil up some willow bark tea. It will help reduce the pain. We'll also heat some more of the stew. Eat a few mouthfuls before you drink the tea." He stirred the coals to life and put some twigs down to start a flame. "You still need rest, but I must ask you to take care of our meal. I'll need to keep watch."

Frank sat up slowly and cursed, blinking eyes that watered. "I can't see well 'nough t' keep watch. Everythin's kinda fuzzy. Best I tend the fire a spell."

Tom returned the boy's pistol then took up position behind the breastworks. "Before you were hit, did you hit any of our attackers?" he asked.

"On'y had one fair target," Frank replied. "Think I clipped him. Mostly I was just throwin' lead."

"Then there's a possibility we only have one whole man to face."

"Yuh hit somebody?" Frank asked with more than a little astonishment.

Facing away from the boy and scanning the hillside Tom nodded. "I'm quite sure."

The reply was so soft that Frank could hardly hear. He placed a few branches on the growing flames.

"And wounded another," Tom added.

"Was that Hank yuh was talkin' to?"

"I believe so."

"Think it was Seth I hit. Hard t' tell." The boy paused a moment, then added, "When I shoot I don't never miss, but I just couldn't hit nothin'."

"Being under fire changes things," Tom advised. "I saw you shoot a deer at well over two hundred yards. You didn't even take a rest."

"Nigh on t' three hun'red," Frank said.

Tom shrugged, his eyes never leaving the line of trees. "If you say so. The point is the deer wasn't shooting back. Tension, avoiding return fire, firing at another human; they all interfere with one's ability."

They sat in silence for several minutes while the flames burned down to fresh coals.

"We have one empty water container," Tom noted. "Do you think you could fill it while I keep watch? We may not get another chance."

When Frank returned to the fire the stew was getting warm and the coffee pot was boiling. He dumped the willow strips into the bubbling water, and pushed the stew closer to the heat, giving it a stir.

"We got us a good chance," Frank observed.

"I have never been a gambling man," Tom responded, "but it is my decided opinion that we have roughly the same chance as a snow ball in hell."

Frank cursed. "We got one dead an' maybe two wounded. Looks a lot better 'n two t' one."

"They underestimated us. They realize their mistake and will treat us differently now. I expect we will find the two wounded are not in very bad shape. It seems to me these men wouldn't push anything that they didn't think was a sure thing. The death of one partner probably made them angry but, once they know what they're up against, I expect they would pull out if the odds were less than three to two."

Frank dished up some of the stew and crawled forward on his knees to pass the plate to Tom. When he had his own plate, he asked, "So what ya figure now?"

"If it was I," Tom replied, "I would climb one of those bigger trees; one that offers reasonably solid support. It would allow the climber to see over our pile of rocks and sticks. A clear shot right into camp. As long as the wind blows no stronger than the breeze we have now, even I couldn't miss."

Frank swallowed the mouthful of stew he had taken and cursed. "He c'n see us we c'n see him. Shoot him out o the tree."

"We will have a moon tonight," Tom said. "It won't be bright enough for us to see a climber, but bright enough for him to get into position. In the morning the other two will attack from each side to draw our attention. While we repel those attacks, the climber will kill us."

There was silence between the two while they finished their supper. Finally, while Frank was scraping his plate clean, he said, "You ain't a real pleasant fellow t' talk to of an afternoon."

Chapter 13

"Seems yuh know a fair bit 'bout these guys," Frank noted.

Tom looked back at the boy from his position by the breastworks. "Whatever makes you say that? I don't believe I've ever known such murderous, immoral people."

"Well, yuh figured out how they was gonna try an' take us, an' they done almost exactly what yuh said. Now you've come up with another plan that makes a lot o' sense. Yuh got t know 'em. 'R yuh readin' their minds?"

Tom smiled and continued his study of the slope and the trees. "Simply a matter of considering the possibilities, and discarding those with the least likelihood of success."

"So, how yuh figure that?"

"Training, I suppose. Perhaps inheritance is responsible in some small way. My father was a major with the Argyle and Sutherland Highlanders. Later he settled in what was Upper Canada, started a family, and became a colonel in the Colonial militia. As his son I was expected to carry on the tradition of military servitude. I was schooled in military academies and colleges, and more than a little of that teaching concerned the tactics of war."

"Thought you was a teacher."

"I was. It upset my father, but he eventually conceded that teaching offered an important contribution."

There was a long pause, finally broken by Frank. "What's all that larnin' tell yuh's gonna happen right now."

Tom could tell from Frank's tone that the younger man was less than impressed with his academic background. He had to admit that the study of tactics was only a beginning and no substitute for experience gained under fire. However, he made no mention of his thoughts and continued with his predictions about enemy actions. "At this moment our opponents are returning from finding their camp has not been violated. They will be angry with the thought that they have been made to look the fools by an

Easterner. Someone among them will present the idea of sniping into our camp. One of them will come to the edge of the woods and engage us in conversation while the others find a suitable tree to make a stand. They will inhabit whatever site they choose during the night and begin their two-pronged attack as soon as the sun rises."

When the explanation was finished, Frank cursed and said, "Yuh done said that already an' I didn't much like it the first time. What I want t know is what we c'n do about it."

Tom swung his arm to indicate their camp. "Defending a static position is always a disadvantage. The attackers have advantages that are only slightly offset by the protection offered by the breastwork—these logs. But we can fight fire with fire."

Frank didn't respond with anything more than a blank look. He poured more tea for himself.

"You find a good spot in the trees near the horses. Not close enough to the horses to draw fire toward them but something up-slope where you can see down into the trees. When the sniper's position becomes evident to you, fire back."

"Maybe pretty hard t' see 'im 'till after he's fired," Frank noted.

"That is quite likely," Tom agreed.

"So that makes the fella out here a target."

Tom nodded.

"How come I'm the one back in the bush? You figure I'm too young t' do muh part?"

"No, I think you and your Spencer are the only pair of us that has any chance of hitting a target that is more than a hundred yards away."

Frank shrugged and grinned. "More 'n a smidgen o' truth t' that. But yuh did mighty well with that Colt when we needed t' throw some lead."

"Thank you," Tom acknowledged. "However, they were less than thirty yards from me with very little cover." He realized that the boy was also talking about his own inability to score a hit, so added, "I've been under fire a few times. Keep that in mind while you're up there. There is no hurry. Make sure of your target."

There was a pause in the conversation while Frank thought about the message behind what Tom had said. He didn't like to dwell on the fact that his marksmanship had suffered during the action so he changed the subject. "I got t' admit though, that Colt rifle shoots mighty quick. Should o' figured they'd be the same as muh Army pistol"

"You haven't told me how you came to have that pistol," Tom noted.

"No, I ain't."

Tom directed his attention to watching the ground to the north. Obviously his approach toward the origin of the Colt had been too direct.

"Well, reckon I'll move muh bed back up into the trees," Frank announced.

"Take the telescope with you. It may prove useful."

When Frank had moved his bedroll and rifle he returned for the telescope and a full canteen. There was a call from down slope.

"Hey, Tenderfoot! That kid run out on yuh?"

"Looks like all that schoolin' might a done yuh some good," Frank said. "Looks like yuh might be right again."

"Might be?" Tom asked with a smile. "Better get back up there and have a look."

Turning his attention downhill, Tom called back. "Why, no Hank. He's right here with me."

"Thought yuh said he was runnin' off our horses."

"No, no, no! I simply stated what I thought he should be doing. But of course, regardless of what I would like, he couldn't do that for we have to stick together in our time of trial. We're partners. I'm sure you understand that, Hank."

"Yuh got a name, Tenderfoot?"

"Certainly! We all have names, Hank." Tom looked around to see that Frank was in position up the hill. "Most of us were given our name by family or church. Some of us have chosen new names for ourselves. Sometimes these new names are chosen to protect those who still carry the old name, and sometimes they are chosen for purely selfish reasons. People sometimes think they can hide behind a new name, but it seldom works."

"So what's your's?"

"Thomas Eastman Simcoe Brash. Most people simply call me Tom."

"That's quite a handle. Most folks settle fer a couple a names an' here you are with four. Must be confusin'."

"Why not at all," Tom responded. He glanced around to see Frank glassing the trees. "You see, I received those names from my ancestors.

Thomas was the name of my father's father and my mother's maiden name was Eastman. Simcoe was a governor with whom my father was associated. You see, I have a history that I am not ashamed of. And you, Hank? What about your name? Is it Henry?"

"Folks call me Hank. Hank Green."

"My, isn't that interesting?" Tom observed. "You come from a very large family. I've noticed there are a great many Greens in the land. And Browns, and Smiths. There's a Green County in Kentucky, and at least two Green Rivers. It must be nice for you to have all that company."

There was a lengthy pause in the conversation. Hank was trying to figure out what Tom had just said. Tom was trying to think of something else to say that would kill time.

Finally, Hank decided, correctly, that what Brash had said didn't matter. "Listen, Tom, have yuh been thinkin' 'bout that deal I offered?"

"You didn't offer a deal, Hank. The word deal implies that each of us has something the other wants, and that we are willing to trade those items. You have nothing I want."

"As I recollect, I offered your life."

"That isn't yours to trade, Hank. It belongs to the Almighty and his instructions are that I am to care for it. I have not received further instruction recently."

"Seems t' me yuh need some help carin' for it. Yuh ain't doin' so good."

"That may be true. It has been some time since I gave thoughtful study to the instructions concerning that question. However, we have been drinking tea and coffee, while eating grouse, duck, trout, and venison stew. How are you doing, Hank? Had any friends die lately? Is everyone in good health?"

"You got 'till mornin', Tom. Then we'll just come in an' take what we want."

"I'm sure you'll try."

Chapter 14

Each of the defenders had four hours sleep while the other kept watch. When the sun broke over the hills to the east, Frank was back in the trees and Tom lay behind the breastwork.

It was quiet enough to hear the sounds of the land. Tom heard a swish-pause-swish sound and glanced up quickly to see a raven passing over. The sounds of flight were momentarily drowned out by the call of a killdeer out on the prairie. A few moments later, from the grove of trees downhill came the drumming of a partridge, which Tom did not believe. There was certainly a multitude of the birds in the area, but it was far too late in the season for mating rituals. The drumming was echoed farther to the west near the stream.

"Get ready, Frank. Here they come."

"Uh-hu. Got their shooter, but I can't get a clean shot."

"He will have to make himself more visible in order to fire."

"Damn well hope so."

There was a flash of movement to Tom's right but he didn't yet commit himself to any one area. The experience of the previous day where he had lost precious seconds concentrating on the wrong target had not been forgotten. Movement to his left also failed to draw his fire. He waited for a much better target than a simple flash of color, a wiggling shrub, or rustling grass.

There were more veiled suggestions of movement, and then the man on the left broke from cover. Immediately, Tom swung his attention to the right, watching only with the corner of his eye for movement on the left. As he expected, the man on the right made the second move. Tom fired, but too quickly. He saw the bullet throw bark and wood chips from the trunk of a poplar behind the moving target.

As he swung his revolving rifle to the left, dirt spouted from the ground two feet in front of his position. The sniper was attempting to make a shot of more than two hundred yards from a station that was undoubtedly swaying slightly. With his first shot that close it wouldn't take him long to find his range.

As he brought his rifle muzzle into position for a shot on the man on the left he heard Frank's rifle speak. Tom's hearing was suffering from the rifle fire so he could no longer hear Frank work the action, but he did hear him curse and knew his young partner had missed.

The attacker on the left lunged from behind a small bunch of willows. Tom had chosen the wrong cover as the man's probable hiding place. He swung the muzzle to the right and fired just as the man dropped. He thought perhaps he had scored a hit.

Swinging back to the other man he heard Frank fire again. The curse that followed had a ring of exuberance.

The attacker on the right had been crawling forward. Tom could see his position by the moving grass. The movement stopped at Frank's exclamation. Back in the trees a scream was accompanied by the sound of breaking branches, the course of sounds punctuated by a thud. The man before Tom began moving back down the hill.

Frank ran down the hill to stand by Tom. "I got the bastard. Second shot an' he come out o that tree like a rotten apple."

"Which, no doubt he was." Tom reached up and pulled down on the younger man's sleeve. "There are still two more out there. Get down or there will be one less up here."

Frank dropped to cover behind the breastworks. There was a light in his eye, but no smile on his face. "I think I just killed a man."

Tom didn't smile, knowing the emotional destruction that faced the younger man. "Maybe not," he suggested. "Perhaps you didn't even hit him but came close enough to knock him out of the tree."

Frank stared through a hole in the breastwork for a moment, then said, "Same thing. Still killed him."

"Perhaps, but I don't have good thoughts about the alternative. Had he remained in that tree for moments longer it would be I that required your anguish. Or, perhaps you feel more inclined toward grief for him than for me?"

Frank rubbed his face with both hands. "Sorry," he said.

Tom was watching his young partner so closely that he almost missed the movement beyond him near the stream. He rolled away from the breastwork, swinging his rifle barrel over Frank's head while drawing the hammer back. As he landed on his left shoulder, he pulled the trigger.

Tom had indeed wounded the man attacking on the left, but not seriously. When the man on the right backed off, Tom had mistakenly assumed that this man had done so as well. This last shot from Tom, a shot that was made in desperation, without aiming, and from an awkward position took the man in the face. He fell back into the stream.

When he saw the man fall, Tom rolled onto his back, rested the Colt rifle across his chest, and stared up into the sky. He breathed deep for a moment, and then said, "Damn, that was stupid."

Frank also stared at the corpse for a moment, and then said, "You're gettin' down right foul mouth. Best watch who you're hangin' 'round with."

Chapter 15

Tom scanned the trees at the bottom of the hill. Back in the bush he could see movement, probably the remaining attacker attending to the one who had been driven from his lofty perch. He rose and walked to the dead man.

"I know of no good reason why we should allow this carrion to poison the stream with his filth," he said, grasped the man's shoulder and dragged him from the water.

Suddenly the after-battle calm was broken by the sound of pounding hooves on prairie sod. A stampede of horses came up the hill from both sides of the lower grove of trees. On their backs sat Indian warriors, stripped to breach clout and moccasins, their bodies painted for war.

Tom had already started back from moving the corpse and saw Frank reach for his Spencer. He knew it was certain death to fire on such a large number. Quickly he crossed the intervening space and placed his foot on the rifle. Frank looked up with surprise, but Tom shook his head. Frank settled back, his expression suggesting that he was ready to accept the obvious outcome.

A few of the Indians held bows but most carried rifles. Perhaps twenty feet from the breastworks the braves pulled in their horses abruptly. They sat silently facing Tom and Frank, all of them in a settling cloud of dust. The two partners noticed that none of the rifles were pointed toward them. The man who sat his horse slightly ahead of the others gave the impression of being the leader. Black bands had been painted across his face, and his torso was painted with red clay. He held his rifle butt against his right thigh, the muzzle pointed at the sky.

Tom searched for some way to open a conversation. He stepped over the breastworks and toward the leader. "Do you know these men who fight us?" he asked, pointing toward the trees behind the braves.

The leader looked around to his followers, his face puzzled. Tom realized the man understood no English.

"Parlez vous le Francais?" Tom asked.

"Oui," the leader responded. "I am happy that it is also with you. There are those of our tribe who speak the other tongue, but I see there are none among us."

"I am Thomas Brash." He turned to Frank and said softly in English, "Stand up." Reverting to French he continued. "This is my partner, Frank Clement."

"I am Red Shirt." He swung his rifle down to point at the corpse, and then returned it to his thigh. "You have done well against these sellers of poison. Why is it that you fight them?"

Tom shrugged expressively, holding his hands out at his sides, palm up. "I am not sure why they attack us. We have little to offer. Perhaps they wanted to steal our horses, or perhaps it is because we saw them kill two Indian people."

"These people that were killed, what did they look like?"

"A man and a woman, younger than you but older than my partner. They had a small tent and three horses."

"And where did you see this thing?"

"On the shores of Old Woman Lake."

Red Shirt nodded toward the horses held in the makeshift corral up the hill. "You did not take their horses."

Tom searched his mind for a suitable answer. "We did not know these people or their ways. We thought perhaps they would need their horses to travel to the other world. It was bad that white men had taken their lives. It would have been wrong for us to take the things they had gathered during those lives."

There was a long pause while Red Shirt studied the white man. Tom could not actually say that he saw a smile appear on the Indian's face, but he was sure a glint appeared in the man's eye.

"You speak well, Thomas Brash. The man who was killed on what you call Old Woman Lake was the son of my sister. They had a son who was in the trees and saw all that happened. He has told me how the young white brave tried to stop the killing, and how a voice came from above. When we heard the shooting during the sun that has passed we came to see if it was the same men. But you have taken our revenge."

Tom expected it was not proper to be anything but sober in the present situation but he could not stop his sober expression from turning to a grin.

The relief he felt, the release from tension was far too great. Red Shirt did not return the smile but the hard look in his eyes softened. Knowing that his young partner would still be wondering when he was going to die, he turned to Frank and said in English, "There was a young boy hiding in the bush when those two people were murdered. He was their son. He told this man, his uncle, how it all happened."

Frank looked up the hill toward the horses as he cursed quietly under his breath. "Then they ain't come t' kill us?"

"Actually, I believe they see you as something of a hero."

Tom turned back to Red Shirt and gestured toward the corpse near the stream. "This is not one of those men who were at Old Woman Lake. He is one of two who joined them to attack us. There is one and perhaps two of them still alive."

"There is one," Red Shirt replied. "We hope that he will live many hours more. Perhaps long enough to think on what he has done. There is another who fell from the tree. We will leave him. He will die before the sun hides behind the mountains."

He nodded twice quickly as if to shake something from his mind, and then continued. "We wish you to be our guests. Come with us. We have buffalo. The village will feast."

Tom could think of no refusal that would not be seen as an insult. "It would be an honor to visit the home of Red Shirt."

"It is only a camp for hunting buffalo. However, you would honor us if you traveled with us as we return to our home. You are welcome in our lodges."

Tom nodded, turned to Frank, and said in English, "Pack up. We have been invited to dine."

"With them?" Frank asked, but turned to the horses.

"Well, it seems to be the only invitation we have had in some weeks. Perhaps we should not be too choosy." He started to make up the packs. Behind him the warriors began to ride down the hill and into the trees.

"We have work that must be done," Red Shirt announced. "I will return to ride with you."

Tom waved his understanding as Red Shirt turned and rode away.

"Where they goin'?" Frank asked

"They are going down to chat with the survivor." He stood from packing and looked down the hill. "I think it is Hank. I expect they will be teaching him how uncomfortable death can be."

Frank and Tom were waiting, their horses saddled and loaded when Red Shirt and two others returned. They said nothing but sat their horses and waited for the two white men to mount. Still without speaking they lead off to the west, expecting to be followed.

Tom rode up beside the leader, despite glares from the other Indians.

"I wonder why you have left your brothers behind," Tom said.

Red Shirt looked over at Tom, glints of light in his eyes, and then faced forward. "They prepare a guest for ceremony. We will honor those who help our people, and then remember those who died."

"I thought you would bring him back to your camp. Surely there are others who knew your nephew and his wife."

"He was known to all," Red Shirt acknowledged. "Others will return with us to this place."

For several moments they rode in silence, and then Red Shirt said, "This man is a trader of poison that kills our people. He is a thief who takes life when there is no battle. He is a coward who fights only with those he believes are smaller and weaker than he. But his body is strong, and his heart is full of hate. He will take a long time to die."

Tom thought about this statement for a moment. Then he said, "It is us that they saw as smaller and weaker."

Red Shirt nodded. "You surprised them. It was foolish of them to continue. My people could not afford such loss. How is it you did this?"

Tom shrugged. "They underestimated us," he replied, and then, at the red man's puzzled expression, continued. "They thought of me as only a man of the east and a tenderfoot. They thought of Frank as only a boy."

Red Shirt almost smiled. "You are not these things?"

"Yes we are. But I have also studied war, and the ways it has been fought through countless generations. Frank is one who shoots very straight for a long way, and has trust for very few."

"He trusts you?"

Tom thought for a moment before replying. "I think not. I think, or rather I hope, that he has some faith in me. I suppose he would not have remained with me, had he not. I think he saw in me someone that could help him, as well as someone who needed his help. But someone has treated him badly and for a long time." He put his closed fist against his chest. "It has left him with a scar, here."

Red Shirt nodded. "Many of my people have such a scar. We have been pushed from our homes by the Long Knives. We have been killed by all men, white and red, because we are the people. The Long Knives still try to push us from the place we live now. And now other men move into this land."

"It must be hard to lead men who carry such memories," Tom observed.

"It is, not because of their memories, but my own. When I was very small, I saw my grandfather shot by a white trader. When I was still a boy I saw my brother and sister cut into pieces by the long knives for which the blue coated soldiers are called. When I was older, traders came among us and brought us the spotted sickness. All our people have seen these things. Once we were many, but now we are few."

"It is a strong leader that can lead two strangers to his camp after he has been treated this way," Tom said. "I understand now the looks of thunder that I received from your men as I rode up beside you."

"That is not why. There will be those, even among the white men, who we can make welcome. The reason my brothers stare at you with darkness is that a war chief is to lead. Few but other chiefs are permitted to ride by his side."

"I'm sorry to have intruded," Tom said and turned his horse away.

"No, no. Stay with me, Thomas Brash. It makes me happy to speak with you. Besides you are a chief. Your tribe is only a tribe of two, but you are the leader."

"Thank you," Tom said, as he urged his horse to continue beside the Indian mount. "I don't know what Frank might think of the idea of me being his leader, but I expect it has been true."

"There are those who follow me and think little of it," Red Shirt responded with a smile.

They rode in silence for a time, then Tom said, "This is a fine thing you do, telling your men that there is bad and good among all peoples."

"It is, but not because I have the heart of a spirit talker. I am a leader in battle. Men do not fight well when they hate. They fight better when they think."

Tom thought about that for a moment, then asked, "When you show an enemy the power of your people, do you not do this where all of your people can see?"

Red Shirt nodded. "When one of us is attacked, it is an attack against all of us. When we show our enemies our power it is the power of all."

"And yet, you have left Hank back there and are taking us to your camp. Why is this?"

"That is the man's name, Hank?"

"Yes, but you are not answering my question."

"It is good to know an enemy's name. It takes some of his power."

They rode in silence for several moments. Finely, Red Shirt said, "You are guests."

Tom nodded. "And you know that our customs do not include torture. You have moved us away from the place so that we will not be upset by the sounds of a long death."

Red Shirt hesitated long enough that Tom wondered if he would answer. Finally, he said, "That is so."

"Then, perhaps your heart is better than you claim," Tom observed. "Perhaps, as well as a war chief, you should be a spirit talker."

Chapter 16

In Red Shirt's teepee a woman sat on a pallet of furs, her eyes on the tanned skin she was stitching. The buffalo skin sides of the teepee were rolled up to allow a breeze so it was easy to see the mats indicated by the war chief.

"It will be my great honor to have you as guests in my home. Leave your things here for we must meet Talking Sky, chief of my people."

In English, Tom said, "Put your bedroll down, Frank, and perhaps your rifle. I notice they all carry knives, so perhaps it will not be an insult to keep your pistol."

Frank didn't curse, but grunted, then said. "Kind o stupid t' pull it out 'round here anyway." He unbelted the gun and dropped it beside the bedroll. "You gonna tell me what's goin' on?"

"At this point there isn't a great deal to tell except that we are about to meet the chief."

"Thought this feller was the chief."

"He's a war leader. If my experience with eastern tribes is any indication, the grand chief will be a politician. Perhaps something of a hunter and a warrior, like this man, but his most important function will be as a justice of the peace."

Reverting to French, Tom asked, "Is this lady your wife, Red Shirt?" indicating the woman.

Red Shirt said something in his own tongue and the woman stood. Then in French he said, "This is my first wife, Walks Fast."

Tom bowed before the woman and said, "Tell her it is my great pleasure to meet a woman of such beauty and the wisdom to join with the honorable Red Shirt."

"Our customs are not as yours," Red Shirt advised. "I can not tell her that."

Tom wondered what taboo he had broken. If he backed away, would it be perceived as weakness? If he insisted that his comments be translated, would it anger his host? He couldn't read anything from Red Shirt's stony expression. He shrugged, his hands out at his sides, and smiled.

Red Shirt said something in his own tongue that brought a smile to the woman's face. She responded and Red Shirt translated. "She says that it is a wise man who can see on a first meeting who chose who. I hope you are happy, Thomas Brash. From this moment until the freezing moon I will have to listen to how slow I was in paying her father the proper price for his daughter.

"Come! We must meet that father now or he will be insulted."

The lodges in the village were placed in a circle, their entrances all facing toward the east and the rising sun. Red Shirt led Frank and Tom toward the largest of these lodges, the one farthest west in the circle. "Within the tent of our chief Talking Sky the council waits. The pipe will be passed. Then Talking Sky will ask you to tell the story of how his son left this life."

"Talking Sky is your wife's father and the grandfather of your nephew?" Tom asked.

"Yes, my sister married the brother of my wife. When the spotted sickness came, few but the family of Talking Sky survived. They had left to live in the mountains and hunt fur. Other clans became no more. My sister and I are all that are left of our people. Many of us joined the clan of Talking Sky so that he is truly the father of all. We are of a different totem so it is permitted that we become… How is it said?"

"That you marry?" Tom asked.

Red Shirt nodded as he paused at the entrance to the teepee and called to those inside. Upon receiving an answer he drew the entrance flap aside and motioned for Tom and Frank to enter. He stepped in behind them and dropped the flap.

The interior of the teepee was oppressively hot, smoky, and suffocating. It was also very dark, despite the completely unnecessary fire. Tom felt a hand grasp his elbow and guide him to a seat. As he dropped down he felt movement beside him and looked to see Frank take a place next to him.

Someone on Frank's left spoke, the voice having the tone of gravel rolling down hill. Red Shirt said in French, "Talking Sky asks if you will smoke with the council of the wolf clan."

"We would be honored to smoke with his people," Tom responded then pressed his elbow against Frank. "The pipe will pass to you first," he said softly in English. "When it reaches you, take a drag and blow the smoke out in four puffs. One to the east, one to west, one to north and one to the south."

"How 'n hell c'n yuh tell which is which in here?"

"Just use right and left, forward and back," Tom advised. "It's the best we can manage."

By the time the pipe was loaded and lit, Tom's eyes were becoming more accustomed to the lack of light. He could almost see those sitting around the circle and watched as Talking Sky drew on the pipe, pointed the stem in the four directions, and then released all the smoke in one puff. The pipe was passed to the man on the left and not to the right as Tom had expected. He could see that the tradition was different with these people than what he was used to, but didn't want to risk confusing Frank with more instructions. He also thought there was a chance their hosts would take offense if he continued to speak with Frank in a language the others did not understand. Besides, in most societies the pipe was an important ceremony and he thought it would be best to maintain traditions he knew and understood.

When the pipe came to Tom he did as he had instructed Frank and then passed it to his young partner. Frank followed Tom's example, releasing the smoke in four directions rather than in one puff. There was a muttering from the others. When Frank passed the pipe toward the chief, another set of hands took it. Tom turned to see Red Shirt completing the ceremony before passing the pipe on to his chief.

Talking Sky placed the pipe on a piece of wood that lay before him and said something.

"Talking Sky notices that your customs are different than ours," Red Shirt said.

"It is the way of tribes far to the east," Tom replied.

"You have made smoke with these people?" Red Shirt asked.

"Yes. As a young boy I knew both Ojibwa and Huron people."

Red Shirt translated the response as Frank whispered, "What're they sayin?"

Tom reached over and squeezed his forearm. "Just a moment."

"Talking Sky says he has heard of these people," Red Shirt said. "They have brothers who came to this land with other white men."

The chief said something further and Red Shirt continued. “Talking Sky welcomes you to his home and says that you are welcome in his village for as long as you wish to stay. He has arranged for you to have a small traveling tent and a woman to cook and clean. What he truly said was a woman to serve you, but I have come to know that many white men think that has more meaning than it has with us.”

“I understand, Red Shirt,” Tom replied. He suspected it would be best if Frank and he left the village as soon as possible so, for the moment he avoided the subject of the efforts made to make them comfortable. “It has been the same with those in the east who are my friends. Tell Talking Sky that I am honored to be welcomed by such great hunters and strong people. We will stay for awhile. Also ask him if it is all right for me to explain to Frank what is happening here. He speaks only English.”

When Red Shirt finished speaking with his chief he said, “Talking Sky is sorry that the young white man does not understand and asks that you tell him what has been said. He also asks if Frank is from the country of the Long Knives.”

Tom knew there was no great love in these teepees for the American soldier and thought swiftly for an answer that would not upset anyone. “There are many from the east that do not speak French and speak only that tongue that is also used by those below the medicine line.”

As Red Shirt replied to his chief, Tom explained to Frank in a low voice what had been taking place. He didn’t know how many of those present spoke English, so at the end he squeezed Frank’s forearm and said, “I also explained that there are many in the east who speak English the same as those from the United States.”

Frank’s only response was a grunt of understanding.

“Talking Sky has heard the story of how his grandson White Bear died,” Red Shirt said, “but it was the story seen from the eyes of the child Little Arrow. He would like to hear how it was for the men at that place.”

“I was not there when the story began,” Tom advised, “but I will ask my friend, Frank Clement to tell the story, and I will tell it to Red Shirt who can then tell it to his chief.”

As Red Shirt translated, Tom turned to Frank. “They want to hear the story of how the people died at Old Woman Lake. When Red Shirt has finished, begin to tell the story. Give Red Shirt and me time to translate during the pauses."

There was silence in the circle of men, their eyes on Frank.

Chapter 17

The brutal killing of the two Indians had been a shock to both Tom and Frank. During the weeks they had been together they had avoided all discussion of the event. Tom found himself looking forward to Frank recounting what had taken place before his arrival.

"I come t' the top o' that hill there an' seen the water," Frank began. "Now, I'd been needin' a drink fer a spell, but I learned better 'n t' run right up without yuh take a look. I slickered down that hill into them trees and slid through, lookin' t' see if there was anybody 'round that might like t' put a bullet 'r an knife into me."

Tom held up his hand for a pause, and then translated in French. When Red Shirt had finished repeating the story in the Blackfoot tongue, all eyes turned back to Frank.

"Now, when I was steppin' light through them trees I heard some voices an' moved over closer to 'em. There was two white men holdin' guns on two Injuns, a man an' a woman. The woman was tryin' to keep her eyes on the ground an' not doin' real well, an' the man was just lookin' them two white fellers in the eye. Looked like the white men'd already been beatin' on 'em. Woman had an eye swellin' up, an' the man had him a bloody nose. He wasn't sayin' nothin', just lookin' at 'em. 'Spect he didn't know what they was sayin', an' couldn' answer 'em even if he did."

Again Tom gestured for a pause and the long process of translation was conducted.

"So then this one feller, Hank it was, made some sign that made it pretty plain them two fellers wanted t'. . . " Frank paused. Tom knew, despite the poor light that the young man's face was bright red.

"Well, anybody woulda knowed they wanted to get under the covers with the woman," Frank continued. "The Injun feller got mighty upset. He jumped up an' spit on Hank. Seth shot 'im."

When the translation had been completed, Frank continued. "Now I wasn't anywhere near ready fer that shot. I sort o' sat there with muh mouth hangin' open. Then when they said they was gonna start in on the woman, I stepped out o the trees an' told 'em I wasn't gonna let that happen."

When he was finished with this translation, Tom took up the narrative. The story went much quicker when only one translation was required. When he reached the part where he had spoken from behind the brow of the hill, the men all smiled. Some of them chuckled.

"What's funny?" Frank asked.

Tom looked a question at Red Shirt.

Still smiling, Red Shirt explained. "When the boy told this story he said the voice of the Great Spirit came from above, and it made the white men stop."

Tom smiled and explained it to Frank.

Frank didn't smile but said, "Reckon we're doin' pretty good. Got 'em thinkin' I'm some kind o' hero, an' at least one o' their kids thinks you're God Almighty."

Tom smiled. "Well, though I agree such a thought is less than flattering to the Maker, I suggest you spend some time with this child. The boy must be very bright, and could perhaps teach you proper respect for your partner."

Frank grunted, then said, "Least I could do is straighten the kid out 'fore he ruins his whole life."

Tom grinned, but it slipped quickly from his face when he returned to the story. He finished with the death of the woman, and how he and Frank rode away from the site.

"You left White Bear and Little Calf," Red Shirt said.

Tom held his hands out, palm up. "We did not wish to insult them by doing things that are our custom and not theirs." He nodded toward Frank and continued. "We do not know the customs of your people."

Red Shirt translated Tom's response then waited while Talking Sky responded. "Talking Sky says that your actions give your words the ring of truth. He says that a white man who gives thought to others is rare. Such a man could learn to live in the ways of truth. He offers you and Frank Clement a place to live and learn as long as you wish."

This was not the sort of offer that Tom wanted. He knew that either he or Frank could unwittingly insult their hosts, and that such an insult might lead to death. That was one reason he had conceded to make this visit; to avoid insult. He knew that insult could be taken from any number of things, but few would be stronger than refusing hospitality and teaching. He also knew that both Frank and he wanted to move on, and would be much safer when they did so. However, despite his attempt to avoid the subject he was now faced with the need to make a response and it had better be the right one.

Tom realized the pause had been too long, and said, "It is a great gift Talking Sky has offered us. My young partner and I have other things we must do, but this offer of Talking Sky is not something to be turned away. We will certainly stay and accept this hospitality for a time. We will talk about if we should stay longer. Give us two days."

When Red Shirt was finished translating, Talking Sky nodded agreement. However, it was apparent from his tight-lipped expression that he was not completely happy with the reply.

Chapter 18

Tom and Frank sat before the teepee that had been set up for their use in a village seemingly short of men. Many of the warriors had returned to offer Hank the special attention they believed he deserved. A few women had ridden with them but the party had been mostly men.

It was not that women were not a part of society or community or that they did not consider the methodical handling of a murderer to be a spiritual duty. However, this was a hunting camp and the women always had work to perform. The daily work of survival, conducted primarily by women with the help of the older children continued throughout the camp.

Not only did survival keep them from the ceremonial dispatch of an enemy but it also kept them from paying a great deal of attention to two white guests within the village. The two white men felt free to talk openly about their problem.

"Don't much like bein' here," Frank admitted. "Might take notions. Like askin' if I'm from the land o' the Long Knives. Find out I come up from that a way, might take a fancy fer doin' t' me what they's doin' t' Hank."

"I wouldn't expect so," Tom responded, a glint in his eye. "You gave support to two of their people. As it developed your attempts were unsuccessful and the two people in question died, but you did try." He gestured to indicate their surroundings. "Considering their lifestyle, I expect hardship and failure are not unknown to these people."

He tired not to smile before he added, "No, if they should decide you need it, they would probably just cut your throat. I don't think they would prolong it."

"Well, ain't that comfortin'? What they got ag'in 'mericans anyway?"

"Well, where should I begin? For a hundred years traders with the American Fur Company joined the enemies of the Blackfoot in war. Since then, settlers have shot them for no other reason than that they offered a target. The American army has attempted to wipe out whole villages at every opportunity. I expect that is why many of them have moved north of the border in these last years."

"Hell they done the same thing t' us!"

Tom paused for a moment to think of a response. He watched several young children playing a game with sticks on the far side of the camp. Several young women pounded dried buffalo meat in the making of pemmican, the food that would keep the village alive during the long winter. In the dirt beside these young women three babies played in the dust.

"Did you have a home at this Fort Union, Frank?"

"Well, best we could, what with Paw gone off t' war an' all."

"It must have been tough. Then you received the news of your father's death."

"Yup, killed at Charleston. Man brought us the news was there when it happened. Moved in with us."

"And became your stepfather," Tom prompted.

"Reckon." Frank nodded briskly. "Never liked 'im. We never had nothin' 'fore he came, an' less after he showed up. Drank up anythin' we put by."

"I guess it's pretty upsetting to have someone move into your home and take it as his," Tom concluded. "When it's all you have, it must give rise to some pretty strong feelings."

Frank nodded and looked around the camp, noting the play and work, the love and laughter. Tom thought he had missed the point and was about to say something further when Frank said, "Reckon I git the gist. We moved intu the Blackfoot home an' told 'em t' leave."

"Well, not exactly. You moved into their country and killed them. And don't be misled, it wasn't only people from south of the border; the Indians throughout this continent have been slaughtered by all those who were not of their tribe and none have been treated harsher by more of their neighbors than the Blackfoot tribes. At least, that is what I am led to understand through my meager study of the subject. The British and French have done their share as have the various tribes mistreated each other."

"I don't reckon I can go that far," Frank objected. "Army just tries t' keep the peace. Don't reckon they go t' killin' fer no reason."

"Yes, I am sure that is their intended purpose as it is the purpose of Red Shirt and his warriors to keep his people alive by eliminating anyone who is or might be a threat. I'm sure the British and French thought themselves quite proper in their actions when they tried to eliminate the tribes in the east." Tom felt he would have to be satisfied with the gains he had made and added, "As with most wars between people it's a matter of not understanding the other fellow, or not realizing that what is right for you might not be right for him.

"So how do you suggest we move on without offending them?" Tom asked.

"We goin' someplace special? Figure I wouldn't mind learnin' a bit about these folks."

"And if they suddenly decide they have had enough of us? I know something, very little mind you, but something of the peoples to the east, but I know nothing of these people. It would not be hard to earn their enmity by transgressing—by breaking some taboo. If we suddenly step outside of what they feel is acceptable, how long do you think we would last?"

"Lot longer than we woulda if you hadn't stopped me pickin' up my rifle back there when they come on us."

"True, we are still alive. But let me suggest that we leave at the first opportunity. We should avoid a mad rush out of camp, thus insulting our hosts, but leave we must. I don't find this a comfortable situation."

Frank shrugged. "Grub we jus' ate was mighty good. Lot better 'n I figured it'd be. Seems t' me I recollect yuh sayin' we didn' have much."

"Yes. Perhaps we should ask to be included in the gathering of some of this food. Extra mouths put a burden on these people."

It was the middle of the next morning before Tom had an opportunity to ask Red Shirt about joining the men on a hunt. It was then that the men returned from the lengthy ceremony that surrounded the death of the whiskey trader.

The sun was nearing the apex of its daily journey when Red Shirt approached the two white men where they sat before their teepee. Frank rocked forward as if to rise, but Tom placed a hand on his arm stopping him.

"As I said earlier, it is quite easy to offend when you don't know the customs," Tom said. "By remaining seated you demonstrate your trust in Red Shirt. By standing you suggest that you are in fear of attack."

"Reckon I am," Frank muttered. "An' I hope your eastern Injuns have some o' the same ideas as these folks."

Switching to French, Tom greeted Red Shirt. "The guests of Red Shirt are happy to see his return. Please join us."

Red Shirt sat and removed a pipe from the bag that hung at his side. Tom produced his tobacco pouch and offered it to the war leader. The three men sat in silence until Red Shirt had his pipe drawing well.

"The whiskey trader died," Red Shirt announced.

"I expected he would," Tom responded.

Red Shirt shook his head. "He died too soon. There was little entertainment, and some are angry. You and the young one who shoots should be careful. Lame Dog has told those who travel with him that the two white men in camp would last long."

Tom watched three women walk past. Each of them carried a bundle and the youngest one looked toward the three men and smiled. Tom glanced at his young partner who was smiling back. "Careful!" Tom said in English. "She may be someone's woman. She is definitely someone's daughter."

Tom turned to Red Shirt and returned to French. "I am flattered that Lame Dog has such faith in our courage. Not happy, but flattered. What wrong have we done to Lame Dog?"

Red Shirt took the pipe from his mouth and looked at Tom, a glint in his eye. "Many things. You allowed yourself to be born with white skin. You did not die. You came to our camp."

"Because I am not of your tribe he wishes to kill me?"

Red Shirt's pipe had gone out. When he had it re-lit he replied. "That has always been the way of our people. It has been our custom."

Tom didn't like the direction this was taking. What Red Shirt was saying seemed to fit in with what he and Frank had been discussing privately since their arrival in the village. However, he was never one to avoid a subject. "This is what all your people want?" he asked.

Red Shirt smiled. "Only those who do not see that the old ways are gone." The smile dropped from his lips and he puffed on the pipe. After a moment he continued. "When we were many and our enemies few, we could keep all others from our hunting. When others became stronger, the Peigan, Sitsika, and Kaini came together as brothers. And now war, and the spotted sickness, and the white man's drink have made even fewer of us. If we kill all those who are not of the people we will soon be no more."

Inwardly, Tom was relieved. "This feeling is strong in your village?" he asked.

Red Shirt tapped the ash from his pipe, and then put it away in his bag. "It is strong with Talking Sky. Many others say that his heart has been made soft by too many hard winters. Some also say that the village is in danger when the war leader supports him in this thing."

Tom watched two ravens fly over the camp. He felt they carried his fleeting feeling of relief with them. "I am sorry that we have placed such a load on Red Shirt."

The war leader held his hands out, palm up. "It is I that brought you here. It was my order to welcome those who helped the son of my sister."

It took Tom a moment to grasp the import of what he said. "And if we do something to anger your people, you will lose much respect."

"Yes," Red Shirt admitted. "And if it should come to be that more of our people agree with Lame Dog than agree with me, I will no longer be war leader."

"On the other side of the mountains there are many white men," Tom said. "They dig in the ground for gold."

"I have heard of both the yellow earth, and the men who look for it," Red Shirt said.

"Perhaps Red Shirt could show me a trail that leads over the mountains," Tom suggested.

For several moments Red Shirt looked through the camp and to the prairie beyond. Then he said, "It is wrong for us to make those leave who have done good things for us. But perhaps it would be best if you went beyond the mountains." He turned his eyes on Tom and continued. "During the cold time we live in the trees near the mountains. We will hunt one more day and then move toward that place. If you stay with us on this move, we will not have disgrace."

Tom nodded, understanding that if he and Frank left so soon after being welcomed into the camp by Red Shirt it would serve to undermine the leadership of both the war leader and the chief. "And when we near the mountains you can show us the trail," Tom finished.

"That is so." Red Shirt stood. "Tonight there will be much food in honor of our guests. Tomorrow we hunt."

Tom stood and said, "It takes much to feed your people. Frank and I would help. Perhaps we could join you on this hunt?"

Red Shirt nodded his eyes troubled. "As you wish, but always watch Lame Dog and where he shoots."

The war leader turned and walked toward his tent, then stopped and turned back. "Great Voice would be wise to have his rifle on the hunt," he said with a smile, "and to have bullets in it."

Chapter 19

During the mid day meal, Tom discovered they had another problem. The young woman who had passed earlier with a smile in Frank's direction was the one who brought food. Tom doubted her repeated appearances were the result of coincidence; a feeling that was supported by her actions while near Frank. She failed to raise her eyes during the few moments she was near, but for his part, Frank had no difficulty admiring her.

When she was out of earshot, Tom suggested that it might be safer to avoid involvement with the local ladies.

"Ain't done nothin'," Frank objected.

"Not yet," Tom conceded. "You will however, recall the reaction of those present when we described the events surrounding our meeting. These people appear to place a high value on their women." He took a bite of the buffalo meat and found it delicious, if slightly rare.

Frank grunted and nodded once. "Reckon so. Looks t' me like they do most o' the work."

Tom nodded, and then began to relate the main points of his conversation with Red Shirt. "So I expect we will have an opportunity to see what the men do in exchange for their fine treatment here in camp." He broke a piece from the flat loaf. He found it lighter than he had expected and with a slightly nutty flavor.

"Best forget 'bout huntin' an' make tracks," Frank suggested.

Tom found himself trying to hide a smile. One day earlier Frank had been in favor of staying long enough to enjoy some of the food. Now he was ready to leave. Undoubtedly he was feeling more pressure from their recent female visitor than he was willing to admit. "Yes, but we can not leave too suddenly. Red Shirt and Talking Sky have spoken for us. If we leave right away, their enemies will say that we are cowards and beggars. These two men have done a great deal to keep us alive, despite the fact that it is counter to their formative teaching. The least we can do in return is give that faith some substance, slight as it may be."

"Thought we was some kind o' heroes." Frank said, not having understood the earlier conversation in French between Tom and Red Shirt.

"True, but people find it much easier to remember what they want. Most people are guilty of that. It might be easy to forget Old Woman Lake and remember the food we ate, if that is what serves one's purpose." Tom went on to explain the feelings of Lame Dog and his followers.

"Which one's Lame Dog?"

Tom shrugged, his mouth full. When he had swallowed he answered, "I have no idea. However, if upsetting us is his pleasure, I am sure he will make himself known."

"Shouldn' have no trouble pickin' 'im out," Frank noted. "Can't be more 'n ten or twelve warriors in the whole outfit."

Tom stopped the few berries part way to his mouth and looked at his young partner. "You haven't been paying attention."

"How yuh figure that?"

"I believe it's because you're young, and spend all your time looking at horses, guns, and girls. There are some pretty girls in this camp."

Frank squirmed but did not respond.

Tom took the few berries, chewed, then explained. "You have to pay attention to the faces you see moving about camp. It also helps that I heard movement in the night and saw the old guard returning to the village. Since then I have done some counting. There are twenty-two warriors, three older men—Talking Sky is one of them—who are past the age of a warrior but probably formidable in a fight, and eight boys who are old enough to be dangerous. There are also twenty-eight women and ten girls. There are only six children, three of them toddlers. I expect this is because they have had several years of hardship that has killed the children; hard winters, starvation, and sickness. Or at least, this is what I surmise from my conversations."

"Where 'n hell they at?"

"The warriors?" Tom asked.

Frank nodded.

"Apparently this land is claimed by several tribes," Tom advised. "We are in enemy country. The others are out on guard to warn the village of an attack. If you had paid attention you would see that the faces change every day."

"Who's the enemy? An' why'n hell would yuh go off intu their country? They all jus' lookin' fer trouble?"

"The Cree are their biggest problem, but Assiniboine and Sioux also claim the area. White men. Anyone. I'm sure you have heard the stories all your life. I mentioned it yesterday when we talked about the reason for the Blackfoot having a strong need to eliminate anyone who is not of their people. I've even heard some of these stories in the east. Who is more hated than the Blackfoot?"

Frank shrugged. "Apache?"

Tom smiled. "Somewhat farther south, but back to your original question. By my reasoning, coming out here in such small numbers is looking for trouble. But they need Buffalo meat in order to make it through the upcoming winter and, as we both noticed, there doesn't seem to be many around this year. If they need food they have to go where that food is to be found.

Also there is the matter of the young man and his wife who were murdered. It isn't usual for them to come this way to hunt. I'm told they often run buffalo over cliffs to the south and west of here, but they came as far as they dared to offer some protection to White Bear and his family." Tom swung his arm to indicate the village. "Or that small part of this larger family, to be more precise. White Bear's wife was an Assiniboine - again, an enemy—and she wanted to see her people once more."

That very afternoon, Lame Dog took a moment to make Tom's prediction come true. It began with the arrival of three braves who rode hard to the edge of camp then walked their blowing horses to Red Shirt's teepee. Making every effort to appear calm and casual, several men moved directly toward the newcomers as Red Shirt stepped out to meet them.

Leaning back to attain some relief from the too-large lunch, Frank jerked his head toward the group and asked, "Any ideas?"

"I expect they are scouts," Tom said. "Perhaps they have found a herd of buffalo for the final hunt."

The tone of conversation in the group of braves seemed to change. Voices were raised and there appeared to be some anger. One of the men broke away from the group and strode toward the two white men.

Frank pushed himself up and Tom thought he was about to rise. "Remain seated," Tom instructed, "and keep smiling."

The man who approached them was truly ugly, his homely face holding all the warmth and expression of a stone. He was made even less attractive by black eyes filled with hate. He stopped before the two white men, put hands on his hips, and stared down into Tom's eyes. In English he said, "White men chase buffalo away. You hunt, you die.

Although petrified by the man's size and murderous glare, Tom forced his smile into a wide grin. Slowly he pointed at Frank, and said, "He hunts, many buffalo die."

Red Shirt stepped close and said something to the murderous brave in their own language. The man turned his head to look at the war leader, and then stormed away.

When the man was out of earshot, Tom looked up to Red Shirt, and asked, "That is Lame Dog?"

"Oui," Red Shirt responded. "What did he say to you?"

"I believe he insulted our ability as hunters. He said we would chase the buffalo away, and if we joined the hunt we would die." He gestured toward the men behind the war leader. "Am I to understand you have found buffalo?"

"Yes, several animals," Red Shirt replied. He looked toward Lame Dog who was disappearing into a tent on the opposite side of the camp. "Perhaps it would not be good for you to come with us. It would give Lame Dog and his followers the chance to shoot you and Shoots Quick."

"Sit with us a moment," Tom suggested. "And describe how it is that you hunt these animals."

Tom and Frank sat at the mouth of a small gully, screened from view by low brush. Their horses had been tied farther back up the draw, well above the level of the plain, but less than a hundred yards from the two men. With rifles close at hand, they watched the land to the north, waiting the arrival of running buffalo.

"Last night I managed to get Red Shirt talking about his earlier meeting with Mr. Green and Mr. Nation," Tom said.

Frank glanced around with a puzzled expression and asked, "Who?"

"Hank and Seth. Red Shirt mentioned earlier that he knew them. Apparently many men, including Hank and Seth came to their camp some months ago. They were looking for an alliance with the Blackfoot."

Frank grunted. "Didn't figure anybody was that crazy. Bad enough tradin' whiskey with 'em. A sight simpler just t' shoot yerself in the guts."

Tom smiled as he watched the horizon. He was happy that Frank had begun his statement with a grunt rather than a curse.

Finally Frank added, "'Spect it's just as crazy livin' an' huntin' with 'em."

"I had the distinct impression you were enjoying the food and the view," Tom noted.

"Ain't no doubt 'bout the food," Frank conceded. "Specially after we run low on grub. Don' expect eatin' them maps o' yours would be real satisfyin'. Not that yuh can't whip up a damn fine meal with nothin' t' make it with. That meal you put t'gether up there in the hills was some fine."

Frank lifted his Spencer and wiped dust from it, put the butt back on the ground and added, "An' there ain't no doubt the view's mighty nice. Mighty pretty gals in that camp."

"For someone who is concerned about the bloodthirsty reputation of our hosts I don't think you could choose a more certain method of putting us in danger."

Frank grunted. "Don't you fret none. Ain't no doubt I'm young an' near as crazy as a stud horse with a new herd o' mares, but I got my mind set on bein' an' old stud."

Tom nodded and grinned.

"So what'd Red Shirt say?" Frank asked.

"He said that many men came to their camp. They were lead by a man who called himself Colonel Coleman. He claimed to be the new white leader of all this land."

"Thought you said this was English?" Frank said.

Off to the north there was the sound of shots followed by a low rumble.

"Yes, part of the Hudson Bay lands," Tom responded. "However, there is talk that the English Parliament will be taking control of it. There is another group that says it will all become part of the new country of Canada. Regardless what is decided, or may have already been decided, there is some question as to who is in charge. The point is such a question of leadership leaves an opening for an enterprising individual."

"Reckon somebody's tryin' t' set up his own country?" Frank asked.

"More likely his own kingdom," Tom responded. "Or his own military dictatorship."

Not sure of the distinction, Frank shrugged. "This colonel feller wouldn't want the news of such a thing gettin' out. You reckon that's why Hank an' Seth went t' so much trouble t' bury us?" The rumble from the north grew louder and the bird songs about them disappeared.

Tom nodded. "Perhaps they knew their boss would be upset to hear of two white men operating independently within what he intends to be his domain. And I dress somewhat differently than the local norm, so it could be they thought of me as someone with official connections. It would make more sense than their going to all that trouble for my meager outfit."

Frank lifted his rifle as the buffalo came into view. Kneeling on his right knee he lifted his left and placed his elbow on it. His left hand cradled the barrel as he sighted at the charging beasts. He raised his voice slightly to be heard over the growing rumble of stampeding hooves. "Time they get in front o' us I'll be out o' bullets. Reckon I can get a few with your Colt as they go by."

"And I will have your Spencer loaded by the time it's empty," Tom assured him.

Frank nodded, took a deep breath, and let it out slowly. At almost the end of that release of air he felt his heart beat, and then squeezed the trigger.

Chapter 20

When Red Shirt and his men rode up on their lathered hunting horses they found twelve buffalo carcasses with the two white men standing up slope and to the east of these bodies

There didn't seem to be conscious effort or thought put into it, but the Blackfoot formed two separate groups. Five men formed around Red Shirt and three around Lame Dog.

Lame Dog's group did not speak, even among themselves, but their expressions and actions spoke volumes. First they studied the buffalo, and then they turned their eyes to the white men. Lame Dog's shock widened eyes quickly filled with hate. One of the men with him leaned over in the saddle and mumbled something. Lame Dog snapped a reply, swung his mount, and rode north. The man who had aroused Lame Dog looked to the other two and shrugged. All three relaxed on their mounts and looked to the pile of meat that would soon be butchered by their women.

Red Shirt's face remained expressionless, but when he rode closer, the two white men could see the sparkle of pleasure in his eyes.

"Bonjour, my brothers," Red Shirt said. He turned to look at the buffalo then back at Tom. "Shoots Quick and Voice From Above have done well. Our people will eat for many moons."

"We have had a good morning," Tom admitted. "Red Shirt and his men have taken other buffalo?"

"We have three more," Red Shirt responded. "With those already drying, there is much meat. Soon we will return to the mountains. It will be a slow journey for there are many loads of meat. Many will have to walk."

"I would be happy to walk if my horse will help," Tom said.

Red Shirt looked at him for a long moment before he said, "Voice From Above can not walk. This may be a good thing in your world, but for you to walk would bring much laughter from Lame Dog." He glanced over at the three warriors who had gathered around Lame Dog before he rode away. "And those who smell his dung. He would force you to fight."

Tom found the prospect of a hand-to-hand confrontation with Lame Dog less than thrilling. He knew that such a battle could, probably would, end in death. Even if it was not his own, the loss of a warrior would do little to make him popular with the rest of the tribe. "I do not wish to fight any of the people of my friend Red Shirt."

Red Shirt's lips twitched and his eyes sparkled with humor. "And I enjoy speaking to my friend, Voice From Above. It will be much better if he can talk back."

Tom looked to loading the chambers in the cylinder Frank had emptied. "Yes, and I enjoy talking with Red Shirt," he said.

Tom was more than a little upset that the war leader had taken for granted that he didn't have a chance in a confrontation with Lame Dog. He was further distressed by the realization that he cared about what Red Shirt thought of his abilities. He had learned to disregard looks of derision when he had left the military life his father had planed for him and become a teacher. He had learned to chart his own course, maintain his own counsel, and ignore what others might think. He took pride in his independence, and the fact that he had left his need to prove his physical skill many years in the past. However, judging by the way he felt about the present situation, perhaps he had reverted to feelings from an earlier life; his indifference to what others thought had been left behind.

"You must join us when we return to camp," Red Shirt said. "There will be much feasting to mark the end of the summer hunt. You have taken more meat this morning than all other hunters have taken in two weeks."

Tom looked up from pouring powder into the chambers and said, "I only helped. It was Frank—ah—Shoots Quick."

Red Shirt nodded. "As it should be. A great chief leads and does not interfere with those who do other things."

Chapter 21

Their evening meal was once again served by the same young woman who had been giving Frank so much attention. This time, however, having set the plates of dried buffalo hide overflowing with roast meat and wild vegetables before the two white men, she did not scurry away but sat on her heels to Frank's left. She kept her eyes on the horizon while the men ate.

"I believe I mentioned that we might have a problem, here," Tom observed. "Something will have to be done."

Frank glanced quickly to his left then turned his gaze toward Tom. "She's just waitin' t' see what we need," he said. "Take th' plates when we's done. We killed a pile o' meat fer these folks. Must figure we're in line fer special treatment."

Tom smiled as he sliced a piece from the delicious Buffalo meat. "It is true that I know little about the customs of the Blackfoot, but I do know a great deal about those of the Ojibwa, and something of the Algonquin and Mohawk. In their camps it would not even cross anyone's mind to supply a special serving mistress for a separate table and certainly not as a reward for good hunting." When he had eaten the piece of meat, Tom added. "No, my young friend, I believe you are being courted. I will ask Red Shirt about it at the next opportunity."

Frank exploded with a string of colorful, if somewhat improbable, cursing. "Yuh don' need t' say nothin'. Ever'body in the whole damn camp'll be laughin' at me."

"Relax, Frank, they wouldn't laugh outright. Snicker and giggle perhaps, but not great guffaws." Tom noticed that Frank was taking this far more seriously than he meant it to be, so added, "Damn it, boy, I said when the opportunity presents itself. I'll ask at the right time and in the right way. I won't do anything to embarrass you. And, as I mentioned, I believe it important we do not upset their social structure in any way. We need to know the proper course. We are living among people with a reputation far and wide for being very fierce, and very deadly."

"The killers o' the plains," Frank agreed. "That there's 'barrassin' all by its own self."

"The key word there is 'living'," Tom responded. "Not only have they not killed us, but they are feeding us quite well. However, should they decide that we, in this case, you, have taken advantage of one of their young women, perhaps the prettiest in the tribe, I might add, it may be just the thing that will give Lame Dog the support he needs to do away with us. Don't forget, not everyone is thrilled with our presence. And we will leave as soon as possible. It's just that it would be a slap in the face for Red Shirt at this time."

"Hell, I 'gree with Lame Dog on that one. I'd just as soon we wasn't here my own self."

Tom did not mention that the younger man's attitude had taken a complete about face since his comments that morning. It was obvious that Frank was uncomfortable with, and knew precisely what, the young woman was doing and it had little to do with clearing the remains of the meal.

Tom finished his meal and placed the wooden plate on the ground. "Pay attention, Frank. They came into our camp and could have easily killed us; they didn't. We were completely out of food, and we are now eating quite well." He nodded his head toward the teepee behind them. "We have protection from the rain, and we didn't have to set it up. As long as we travel with this group, we will not be killed by another group unaware of our great worth. If we take our time, we can probably leave these people with a packhorse loaded with food. Count your blessings."

Frank smiled. "Our great worth?"

Tom smiled in return. "All a matter of one's point of view."

Frank placed his plate on the ground and the girl rose, collected both plates, smiled at Frank and left.

"Mighty pretty gal," Frank observed. "But she's damn young. Too damn young fer marryin'. Me too."

"There probably isn't a woman in camp over fifty," Tom observed. "They marry young and die young. The men are permitted to marry when they become warriors, which you have done by fighting Hank and Seth. On top of that, you're a rich man."

"How yuh figure that?"

"Red Shirt tells me there were five horses in the grove where Hank and Seth and their partners met their end. The saddle and horse you have been riding are yours as well as a packsaddle and another horse. The spoils of war."

Frank stared at Tom for a moment before he asked, "What'd you get?"

Tom made a dismissive gesture with one hand. "I already have all I need." Then added hastily, "Except provisions."

"So the horses an' saddles 'r our share an' yur givin' it t' me," Frank concluded. He picked up a small twig and began poking the dirt. "Ain't hardly right."

Tom produced his tobacco pouch and began to load his pipe. "I have horses, which are presently receiving the rest and food they have needed for several days. You didn't have horses, and the only other thing we require is food."

Frank broke the few minutes of silence. "'We, huh? 'Bliged."

"No obligation," Tom responded. "Except that you look after them, as I know you will."

The young Blackfoot woman appeared before them again with a mug made from Buffalo horn in each hand. She handed one to each white man and sat on Frank's left as before.

Tom sipped the steaming liquid. "Tea," he observed. "A little bitter, but somehow the perfect thing. A very good woman you have there."

Frank almost choked and did manage to spill some tea. He cursed at length and added, "She ain't muh woman, damn it!"

"As I said, I'll try to straighten this out with Red Shirt."

Frank wasn't paying attention. His gaze was on the hunters gathered near a large fire at the center of camp. "Here comes trouble," he observed.

Tom looked up to see Lame Dog bearing down on them. As the warrior drew near he began to shout in the Blackfoot torque, and then stopped before the young woman. As quick and as hard as the kick of a horse, the back of his hand struck the girls cheek, driving her into the dirt as he bellowed.

Lame Dog drew his foot back to kick the girl, but stopped with that foot in the air. As if by magic, the muzzle of an Army Colt revolver was pressed against his face just below his right eye.

Those who had been moving rapidly toward the commotion stopped in mid-stride. The noise made by the camp preparing for the feast and celebration of the hunt abruptly ceased.

Tom Brash was the first to find his voice. "Let us all calm down," he said, stepping around and in front of Frank. Slowly he put his fingertips against the barrel of the revolver and pressed it away and down.

With the gun no longer pointed at his head, Lame Dog began to swell up like a bullfrog with much to say. Red Shirt stepped forward, speaking softly. While he spoke, the war chief gently pressured the warrior away from Frank.

Calmly and quietly, Tom said, "Put the pistol in the holster, Frank. Go back and sit before our lodge."

Frank cursed as he sheathed his weapon. "Son o' bitch makes a move agin'. . ."

"This is by no means over," Tom interrupted. "The young lady may have, or perhaps it appears she has, committed some wrong in the eyes of the camp. I expect Lame Dog has committed a wrong by striking her in public. And you, an outsider, have almost cost the tribe one of those who supply food and protection. Go and sit down, as I suggested, and we will soon see where this will lead."

Frank grunted and grumbled, but did as instructed.

Tom turned to see Red Shirt and Lame Dog in animated, if somewhat subdued discussion. Lame Dog seemed to have recovered from looking at death for some of his usual air of bravado had returned. When the discussion was completed, Red Shirt turned and stepped toward Tom as Lame Dog crossed his arms and stared at the white men, his eyes full of hate.

"This is not a good thing, my friend," Red Shirt said in French.

"There were several things here that where not good," Tom responded. "Do you speak of the mistreatment of the young girl, or the need for a visitor to stop this mistreatment?"

The concern in Red Shirt's eyes flickered for a moment, and then he said, "Lame Dog has demanded his honor be restored."

"His honor?" Tom asked. "Is there any honor for a man—a warrior—who beats a child?"

Red Shirt studied the white man for a moment. "He is the brother of the girl's mother. She has no father. The girl must follow."

Tom studied Red Shirt's face. The war chief's expression was stony, but Tom did not feel he was looking into the eyes of an enemy. "This is your custom."

"It is our way. But I agree Lame Dog has not done it well." He held his hands out, palms up. "Perhaps I only see this because he has caused me trouble."

Tom was afraid to ask the question, for he had an idea what the response would be. Finally, he continued. "So, what must be done?"

"Lame Dog says the insult must be wiped out. He will fight Shoots Quick until there is no more insult."

"Unto the death," Tom responded. It was not a question.

Red shirt shrugged. "Is there another way to remove an insult?"

Chapter 22

An idea was beginning to form in Tom's mind. He motioned Red Shirt to follow and the two men walked between the lodges and out onto the prairie. "This fight will be with what weapons?" he asked.

"It is Lame Dog who is insulted. He will choose knives."

It was as Tom had suspected. Few men could match the boy with a firearm, and certainly no one in the village. However, with a knife almost any warrior would kill him. Tom doubted if the boy had any experience in hand-to-hand fighting, and he certainly didn't have the size or strength. On the other hand, Lame Dog was probably very experienced. He was certainly strong. "Lame Dog is insulted because Frank has interfered with his handling of the girl. Is this correct?"

"Oui," Red Shirt replied. "He is her mother's brother, and the eldest male of the family. It is his duty to protect the girl, and no one else must interfere."

"He is not insulted because Frank pointed his pistol in his face?" Tom asked.

Red Shirt's eyes twinkled. "That also may be true, but Lame Dog must not admit this. A warrior must face death and laugh at it."

Tom stopped and turned to face the war chief. "I do believe I am insulted," he announced.

"You?"

"Yes. In our group of two, I am the elder. It is I that must teach Frank, Shoots Quick, the proper way to treat other people. It is my duty to see that he knows how to behave while we are with the great people who have been our hosts and brothers. I have taught Shoots Quick to treat the woman in Talking Sky's village as he would treat his own sister or mother. But by his actions, Lame Dog has suggested that my people are no better than dogs. He is saying that my people would steal a maiden from our hosts and brothers. This is a great insult."

As Tom spoke, Red Shirt's puzzled expression turned into a smile. "You have been greatly injured," he responded. "I must explain this to the village. When the fight with Shoots Quick is over, Lame Dog must face Voice from Above."

Tom shook his head. "No. The insult to me came first. Lame Dog berated the girl because he did not trust us to care for her. It was only after this that Fra...Shoots Quick drew his pistol and interfered. Therefore, it is my wound that must be healed first, before the wound of Lame Dog."

Red Shirt nodded. "And it is your choice of weapons and you will choose pistols."

Tom could not imagine that. With a rifle he was a better than average shot but with a pistol he worked hard to be only fair. He would have to be close enough to Lame Dog that both of them could die. "No. I care not for the weapon. Lame Dog may choose as he wishes."

"But he will choose knives."

Tom nodded. Red Shirt had already suggested that knives would be the choice.

"He is very good, and very strong," Red Shirt warned.

"I expect he is," Tom admitted. He began to walk slowly toward the village.

"This is not good," Red Shirt said. "The boy does things too quickly, without thinking. If you are not there to protect him, he will not survive."

"And if I allow Lame Dog to fight the boy?"

Red Shirt shrugged. "If the strong survive they will help to make others strong."

Tom smiled. "Survival of the fittest."

"Nes pa?"

"In England, across the sea in another land, there is a man who is teaching this idea. There are many leaders who say that he is wrong."

"This is silly," Red Shirt responded. "It has always been so. The strong defeat the weak. The strong make stronger children. It has always been so. And it should be so now."

"I think you are my friend, Red Shirt. I know you are worried about me, but perhaps you should worry about Lame Dog?"

"I have seen him fight."

"Yes. I am sure you have."

Chapter 23

News of the challenge had traveled to every ear. The entire village was grouped near the large pile of wood that had been earlier set for a festival and would now cast light on a battle. With Frank between them, Tom and Red Shirt walked through the hushed throng to the open area in the center.

The area set for the battle was about thirty feet in diameter. On one side the fire had been lit and was licking its way into the wood. This seemed a waste to Tom for the fire would have burned down by the time the sun fell below the horizon. It must be a ceremonial thing, he decided, for no one could expect the fight to last from late afternoon until dark. The people of the village formed a semicircle, the fire at both ends of that arc. On one side of the circle, the fire to his right, stood Lame Dog, his exposed flesh glistening with grease and highlighting the bulges and ripples formed by his muscles. On the other side, the fire on his left, Tom had a long, woolen coat draped over his shoulders.

Red Shirt stepped forward and spoke in his native tongue. Lame Dog replied and for several moments the two warriors appeared to be arguing. Tom suspected that much of what was being said was for the benefit of those listening, and had little to do with improved communication between the two participants.

Another voice spoke from the crowd. Talking Sky stepped forward, his open hands held high. He made a short statement and his hands dropped.

Red Shirt turned from the confrontation and reverted to French. "Talking Sky agrees. It is Voice from Above who suffered first insult. When the matter is settled between you and Lame Dog, then the matter with Shoots Quick will be settled. You have the choice of weapons."

Tom shook his shoulders and the wool coat fell to the ground. Under it he wore only his high boots, pants, and a belt around his waist, which held up a sheathed knife. His exposed torso glistened with bear grease slathered on by Frank at the suggestion of Red Shirt.

His two aids had been somewhat surprised when Tom removed his shirt. It wasn't so much the wicked white line of scar that ran down his left arm from shoulder to elbow or another from right shoulder to left hip but rather the tightness of his skin. What Frank thought of as a "fat" teacher was nothing of the kind. He was very square, but not as soft as they had suspected. In fact, the tenderfoot was in very good shape. There was, however, no sign of the rippling muscles such as could be seen under the skin of his warrior opponent.

Calmly, Brash drew the twelve-inch blade from the sheath at his waist and stepped into the circle. His heels came together and his head and shoulders bent forward in a quick bow.

Lame Dog smiled, dropped into a crouch and shuffled forward on bowed legs. The knife that he had held along his thigh came up and weaved back and forth like the head of snake about to strike.

Tom held his knife near his thigh, but out a few inches, the tip pointing at the ground. As Lame Dog shuffled to his left, Tom turned slowly to his right, still standing straight but always facing the warrior.

In the first row of the encircling crowd, Red Shirt could see that the white man would soon die. He stood in one spot, his knife not ready for the attack that would soon come. He was not even balanced for the charge, his feet together.

Beside the war chief, Frank could also see that Tom was not ready for this battle. He wanted to draw his Colt and shoot the Blackfoot, but Tom and Red Shirt had taken his pistol and belt so that he wouldn't do anything rash. To keep his hands busy he hooked his thumbs into the rope that served to keep his pants up.

Suddenly, Red Shirt noticed that something had changed. The white man's feet were spread, the left foot well behind the right. Red Shirt realized that as Tom had turned he had been allowing his feet to spread into a more stable position.

Suddenly, Lame Dog whipped his knife forward at Tom's belly. There was a clang and the two fighters stood facing each other, their knives locked at the hilt.

There was a murmur from the crowd, none of whom realized how Tom had blocked the charge. Although few could understand him, Frank spoke for everyone when he said, "How 'n hell did he get that knife out there so fast?"

Tom smiled, spun his forearm in a swift circle, and jumped back. Lame Dog was left standing alone his knife hand to one side and his torso exposed. Six feet away the still smiling white man resumed his feet-together stance and dropped his chin in another slight bow.

Several in the crowd chuckled. Over the murmur they made, someone could be heard laughing.

Lame Dog let out a blood-curdling scream and charged. Tom jumped aside, slapped his opponent's knife away with his left hand, and swung his right leg at the other man's feet. As Lame Dog stumbled, Tom swung the butt of the knife handle against the base of the warrior's skull.

Lame Dog ducked his head and went into a roll, springing to his feet near the surrounding crowd and facing the white man. He shook his head to clear vision blurred by the blow.

Once again Tom placed his feet side by side and bowed.

A growl grew in Lame Dog's throat and became a roar. He charged across the circle, legs spread, his knife hand well before him.

Swift as a cat, Tom's feet spread and his own knife came forward.

The crowd saw only the flash of steal in the firelight. Several times they heard the clang and crack as the blades met. Then the white man jumped past Lame Dog, who went down.

It seemed that Lame Dog was a little slower rising. When he turned, the watchers saw a long line of blood coming from the upper arm on his knife side. The murmur of the crowd rose to a rumble.

The white man no longer went into his upright stance, but stood with legs spread waiting for Lame Dog. He had a red mark on the back of his hand, but aside from his heavy breathing showed no other signs of combat.

This time Lame Dog moved forward much slower. His breathing seemed no louder than the white man's but he had been working much harder than his opponent. Once again he circled to the left, which forced the white man to turn to his right.

Lame Dog's knife flicked forward. Tom parried with his knife. As the knives touched, Lame Dog's left came forward like the strike of lightning. The dirt on his palm allowed enough grip on Tom's greased, right wrist, and he pulled, releasing enough pressure on the locked knives that he could free his own. His weapon free, he drove it at Tom's exposed stomach.

The noise from the crowd rose to a roar.

It was a good move, and the white man should have been disemboweled. But the move put Lame Dog slightly off balance, his right arm at the fullest extent of its reach.

Tom dropped his knife and spun his wrist within Lame Dog's grip. Grasping the warrior's wrist he spun and turned. Lame Dog stumbled forward and Tom transferred the grip on his wrist from right hand to left, and then jammed the heel of his right into his opponents elbow.

Those near the front of the crowd heard the arm break, even above their own noise.

Tom dropped and rolled away from the falling warrior. When he sprung to his feet, his knife was once again in his right hand. There was an angry red line just under his navel to show how close Lame Dog had been to ending the fight.

On the other side of the circle, Lame Dog also rose to his feet. He too held his knife. But his left arm hung useless at his side. The noise from the crowd was deafening.

"Red Shirt, you need all the warriors you have," Tom shouted in French. "If Lame Dog wishes, I will accept his apology."

Lame Dog's eyes flickered toward the war chief, then back to his opponent. He screamed and charged, his knife held forward like a lance.

Tom slapped the knife aside with his left and made a back-handed slash with his own weapon.

The noise from the crowd suddenly dropped to a murmur.

Lame Dog's momentum carried him almost to the surrounding crowd before he fell. The ground was covered with blood. It appeared he tried to rise, then dropped and remained still. Very quickly the blood stopped flowing from the deep gash in his neck.

Chapter 24

Tom's gaze remained on the body of the warrior. For several moments the crowd was silent, but then whispered conversations began as people looked at the body, then at the victor. Tom turned and walked away, the crowd parting as he approached.

Frank ran up to his partner and threw the heavy coat over shoulders covered in sweat and mud. The only indication that Tom appreciated or wanted the cover was his left hand trying to pull the lapels together. Finally he dropped the knife and held the coat with both hands. Frank stopped long enough to retrieve the weapon.

At the entrance to their teepee, Tom paused, but did not turn, his eyes on the wall of cured buffalo hide. "I need some time, Frank." He stooped and entered.

"Uh, yeah, sure," Frank said to no one. He dropped on the ground near the tent opening and began driving the knife into the earth, cleaning it of blood.

Tom sat alone in the lodge for more than an hour. When they had first entered the Blackfoot camp he had done so only to avoid being eliminated by Red Shirt's warriors. During their stay, however, he had come to enjoy his discussions with the war chief, and considered the man a friend. Now he had killed one of the members of the band, a warrior that the war chief needed to protect and feed his people.

In his mind he saw Lame Dog charging, the picture as vivid as if it were happening again. He saw the tip of his knife slice through the side of the man's neck. He saw the body as a massive river of blood flowed into the dust.

Could he have avoided the fight? Once the battle was joined, was there some way he could have avoided killing? Did he give enough thought to Red Shirt's need for warriors? Did he kill the man because he didn't like him? Did he kill Lame Dog because the warrior reminded him of white men he found equally repulsive? Did he kill him simply because he was a Blackfoot, a people feared more by the white man than any other?

Thomas Brash had often fought, had killed, and had sent men to their deaths. That was war. That was British and other Commonwealth soldiers firing against an opposing force on the field of battle. That was uniformed men firing at available targets or muzzle flashes. That was feeling sorry for the families and friends of comrade and enemy dead while feeling guilty and relieved that he wasn't one of them.

What he had just done was an entirely different thing, with an entirely different churning in his guts when it was over.

The picture he saw in his mind changed to one from more than a decade earlier. Hundreds of bodies lay on the field before him. Many of those bodies were corpses and many more would wish that they, too, had died. While still fighting for life, many of the wounded would soon join those more fortunate comrades whose pain and fear had been cut short by blast, bullet, or saber. Most were even younger than the young Captain Brash, who was also wounded, but would live. The pain of the saber slashes on his arm and back were nothing compared to the pain he felt for having ordered these boys into battle and to their death.

The next scene was from a year later and more than three thousand miles to the east. Fourteen men died trying to protect their major as hundreds of screaming tribesmen came at them in waves. One of those to die was a man whose service to Queen and country had been longer than the entire life of the major.

The third scene was from Upper Canada. He watched as three pine boxes were lowered into the muddy ground. The driving rain threatened to fill the graves before the men standing by with shovels could complete their work. Before the coffins disappeared from view the picture was replaced by a large, frame, farmhouse, flames roaring from every window and door.

Finally he rose, allowed the coat to fall to the ground, and dressed. Stooping and stepping outside he found Frank sitting on a buffalo robe to the left of the lodge entrance while flipping the large knife into the air and watching it drop to the earth.

"Thank you for allowing me some time alone, Frank."

Frank grunted, and then added, "Ain't nothin'."

Tom took a seat next to Frank on the robe and they sat in silence for a moment, save for the swish of the knife flipping through the air and the 'thunk' as it hit the turf. Day was fading fast and the large fire near where Tom had fought was quickly becoming brighter despite the disappearing fuel.

"How gawd damn long we bin trailin' t'gether?" Frank asked, and then flipped the knife again.

"I would have to check my day book to be sure, but I believe it has been twenty-eight days," Tom replied, then added, "Your actions with that knife are beginning to make me nervous. Is it not a little too dark for that game?"

"Maybe is." Frank retrieved the knife and ran the sides of the blade over his tattered pant leg. "Damn near a whole month, an' you left me thinkin' yuh was a teacher."

Tom looked at the young man whose silhouette shone in the firelight. Finally he said, "I believe I mentioned that I had been a soldier. More than once, actually."

"Huh. Paw was a soljer, but he never had no trainin' like you."

"What makes you think I've had special training?"

Frank shrugged. "Plain as the sun on a hot day, way yuh handled Lame Dog. Yuh had yuh some trainin'. An' I bin thinkin' back t' our little shoot-out in the trees. Yuh set that up mighty neat. An' as I recollect, yuh said somethin' 'bout tac'ics. Heard off'cers sayin' that back t' Fort Union."

"Fort Union is an army post?" Tom asked.

Frank shook his head. "'Merican Fur Company. Al'ays soljers 'round, though."

"So, your father worked for the American Fur Company?" Tom asked.

Frank shook his head again. "Soljer. Sergeant. Went off t' fight fer the Union. After a spell they come an' tol' us he was killt. Tol' Maw they'd move us back east, but somehow she was sceered o' that. So she got a job up t' Fort Union. An' yuh still ain't said nothin' 'bout not bein' no teacher."

"Well, I am a teacher," Tom responded, then gestured toward a group of Blackfoot men gathered near the fire. "For the first twenty-six years of my life I was raised to be a warrior in my world. A soldier."

"Why'd yuh quit that an' go t' teachin'?"

Tom smiled. "I thought that was the sort of thing one did not ask out here?"

Frank slapped the blade of the knife into his palm and looked away.

"To answer your question," Tom continued after a short silence, "I found teaching to be very rewarding. For eight years, at least. The basics, primarily, but I did have two students go on to normal school."

"Basics?"

"Reading, writing and arithmetic; the fundamentals of government, history and geography."

"That ain't normal?"

Tom chuckled. "No, well, yes it is, but normal school is for students who wish to advance in other than military studies. Many graduates of normal schools go on to become teachers, or go on to universities."

"So what's this 'bout bein' a soljer?"

"I come from a military background. My father was in the Royal Army, as was his father and his father. I believe I mentioned that. My uncles have all been in the service, on sea or land, for England, Spain, or Germany. It was expected that I, too, would serve in this manner, but I . . . well, I became dissatisfied."

"So yuh went t' teachin'."

"Yes, and I found it most rewarding. One of the main reasons I left the army was to raise a family. I thought that it was more important to be a father and part of the development of my children, an area where my own father was conspicuous through his absence. As appears to be the case with you." He paused for a moment, hoping Frank would add something, but the young man refused to take the bait. "However, my family is gone and all that remains are my students."

"Family?" Frank asked.

For several moments Tom did not respond. Perhaps at another time he might have refused to answer. There had been a time when he thought of little but his family and saw nothing in his imagination but their faces. During the past few months of travel he had managed to drive those images into his subconscious, and resisted anything that might bring them back to their former dominance. However, triggered by the hand-to-hand killing of an Indian warrior, thoughts of his family were once more strong and vivid. "A wife and two children," he said.

"Died, I reckon."

Tom nodded. "Cholera."

During the long pause that followed they listened to the talk around the fire and the distant wailing from the east side of the camp. This wail was joined by a course of blood curdling cries from the group near the fire.

"Death song," Tom noted. "I wondered what was missing. No one was singing a death song for Lame Dog."

"Seems nobody liked him much," Frank responded. "Yur pal had t' go 'round an' hire folks t' sing."

Tom was not particularly surprised by Frank's information. He had seen a few men accompany Lame Dog, but only when it appeared there might be something specific to gain from such association. There was something else about the young man's observation that nibbled at the corner of his consciousness, but he couldn't place his finger on it.

"Off'cer?" Frank asked.

Tom thought of another method that might bring information from Frank and said, "This is not a part of my life that I generally discuss. I have also been led to believe that it is not necessary to speak of one's past, here in the west." He didn't think it necessary to point out that Frank had been one of those who had made that clear. "However, as you have pointed out, our knowledge of each other is sorely limited, despite our association.

"In response to your inquiry, I retired with the rank of major. In the Royal Army this is unheard of at the tender age of twenty-five, twenty-six when I retired. A few people have achieved rank at an early age, General Wolf for example." Tom paused, thinking how he had changed. For ten years he had denied his military history and here he was bragging about it. "But the Crimean stupidity decimated the forces. Not only did I receive two field commissions, but there was no one to take my place when it was over. And I started young, of course."

"Yuh was in a war?"

"Yes."

Frank did not respond to the obvious challenge to add information about his own background, but when it became apparent that Tom was not about to add anything further, Frank took the knife by its blade and held it toward Tom. "This here knife, now, its kind o like my Bowie. Pretty near the same length, but she's kind o got a curve to 'er, an' the back o' the blade's sharp maybe a third o' the way back from the tip. 'Nother thing I noticed, don't seem t' matter how I throw it, she seems to land on the tip. Ain't no Bowie."

Tom took the knife and sheathed it. "It was made to my order in Seville."

"Spanish."

"You've had some geography."

Frank shrugged, and then realized Tom probably couldn't see the gesture. "Listen and learn."

Tom saw it as an opportunity to practice his chosen profession. "For more than four hundred years the Moors occupied most of Spain. They brought many things with them, including knowledge of the working of iron. This knife is the result of perhaps a thousand years in developing the art of making such instruments."

"Reckon that's fine," Frank responded, "but yuh still figure t' head on west, you'd best figure what t' do with the women."

"Women?"

"Lame Dog's sister an' the girl. Gal that brung us 'r meals an' started all this." He waved his finger toward the camp in general. "Talk seems t' have it that they's yurs t' look after."

It dawned on Tom what had bothered him about the information Frank had given him about Red Shirt having to hire mourners. "You speak Blackfoot?" Tom asked.

Frank shrugged. "Word here 'n there. Hear some o' it 'round Union time t' time, an' I been listenin' since we bin here. An' listenin' t' yer Froggy talk with the War Chief."

Tom shook his head. "A year ago I would have given almost anything to have a student who could absorb things that way. It's like a blotter picking up ink. A week in this village and you're already speaking two languages."

Frank grunted. "Be speakin' this here heathen' Injun long time 'fore I'll be talking Frog. You an' that there war chief seem t' use a whole lot a talkin' t' say mostly nothin'."

Tom smiled. "It's amazing that you can pick these things up, but even more so when one considers your prejudice."

Frank cursed. "I'm a real ring-tailed terror," he said, not really understanding what 'prejudice' Tom was referring to. "What 'bout the women?" he asked.

Tom let his breath out in a long, explosive sigh. From his knowledge of some eastern tribes, he could see where it might be true that he was expected to care for those who had been under Lame Dog's protection. Perhaps because the Peigan people believed that to the victor go the spoils, or to the victor goes the responsibility. From what he had seen of these people, he expected the latter would be the case in this instance.

"Well, that's something we'll have to stop. Somehow."

"What's this here 'we,' Englishman?"

"All right then, I. And I may be a subject of the British Crown, but I was born in the Canadas."

"Can't see nothin' wrong with some gals comin' 'long t' cook an' such."

Tom shook his head. Frank was expressing an attitude that seemed to be growing stronger, despite changes in the world that had been brought on by the actions of people like Queen Victoria and Florence Nightingale. "There are several things wrong with it, Frank. One, we will be unable to outrun pursuit such as we did a few weeks ago. We could be trapped in the mountain passes, and instead of two of us freezing to death, there will be four. But most important, these women have a life here with the prospect of children who will become part of their society. If they come with us it will be to a new world, a new society, and the eventual death of all they have known. And of themselves."

"On'y women," Frank protested. "Injun women, at that. 'Sides, our way's 'l wipe 'em out anyways."

"Who's way? Mine or yours?"

"Yuh know what I mean. White man's ways. More 'fficient."

"From your use of the word efficient I can only assume you have been listening to some damn fool. At this particular moment we are living in an Indian house, eating Indian food, by an Indian fire. It appears that our ways have been inefficient, so we have been forced to resort to other means."

Tom paused, realizing that he was becoming upset, and making an effort to control his anger. "These are people, and their women are people. Their world is different than ours, but it is still a working world."

"Dam'est thing I ever heard," Frank responded. "Next yuh'll be wantin' 'em t' vote!"

"That time will come," Tom responded. "Perhaps not for another hundred years, but it will come to pass.

"And how can you say they are so very different?" Tom asked. "As long as Lame Dog appeared to be strong he had followers. As soon as he's dead, all those followers suddenly disappear. Seems to be the same politics we put up with in Kingston, or your people have in Washington."

Chapter 25

Tom was loading his pipe when Red Shirt appeared from behind the guest lodge. Holding his pipe and tobacco in one hand, Tom gestured toward the buffalo robe with the other.

"I can not stay," Red Shirt responded, then inclined his head toward the fire. "I must see to the last journey of Lame Dog."

Tom looked to the fire, at the ground, and then at the war chief. "I am sorry, my friend. I have cost you a warrior."

"It is a strong thing to fight man to man," Red Shirt responded, also looking toward the fire.

"Your command of the French tongue is not as good as I had thought. Strong is not the word I would have used."

Red Shirt shifted his gaze to the white man, eye to eye. "I do not understand the white man. I have killed many men in battle, and it is good. If we do not kill our enemies, they will kill us, and then our children. Some white men are only happy when they kill my people and you . . . it is like you have killed one of your . . . " His voice trailed away, and then he added. "It is easy to die. It is harder to live."

There was silence for a moment, and then Tom rose, looked the war chief in the eye and said, "Please sit down."

Frank rose and moved away into the dark as the two men sat. When they were comfortable, sitting cross-legged on the robe, Red Shirt returned to the subject. "This is not the first man you have killed." It was not a question.

"No, but those times before, always in battle. This time I have killed a warrior of your people. A warrior that my friend Red Shirt will need to protect his people."

Tom remembered the tobacco pouch in his hand and resumed the loading of his pipe. "In my world we are taught that we should care for our brothers," he said.

From under his blanket Red Shirt also produced his pipe. "It is the same with us. We must help each other if our village is to grow and be strong. But it is not for me to live the life of Lame Dog. When he stays within the laws of our people, I must support him, but I do not live his life."

"And you do not take his life, for he is a strong arm in your defense," Tom responded, and then passed his tobacco to Red Shirt. Switching to English he called out, "Frank, could you go to someone's fire and borrow a light for our pipes?"

"Sure 'nough," Frank responded, and walked from the dark on his errand.

Tom reverted to French and continued. "I am upset that Lame Dog died. As you know, at the end I tried to stop it. You can not afford to lose warriors."

"This is true," Red Shirt admitted. "When we are hunting, we need every hunter if our children are to live through the cold times. Our enemies are many, and when they come to take our women, our horses, and our lives, we need each good fighter. But sometimes good hunters cost more than what they supply. Sometimes good warriors start more wars than they finish.

"At the end, Lame Dog knew that you did not wish to kill him."

"He spoke French?" Tom asked.

Red Shirt shrugged. "It is not needed to understand what you said to me. But he could not live with the shame of being beaten by a weak, white man, even though he knew he could not beat you with a broken arm. So he charged, knowing that you would do what the Great Spirit wants you to do. To live."

Frank returned with a flaming brand and placed it in the nearby fire pit. Both Frank and Red Shirt lit slivers of wood and touched them to their pipes.

Frank stood near for a moment, and then faded into the dark.

They drew on their pipes for several moments. Finally Red Dog rapped the ash from his into the fire pit. "Lame Dog did die at your hand," he said, "but not because of you. He died because he did not think ahead, and because he was lazy."

"He was thinking ahead far enough to outwit me on more than one occasion," Tom responded. "He came very close to leading me into serious mistakes, even though my training is, or was, far superior to his. As for being lazy, he seemed to be working quite hard to kill me."

"I have not said it well. . . ." Red Shirt shrugged. "He did not have his own vision. He thought only that he would be war chief, for he was a great fighter. But a war chief must know when not to fight so that his people always win. And many other things. But he was too lazy to learn these things that he did not understand. Instead he thought only to be rid of the war chief and fill his place.

"He did not care that Laughing Brook had eyes for a young man. If she was to go with a man, perhaps she would take her mother to the new wickiup, and Lame Dog would not have to care for the woman of his brother. It is true that he would not like this new husband to be a white man, but, even so, it would make things better for him. He did not attack the girl in front of this lodge because he cared about the time she spent here. He attacked her because he thought the white men would fight.

"It was I who brought Shoots Quick and Voice From Above into our village." Red Shirt struck his chest with a closed hand. "It was I who spoke for them in council." Once again he struck his chest. "It was not Laughing Brook or the white men who Lame Dog attacked outside this lodge, but Red Shirt. And when Voice From Above stepped forward, it was good for Lame Dog, for he could accuse my guests of destroying the families of our village. He could blame me for bringing the sickness to our people. He could banish me and become war chief, at the same time proving what a great warrior he was by killing two weak, white men. He was too lazy to understand that a killer is not a warrior, and a warrior is not a war chief. It is easier to earn a place at council by a life of work than by trying to kill two white men."

Red Shirt stood. "All that was the property of Lame Dog is now yours. Laughing Brook is to be the woman of a Kainai warrior, and she must be kept ready for this joining." Red Shirt paused to allow Tom to think about what he had just said, and then added, "His horses are your horses, his lodge is your lodge, and his sister, Looking Back, is your woman."

Suddenly, Tom sensed a way for him to maintain his sense of Victorian propriety. "I will try to be a good brother to her," he reasoned, "but after the killing of her brother, her husband's brother, it would be best if a few days should pass before I take his place in her life."

Red Shirt almost allowed himself to smile. This was a strange white man. "Perhaps Looking Back will be your sister, perhaps not." He moved toward the fire, and then turned back. "You fought very well today. How did you learn these things?"

"I was raised to be a warrior in my world. A soldier."

Red Shirt nodded. "You learned well." He turned, and walked away.

Chapter 26

Tom dropped off to sleep immediately that night. It was not restful however, but broken by dreams of cavalry charging into heavy artillery fire, a farmhouse near Kingston going up in flames, and a charging Blackfoot warrior. A thin band of gold on the eastern horizon greeted him when he stepped from the guest lodge.

At first he was disoriented. Instead of two dozen lodges, he saw only half a dozen in the early light. Then he saw people packing horses and travois. Off to his right, two women were rolling a lodge cover into a tight bundle. With the coffee pot and his one remaining bar of soap he walked off to the stream.

When the water was boiling he dropped a handful of coffee into it, replaced the lid, and stuck his head into the lodge. "Time to roll out, Frank."

It was perhaps thirty seconds before Tom's call was answered by a long string of curses. "What's yer damn hurry?" Frank added.

"The women are striking camp. They'll want to take our lodge away soon. You may find yourself dressing in the great outdoors."

When Frank stepped outside, still tucking in his shirt, Tom handed him a cup of coffee. The sun had not yet broken over the hills to the east, but there was plenty of light.

"Over t' Union, folks call 'em lazy Injuns" Frank observed. "Shiftless an' such. But when they gets after doin' somethin' they get downright sudden."

Tom shrugged. "Their ways are not ours."

Tom guessed that the woman approaching them had seen only a few less years than he. It was hard to judge with these people, but he guessed her to be about thirty, and although she had the warrior look to be found in the faces of all her people, she was quite handsome. She placed two wooden bowls by their fire, smiling coyly but never looking directly at Tom. She turned and walked away as silently as she had arrived. He realized that the woman's smile turned her from handsome to very pretty.

Tom's gaze was on the departing woman as Frank inspected one of the bowls.

"Sum bitch," Frank exclaimed. "Kind o like boil oats."

"Porridge we call it," Tom said as he picked up the other bowl. He tasted it and added, "It's not porridge, but certainly some sort of boiled seed."

They ate in silence for a moment, and then Tom asked, "Perhaps you could retrieve our horses once you've eaten?"

Frank nodded. "Quite a bunch of 'em, now."

With other things on his mind, Tom had not been thinking about their growing herd, but now realized that the young man was right. They had his original three, two more from the white men killed in the trees, plus whatever animals had been the property of Lame Dog.

"While you are bringing in the horses, I'll try to find Red Shirt," Tom said. "We have two saddles from those killed in the hills. Pick out the one you prefer for yourself and we'll give the other to Red Shirt. I'll also offer our animals for use in packing the extra meat."

Frank entered the lodge, threw the two saddles outside, and then followed them. "This here's an ol' Army saddle,'," he said, touching one with his toe, an unnecessary observation since it was clearly stamped with the CS of the now defeated southern states. "Folks see me on that they's likely t' think I'm a Reb. One t' give t' the war chief. Other one's a stock saddle. Ain't very old, neither. Maybe someday I'll go t' chasin' cows 'r breakin' horses."

Tom nodded agreement, though due to his own background he thought the Confederate saddle looked more comfortable and would have chosen it despite the markings.

Frank picked a bridle from the equipment and began to move off, then stopped and turned back. "Woman that brung us the gruel?" he said. "She'd be Looking Back, woman Red Shirt was talkin' 'bout. Yours now."

"I can't own a person," Tom protested, but it was to a rapidly disappearing back.

Tom found Red Shirt sitting before his lodge combing his hair. The war chief gestured toward a buffalo robe that lay near and showed signs of someone having just risen from it.

"You will need the horses of Lame Dog to move," Tom observed.

"They are no longer part of the wealth of the tribe," Red Shirt observed, "but it is good that Voice From Above offers them for our use."

Tom had not come with it in mind, but the war chief's response suddenly gave him a way to change his standing concerning the Indian women. "With my people, wealth goes to the closest relative," he observed. "For us, then, the horses should be the property of Looking Back, and therefore, still part of the wealth of the tribe." This was not exactly true, since women in Upper Canada were little better than property themselves.

Red Shirt did not respond while he braided his hair, and then said, "The council must speak of this. For now, I thank Voice From Above for the use of these animals."

"And you must use our other horses," Tom added. "We will need only three to carry our own things. That will leave two animals to carry the extra meat. And, if you will come to the lodge, there is another thing we must speak of."

Red Shirt's black eyes followed the white man as he stood. He tied a strip of rawhide around the final braid to hold the end, and then stood to follow the white man.

As they approached the small guest lodge, Tom could see three riders approaching, one of them Frank. They were herding close to thirty horses.

"While Frank and I halter three of them, perhaps you could ask your young men to take the others where they can be loaded?" Tom asked as he picked up halters and lead shanks.

The Indian ponies did not like the smell of the white man as he moved slowly among them, shifting and turning and making it hard for the three outriders to hold them. His own three horses, however, stood calmly as he approached, and one mare reached out to nuzzle his arm with her nose.

Tom noted that Frank was mounted bareback on one of the horses taken from the white men. "Let that one go with the rest of the herd, Frank. We'll use these three for now."

Slowly, so as not to excite the herd any further, Frank slid from the animal's back and slipped the bridle off.

When Tom had led the three animals from the herd, the two young Indian boys pushed the rest of the herd around the camp to where several women were packing and loading. He dropped the halter shanks on the ground, confident that the horses would not move far, and then approached the pile of gear before the lodge.

"Frank, I think we should do this together," Tom said in English. "Grab the other end of this saddle and we'll present it to him."

As they lifted the saddle, Tom switched to French and said, "This is the saddle made for a white soldier far to the south. It is now a gift to a great warrior in this land, Red Shirt."

"I can not accept it, for I have brought nothing to give in return," Red Shirt objected.

"You have given us food and lodging," Tom responded, gesturing toward the small lodge that was even then being dismantled by three women, "and you have given us friendship."

"Not t' mention 'r lives," Frank added quietly, in English.

Red Shirt's eyes sparkled and his lips twitched, but he did not smile. He took the offered saddle and stepped back. "Red Shirt will remember this gift, and today he will ride it." He turned and walked away.

As the war chief walked away, Tom let the smile fall from his lips, and then let out the breath that he had been holding in a long sigh. "Young man, I do believe you have just pushed our luck." He turned to saddle the horses.

"Little, maybe," Frank responded. "But now we know he un'erstands a little 'merican."

"As opposed to English, you mean?"

Chapter 27

During the time they had lived in the village of Talking Sky, Tom and Frank had been housed in a guest lodge set up on the south side of the camp circle. It was similar in all respects to the family lodges, including having a buffalo-hide wall, but it was slightly more than half their size. Tom could not believe that the village would go to the trouble to carry an extra structure on a hunting trip and suspected it had originally been intended to house White Bear and his family whom Talking Sky had expected to meet in the area. However, when the camp was set up after their first day of travel, Tom and Frank found a full-size lodge in their accustomed place with the 'guest' lodge set up slightly to the rear and east, almost, but not quite, outside the circle formed by the village.

They were only slightly confused by this new location for they were travelers living in a strange world and learning to adjust quickly to changes. They began to lead their animals toward the smaller lodge when Looking Back stepped from the larger structure.

She turned and gestured toward the opening with an outstretched arm. "Lodge—Great Voice," she said in halting English. She swung her other arm toward the smaller lodge. "Shoots Quick."

Suddenly Tom's face felt like it was on fire. His stomach felt much the same as it had when he had stepped between Frank and Lame Dog. He realized that all his efforts to dodge his responsibility for this woman through hints to Red Shirt had been less than effective. Perhaps it would be best to try a more direct approach.

"Is it proper for me to enter this lodge when Lame Dog has only just been sent off to the other world?" he asked

The woman's black eyes leaped to life with the glint of fire. "I ugly? Lodge no good?" She paused, took a deep breath through clenched jaws, and then added. "I cut hair. Burn lodge. Great Voice—many skins. Make new lodge."

"No, no! Stop!" Tom realized that he would have to face up to something he had been sure he could avoid. "We must speak of this. Wait," he added, holding up one hand toward the woman.

Turning to Frank he found the boy wearing a very wide grin. "You may find this amusing, but it will prove devastating for this woman. And more than a little upsetting for our plans."

Frank's smile disappeared but with evident difficulty.

"Please see that the horses are fed," Tom continued, "and then bring them in close for the night. I'm sure we will be moving on again quite early."

"Sure 'nough," Frank responded, taking the reins of Tom's mount. "Yu all get some rest now," he added, turning away. "Don' wanna see yuh too tired fer travelin'."

Tom bit back a reply and let the boy leave, then turned to Looking Back. He held his hand toward the door of the lodge. "With our people, the woman must enter first."

"Make trouble," she responded.

Tom held his ground, his hand still held out toward the entrance.

Looking Back shrugged, ducked, and entered.

Tom found that the rear of the lodge had been rolled up to allow air to flow and light to enter. A single sleeping pallet had been laid, and a fire prepared, but not lit. He sat to one side, well away from the sleeping pallet at the back, and gestured for Looking Back to sit.

"This is a very fine lodge and you are a very pretty woman," he began. "But with my people, man and woman do not, ah, spend the night together unless they are married."

Looking Back swung her hand about the lodge. "My things, your lodge. Your woman."

"That's another thing," Tom continued. "This was the lodge of Lame Dog. Now that he is gone, it should be your lodge."

Looking Back shrugged. "Your things, my lodge. You my . . . . man?"

"Husband," Tom corrected without thinking. "No. I mean, these things of Lame Dog's should now be your things. You should be a rich woman in this tribe. You should have the power to do as you wish."

For perhaps a moment Looking Back stared into the pile of tinder where a fire would be lit to chase away the chill of the coming night. "This way ver' bad. Man bring meat and fight enemy. Woman cook meat, make lodge." She pointed at the roof over their heads. "Is good way. If no one kill enemy, then enemy kill us. Bad plan. Man own lodge and care for woman.

Man die in fight, huh, with the people, then winner has all that comes from one who die. That way, woman always have home. Is care from enemy."

"Is it right to move with a new man when the other has only just died?" Tom asked.

Looking Back shrugged. "Lame Dog not my man," she said. "Brother to my man, my hus-ban. When Cree kill my hus-ban, Lame Dog try be my man, but he not Lame Dog. He what dog leave in pile all over grass. Hit me many time. One more time an' Great Voice not have to fight him."

By reading the glint in her eye as she said this last, Tom found it easy to believe that she would have killed Lame Dog, given the chance, despite what it may have done for her standing in the village.

Suddenly the smile that had startled him before lit up the woman's face. "You 'fraid," she said. "Long time, no woman." She reached over and patted his knee. "Go. Smoke with Red Shirt. Then food ready." She rose, left the lodge, and began to prepare a cooking fire outside.

Tom found Red Shirt's lodge in its usual place on the North West side of the camp circle next to the lodge of Talking Sky. Red Shirt sat on a Buffalo robe in front of his lodge while his women hovered over a fire before him.

"Would my friend join me in a pipe before his evening meal?" Tom asked.

"I would," Red Shirt responded, drawing his pipe forth. "And would my friend join me at the evening meal?"

Tom shook his head as he sat and drew his pipe and tobacco pouch. "I suggested to my friend, Red Shirt, that it would be best if I was to remain a single man, but perhaps he did not hear. Now I must return to my new lodge."

Red Shirt's eyes twinkled as he stoked his pipe. "I am only a war chief. I am prepared to face our enemies even should they be so many as the blades of grass upon the land. We have many enemies, and I have faced them many times. This has taught me many things. I have learned when to fight and when to run." He rose, moved to the fire, picked a small coal with his bare fingers, and dropped it in the pipe bowl. When he had drawn the pipe to life he shook the coal from his pipe into Tom's, and added. "It has also taught me not to stand in the path Looking Back has chosen."

When his pipe was going well, Tom removed it from his lips. "Well, I must return for the meal she is preparing. I expect it would be unwise to miss the first meal."

They each drew from their pipes for a moment, then Red Shirt said, "It is a heavy load you must carry, my friend. She will cook you a meal in your own lodge. She will pack that lodge and see that it is carried to the next camp where she will have another meal for you. Tomorrow she will bring you food during the march, and soon she will make you fine leggings and moccasins to replace these white man rags that you wear. Tonight, when the air is damp and cold, she will warm your blankets. It is a hard thing, I know, but as we reach manhood we learn that life is not always easy."

It was easy for Tom to smile in response, even though there were things on his mind that he could not release. How could he say to his host that he did not wish to stay with his people? How could he explain the dislike Looking Back would face in the white man's world? In his old world he might find a man just like Red Shirt to whom he could confide such worries and many more. Some things he could say to Frank, but his traveling companion was just too young and inexperienced. Perhaps that wasn't exactly true or fair for the boy had gone through things of which Tom, thankfully, knew very little and had not seen. However, Tom was feeling very alone at the moment which, he noted, was particularly ironic since he had come west to be exactly that; alone.

"It is true, my friend," he said. "I have seldom been treated as well, or made to feel as welcome as I am in the village of Talking Sky. But I fear I do little in return. I do not deserve such fine treatment."

"You protect our people and bring us meat," Red Shirt responded. "There is nothing more to be done."

They drew on their pipes for a moment, and then Tom said, "I did not think there were many in the village who spoke English. How is it that Looking Back speaks the language of my father?"

Red Shirt visibly bristled. Tom was trying to think of what it was that offended his new friend and how to counter it when the war chief responded. "Many of my people have some words of the tongues of all our enemies. But many of the Lakota people speak your language for they have been many years with the Long Knives."

"Looking Back is Sioux?" Tom asked. "She is not of your people?"

"She is the daughter of Talking Sky," Red Shirt replied. "When she was no more than two winters she was taken by the people of Man-Afraid-Of-His-Horses. It was more than ten winters after that when we took her back." He pointed with the stem of his pipe to a drawing on the wall of his lodge. It showed a half dozen mounted warriors, some with bows and some with firearms shooting into a group of figures gathered around a fire. "This was near the river called Mary-as by the Long Knives."

"The way has been hard for your people," Tom observed.

Red Shirt shrugged. "We also make it hard for others. It is the way our people live on, and the way of our enemies. But if we make ourselves ready for what is to come, if we have friends like Shoots Quick and Voice From Above, then perhaps we will live through the future, and our enemies will not."

Tom tapped the ash from his pipe and stood. "I am glad that Red Shirt is happy with what I do. Perhaps one day I will also be happy. Good night."

Before Tom had taken two steps, Red Shirt called, "Voice from Above!"

There was a gravely, serious sound to the call, and Tom turned to face the war chief.

"Tomorrow we will travel far," Red Shirt continued, his stare boring into Tom's eyes, "and the day will be very hot." Suddenly his face split into a wide grin such as the white man had never seen on the stoic face. "Try to get some sleep."

As he turned away, Tom found that his grinning face was once again on fire. He also discovered that the cold pit of fear had once again opened up in his belly.

Chapter 28

It was a damp, cold morning, mist obscuring anything outside the camp. It had finally rained and the ground was slick with mud.

Frank saddled their animals but was still not comfortable making up the load for the pack animal, preferring instead to leave that for Tom Brash. Should Tom's goods land on the ground it was better that he, and not Frank, had tied the load.

Tired of waiting in the chill air, Frank strolled casually around the larger lodge where he found Tom sitting by a small fire with a steaming cup in his hand and a peaceful look on his face.

"Good morning, Frank," Tom greeted in his usual calm way. It was hard to tell, but somehow the older man seemed more subdued.

"Didn' think yuh had coffee left," Frank noted.

"A little," Tom responded, "but this is mostly chicory." He grasped the pot and poured some into a second tin cup. "Help yourself," he suggested.

Frank took the cup and sipped, scalding himself, as always, on the rim. He realized that the coffee pot and the cups came from their own gear. The older man must have retrieved them before he woke up. "You bin up a spell," he noted.

Tom's smile was only a flicker. "Most of the night," he admitted, then sipped his own brew.

The night before, Frank had been looking forward to teasing the older man. Perhaps getting in a few ribald jokes and comments about the extent of Victorian principals. But now he felt like an intruder and slightly embarrassed. He squatted down by the fire and sipped the chicory brew.

When they had sat in silence for a few moments, Frank heard movement within the lodge. "Help pack the lodge?" he asked.

Tom shook his head. "They take exception to men interfering in their work. We can help load it on the travois when they're ready." He realized that such a suggestion was completely out of character for Frank. Perhaps some of their conversation was showing some effect.

Frank took another drink. "Packhorse ready t' load," he advised.

Tom set his cup by the fire, nodded, and rose. "Then I suppose I should get to it."

During that second day of the march, Looking Back rode a pony beside the two horses each of which pulled a travois that held all their goods. The girl, Laughing Brook, watched the two draft animals while her mother worked with buckskin on the back of her mount.

Frank had made friends with a young brave who was in charge of the horses and spent most of his time riding with the herd. During the afternoon he rode up to the main body. The early morning rain was only a memory and dust settled around them as he pulled his horse to a walk beside Tom. "Damn woman don' never stop," he said.

Tom glanced back to see Looking Back working away as her mount walked along without direction. "There's always much to do. Woman do all the work of maintaining the village that we have been living in."

"Shouldn' be tough," Frank said. "On'y half as many men as woman. Tougher fer the men t' feed all them mouths."

Tom looked directly at his young partner and realized he had been serious. He thought they had already had this conversation, but apparently Frank didn't understand fully what had been said. Before he could respond, however, Frank continued. "Thought we'd be stoppin' fer the hot o' the day. Did yes'erday." He took the large brimmed hat that had once belonged to a now dead whiskey trader from his head and mopped his brow with the sleeve of his shirt.

"Perhaps they have a specific sight in mind for tonight's camp," Tom suggested.

"Reckon," Frank conceded. "Movin' a town like this, they don' cover near as much groun' as me an' you do by our own selves. Time t' time I 'spect yuh got t push 'er a bit if'n yer gonna get some place. But with all the bodies, the sun straight up, an' the dust, why she gets down right uncomfortable."

They rode in silence for a few moments before Frank added, "Ain't our place t' call the shots, but it'd be nice to know."

"We eat well and travel without fear of attack," Tom noted.

"Not t' mention havin' a nice warm place t' sleep," Frank added with a grin, then turned his mount and rode back toward the horse heard.

Late that afternoon they halted near a small stream. There was good water, two benches of perhaps thirty acres covered with good grass, and a line of trees to break the constant breeze from the west.

There was also a stranger and his horse waiting by a small fire when they rode down the slope. He was a small man, no bigger than Frank, with a battered derby hat pushed back on his head. His clothing consisted of moccasins similar to those worn by the Blackfoot, fringed, buckskin leggings and breechclout, a red flannel shirt covered by a vest made from the hide of a spotted calf. He wore a wide belt from which was slung a holster holding a Colt Army .44. The weapon was easily recognizable since much of the top of the holster had been cut away, and only the hammer thong kept it in place.

Lead by Red Shirt, many of the warriors broke from the moving village and charged the stranger. When almost upon him, many of the younger braves swung from their moving mounts and surrounded the small stranger, smiling, hugging him, and all speaking at once. Tom watched it all with interest but did not feel he should interfere in what appeared to be the greeting of an old and valued friend.

Later, when the camp was set up and the cooking fires working their magic, Red Shirt approached, accompanied by the stranger.

In the accepted manner, something to which he was only now becoming comfortable, Tom remained seated.

"My friend, the great Kainai warrior, Bear Child," Red Shirt announced.

"If he is a friend of Red Shirt he must surely be a great warrior," Tom replied, "and I would be honored if two such men should smoke with me."

Tom had just seen Looking Back tending the pot over the cooking fire, but suddenly she appeared from the lodge with a Buffalo robe that she spread on the grass. The two warriors sat and pulled their pipes from their robes.

As Tom passed his tobacco pouch, he asked, "Does Bear Child speak French?"

"Can hear it," the newcomer responded in English. "Don' speak much."

"That is good," Tom said. "It is always better when people understand each other."

Bear Child finished filling his pipe and passed the pipe to Red Shirt. "Some time I un'erstan' white man an' is not good," he said, and then smiled.

Tom smiled in return, and then said, also in English, "With me it is more often that I don't understand, for I am new to this land. For instance, I do not know the name of your people, the Kainai."

"White man call us Blood injun."

Tom nodded. "One of the peoples who the white men call Blackfoot."

Bear Child nodded.

Tom turned his gaze to Red Shirt and returned to French. "I am sorry, my friend. I do not wish to leave you out of the talk."

Red Shirt finished lighting his pipe and shrugged as he passed the lighted twig to Bear Child. "It is better that our guest is made welcome."

They sat in silence, the warriors smoking while Tom filled and lit his own pipe. Finally, Red Shirt said, "Bear Child brings us bad news. The traders of fire water come this way. The Long Knives come with them."

"They will not come into this land," Tom said, but knew it would not have been a subject of discussion unless Red Shirt was concerned.

"Mad 'bout trader you kill," Bear Child advised. "Man call himself Colonel push 'em. Make so'jers come until they find bad Injun an' kill 'em."

Chapter 29

They smoked in silence for a few moments while Tom considered both the information and what it might mean. It was the type of thing he had feared. These people had saved his life, fed him, sheltered him, and now he slept with one of their woman. Although they might see him as being different from the Long Knives, he still knew he was white. The American troopers were white. He had no wish to be between the two.

"What is it you wish of me?" he asked in French, mentally cringing at the response.

"We have many enemies," Red Shirt responded, "and every day our village is smaller. If we have more enemies, even more of our people will die. But when our enemies attack, we must fight them, or we will be no more.

"For many years we have tried to stay north of the medicine line, for the Long Knives do not follow us here. Now Bear Child tells us that this line will no longer protect us. But you are a white man. One time you were a soldier for the Great White Mother. Is there some way to stop the Long Knives from coming into this land?"

Tom nodded and smoked in silence until his pipe was empty. As he tapped the ash out he asked in English, "How many?"

Bear Child flashed his fingers three times. "Thirty so'jer," he flashed his fingers once, "ten trader."

Tom had not met many Indians who used numbers in this way and was mildly surprised. "Surely they don't expect to face the Blackfoot confederacy with only forty men?" he asked.

"People all spread out," Bear Child said. "Many small family. People of Talking Sky many days ride from their brothers. They know it is village far to the east of their own land who kill traders. Catch 'em before they get back."

Tom reverted to French. "This is not your country?" he asked Red Shirt, mostly to stall for time since he already knew the answer.

"All our country," Red Shirt responded.

Tom almost smiled, but stopped himself in time. "And who else claims it as their country?"

Red Shirt's eyes twinkled. "Many peoples."

"Many people claim this land, but only Cree have many numbers," Bear Child interjected in English.

"So, forty men plan to attack twenty warriors and their families," Tom concluded in French. He looked around at the camp. It was not a good position to defend against trained cavalry. "You are sure they will come north of the border, the medicine line?"

"The trader Coleman say he is now chief in this land. So'jer can come because he ask them."

Brash was not particularly surprised that someone was laying claim to the area. Red Shirt had already recounted how Coleman had approached the Blackfoot for support, but there was other support for such a story. For some time the Hudson Bay Company had expressed a desire to give up some of its responsibility in Rupert's Land, particularly the area in the south where they harvested few furs. Eventually, someone was bound to take advantage of the perceived absence of leadership. "Are they close?" he asked.

Bear Child shook his head. "Ride today from Fort Benton. Seven, maybe eight day."

"And how will they find the people of Talking Sky?"

Bear Child shrugged. "On'y so many river. Follow trader trail north to Milk River, then along it to east. No see village or dust, wait at Pakowki Lake."

"How far is this lake?" asked Tom.

Bear Child shrugged again. "Maybe one day more."

"So we can meet them somewhere on the Milk River," Tom concluded. He reverted to French. "Something may be done," he said. "I will have to form a plan. We have time, so let me think on this, and at tomorrow's camp we will study my maps together."

Bear Child nodded. "It is good," he said, making a horizontal slashing motion with his hand to indicate the subject was closed. He stood, said, "I go now," turned and walked away.

"He has many friends in our village," Red Shirt said, then sucked on his long-dead pipe, tapped the doffle from the bowl, and sucked on it again. He started to put it away, then rubbed the bowl and sucked on it again. Finally, he said, "A promise was made to Bear Child."

"My friend appears anxious," Tom noted. "There is a problem with this promise you speak of."

"Many of the horses you now have were given to the man who once owned them for the hand of Laughing Brook."

Lame Dog promised his niece to Bear Child and was paid a bride price of several horses, Tom concluded without actually saying it for he new that some people made a point of not speaking a dead person's name. "Is there some reason why this promise should not be kept?" he asked. "If your people are unhappy with this union, perhaps the horses should be returned to Bear Child."

"It is not the people who must be happy," Red Shirt responded, "it is Voice From Above."

"It is not my place to interfere." As he said it, however, Tom wondered if the girl had any desire to be married to the homely little Kainai warrior.

"Shoots Quick has sat with the girl," Red Shirt noted. "This was the cause of a battle to the death. Perhaps Voice From Above would like this union better than one with Bear Child."

I can think of few things I would like less, Tom thought to himself, but said, "It is not my place to decide this. I will speak with Frank, Shoots Quick, and with the girl and her mother. When I have spoken with them, I will speak to Red Shirt."

"And I will speak with Bear Child," Red Shirt added. He rose and walked away to his own lodge.

After their evening meal, Frank and Tom sat near the fire drinking some kind of herb tea and quietly enjoying the sunset. Looking Back stopped beside Tom, her eyes down, and said, "I wish . . . speak Great Voice."

"Certainly," Tom said, but the woman had already walked on and was entering the lodge. He rose and followed her.

Inside the lodge, Looking Back stood with a bundle in her arms. When Tom stood straight, having crouched to enter, she shook the bundle loose to reveal fringed leggings, hunting shirt, and breach clout. "I make for husban," she said.

Tom reached out and took the clothing. This is what the woman had been working on all day. The buckskin was soft as velvet. "Looking Back, this is a wonderful thing you have done. I will be proud to wear the work of your fingers."

"You put on," she ordered. "White man things wore out."

When Tom returned to the fire and his tea, he was dressed the same as the warriors except for his wide brimmed hat. He carried another bundle of buckskin in his arms.

Frank set his cup down and cursed with a great deal of force and color. "Yuh sure by damn fittin' in," he declared. "Even got fancy beaded moc'sins. Finer 'n anybody else in the village."

Tom leaned over and set the bundle of skins on the younger man's outstretched legs. "Then we'll both be the fashion leaders of the camp," Tom informed him. "She made a similar set for you. This should be particularly thrilling for you. My clothes—white man's clothes, as she calls them—are worn out, but yours are non-existent."

Frank jumped up and shook out the garments, holding them up in front of himself. His grin spread from ear to ear. He almost tripped over his tea cup, spilling it. Quickly he stooped to pick up the moccasins that had fallen to the ground and were in danger of soaking up the tea.

"Looks like they'll fit," he said.

"I'm sure they will" Tom said. "They were made for you. Mine fit and feel wonderful. But the way to find out is to run over into your little lodge and try them on."

Chapter 30

The ride to Pakowki Lake was another long push without a midday stop. Once again Frank rode away from the horse herd and up beside Tom.

"Hotter 'n hell," Frank said.

"I'm sure I was there once and it wasn't this hot," Tom responded.

Frank swung his gaze around to where Looking Back was still riding and sewing. "What's she doin' now?" he asked

"Probably making another outfit for us. Plus we will need high-top moccasins and outer moccasins for the cold weather to come."

"Too damn hot t' be thinkin' 'bout cold. . . ." Frank stopped. "Fer us? Yuh mean she's makin' some fer me? Ain't never had but one set o' clothes in muh whole damn life."

"Well, that really hasn't been all that long," Tom noted. "All the same, it is time you learned to give some thought to what is over the next hill."

Frank looked at him for a moment as their horses shuffled along. "'Nother hill," he said.

Tom smiled. "No. What I mean is, you should give some thought to what you are going to wear when your present attire is dirty, or ripped, or simply worn out."

Frank fingered the sleeve of his hunting shirt. "Reckon I'll get me some Blackfoot woman t' make me some more. Ain't never bin togged out like this. Hell, ain't never had a whole suit made for me neither."

Tom knew that Frank had no intention of staying longer than necessary among the Blackfoot and was only trying to cause unnecessary worry so he refused the bait. Instead he asked, "That reminds me, do you have designs on the girl?"

Frank's expression became puzzled again. "Huh?"

"Laughing Brook."

"I figured yuh was talking 'bout her, I just don' know what yuh mean by de-signs."

"Do you plan to move her things into your lodge," Tom said. "I suppose I mean to ask if you intend to marry the girl, although the Peigan notion of marriage does seem to differ somewhat from mine."

"Hell, no! Whatever would give yuh that idea? Be a lot o years 'fore I get hitched. Kind o pretty an' all, an' I sure do get t' feelin' randy when she gets up close, but I'm kind o' partial t' muh scalp, too."

"Good, then she will marry Bear Child," Tom said. "I was hoping you would say that, for I don't think we need any greater commitment to these people than we already have. But some of the tribe thought there was some question about the promises made by Lame Dog since I have taken over in his place."

"Hell, yes. Let's get us on over them mountains an' intu that there gold country. Trade some o' them hosses fer some riggin' an' go to pannin' gold. Muh partner's got him a woman now t' keep the grub comin'. We c'n hunt gold from can see t' can't."

"So you do have a plan for the future," Tom noted dryly.

"Huh. I see what yuh mean 'bout the next hill. But there ain't no plannin' when yur talkin' 'bout gold. Most ever'body wants t' get rich."

"Well, that, as far as it goes, is true," Tom responded. "However, few people can agree on what the actual meaning of rich might be. Is it more important to have gold and jewels, or is the man with companions, contentment, and calm the one to be envied?"

Frank cursed. "Dumb damn question. Man's got him the money he can buy him some calm."

"And how much will that take? A thousand pounds, ah, dollars? A hundred thousand?"

"Yup. Hun'erd thousand aughta do 'er."

"Most people in this world have a dollar or two in their pocket and want the thousands you speak of. Will you be calm knowing that so many people will be trying to take your money away from you?"

They rode in silence for several minutes. "Reckon I don' wanta have t' shoot that many folks," Frank admitted. "Yuh sayin' we hadn't aughta go t' pannin' gold?"

"No, I think it's an excellent idea," Tom replied. "However, it is not my intention to begin such an endeavor with the idea of attaining great riches, but rather for the experience and knowledge that will surely develop. From what I have seen and heard, few of those who work for the gold are the ones who become rich. If they are lucky enough to get a good claim, they may make a very good living as long as the gold lasts, but few become rich.

Those with the first good claims that are sold to big developers, or those who supply the miners are the ones who do well."

Frank cursed. "Well, she's a might late t' be findin' the first claim an' I don' wanta be no store keeper. An' why yuh wanta pan gold if'n there ain't no money t' be had."

Tom spent a few moments thinking of an answer that Frank would grasp. Finally he asked, "Frank, what have you done in your life?"

Frank shrugged. "Ain't done much o' nothin'."

"Frank, you walked alone across a long stretch of prairie where older, experienced men have been killed by the elements. You faced two tough, seasoned killers, and eventually escaped them. You've lived in an Indian lodge, which very few whites have done, and you've hunted buffalo. Perhaps it doesn't mean much to you now, but in a few years it will be quite an exciting memory."

Frank shrugged again. "Well, that all may be so. Maybe someday it's gonna be a story t' tell. But what's that got t' do with anythin'."

"You must have heard people telling stories about the riches they made in the California gold fields."

Frank turned his head to look at Tom, and grinned. "Yuh mean all them stories was just big windies?"

"Oh, they may have panned gold. Some may have made more money in a day than they did doing anything else. But it seems the quantity of gold gets larger with each telling."

"Well, hell, lets move on over them mountains an' pan us some good stories," Frank said, then laughed. "Don' get no gold, least we can put on a good show." He poked his horse with his heels and rode away toward the herd.

Tom watched him ride off, then said aloud, "That's it. That's the answer. Put on a good show."

Chapter 31

While the women set up the village, Tom met with Red Shirt, Talking Sky, and Bear Child. Two other warriors Tom didn't know stood in the group he and Frank approached, but no one introduced him, perhaps too preoccupied with thoughts of the approaching U.S. cavalry to realize that the two white visitors had actually met few of the people they lived and traveled with. Frank stopped and stood alone just outside the group gathered between the camp and the lake.

"We will meet the American soldiers in about two days?" Tom asked in English.

Bear Child nodded, then added, "Maybe three."

Tom drew an east-west line in the dirt with a stick. "This is the Milk River," he said in French, then drew a crescent on the north side of the first line while Red Shirt translated. "We need an area like this," he tapped the curved line at various points, "with high hills all along this line." He put the point of the stick in the center of the half circle near the line that represented the river. "This area should be big enough for a village. Perhaps two villages."

Red Shirt was puzzled. "We do not have two villages," he protested. "Only one."

"We won't be setting up the village there; we only need an area of that size. It would also be nice if this area was not too difficult for the Americans to find and approach." He put the point of the stick on the south side of the line representing the Milk River. "They will be riding the south side of the river?" he asked.

Bear Child nodded. "Maybe scouts on north."

Tom switched to English and spoke directly to Bear Child. "Is there such a place as I describe?"

The Kainai stepped forward and took the stick from Tom. With his moccasin foot he rubbed out Tom's drawing and drew a line toward the east with a jog in it. "Milk run east, then north, then back east and some south." He put the point of the stick just past the point where the river began its run southeast. "There is place you want here." He turned and pointed southwest with the stick. "There. Maybe one day ride with no village."

"Can you and one other warrior ride with us?" Tom pointed at his young partner. "Shoots Quick and myself."

Bear Child looked at him with a puzzled expression. "Only four? No more warrior?"

"We will need more warriors than are here when we meet the soldiers," Tom admitted, "but four of us must be there early to prepare for their arrival. Then one must come back and lead the rest of the village into place so that we can have a proper greeting for these men who visit our country."

Bear Child turned to Red Shirt and spoke in their language. One of the other warriors joined in as Tom stepped back to let them speak without interruption.

"Good Young Man sez you're gonna get two warriors in a trap," Frank said quietly. "Sez the Long Knives'll kill the two warriors in place o' the whiskey traders got killed over t' the Cypress Hills. Red Shirt's on your side, an' Bear Child sez yuh got somethin' up yer sleeve an' he's fer givin' it a go. Think that done it. Seems this Bear Child fella swings a pretty big stick here 'bouts."

The four warriors turned to Tom and he stepped forward.

"Voice From Above, we will hear your plan," Red Shirt said. "Then we will decide."

"My plan is very rough," Tom admitted, again in French. "But the soldiers have broken the laws of the Great White Mother. They know that and it will be bothering them. We will use that against them. This means nothing to the traders, but if we can turn the soldiers and traders against each other, we may have a chance. I will try to do this thing as the soldier of one nation—as the soldier of one people talking to a soldier of another people."

He stopped, looked out over the lake, and then shook his head. He had only the vaguest of plans, and it would all depend on how willing the American soldiers were to communicate. Would they all be veterans of the civil war, tired of battle, and eager to avoid a fight? Would they all be young, depending on the traders for whiskey, and willing to do anything to support them?

"I will need the help of forty warriors," Tom advised, then began drawing his line and half circle again.

Bear Child and Red Shirt spoke at the same time, one in English and one in French to say that there were only twenty three warriors.

Tom put the point of his stick near the straight line that represented the river. "I will be here so the soldier chief must come to meet me. Red Shirt's warriors will be here," he put the stick on the curved line, "too far away for the soldiers to see them clearly. If they are dressed like warriors, and look like warriors, the soldiers will think they are warriors."

Bear Child grinned.

Movement in camp woke Tom. He had first learned about the Blackfoot guards by seeing someone moving about in camp, and he now slept right through it. But this was different. It sounded like several people. He rolled from the pallet of buffalo hides, rose, and dressed.

Stepping out of the lodge he looked up at the big dipper to see that it was well after midnight. The night was very dark, the only light from the distant stars. Someone stepped around the lodge. Tom turned, whipping out his Spanish knife.

"It is Red Shirt," the war chief said, his voice low.

"Why is my friend wandering in the night?" Tom asked.

"Running Bull has found one of his scouts dead. He was scalped."

"Cree?"

"Yes. They have been following us for two days. They have come in over the body of the dead scout and will now be close to the village."

"Why would they attack now?" Tom wondered.

"Only they can say," Red Shirt responded. "Perhaps they only now are large enough in number. Perhaps they know of the Long Knives coming and wish to take our scalps before the white man. But they are here."

Tom put his hand on the war chief's shoulder. "Use your men wisely," he counseled. "Shoots Quick and I will hold this side." Then he had another thought. "Do you plan to bring the horses into the circle of lodges?"

"They have been sent for," Red Shirt replied, then disappeared into the night.

With the help of Looking Back, Tom and Frank prepared to welcome their uninvited guests. Frank collected all the .44 rimfire he had for his Spencer, and Tom checked his stock of powder and ball. They made sure Looking Back knew how to load all their weapons.

"Still don't make a lot o sense t' me," Frank commented.

"What doesn't make sense?" Tom asked.

"Forty some people wanderin' around in enemy country, less 'n half of 'em fighters."

Tom shrugged. "I've been giving that some thought. Remember a young fellow putting the muzzle of his pistol in the face of a Peigan warrior? True, it all happened very fast, and with little thought, but was it not a silly thing to do? Were there not several Peigan warriors standing around at the time, more than the number of loads in the pistol? Was there not some pride involved in that action?

Frank nodded. "I reckon," he admitted.

"I believe it is the same with the Peigan," Tom continued. "It's a matter of maintaining their self assurance, pride, whatever you wish to call it. They face very bad odds in their efforts to survive. All of the other tribes, the Americans, everyone is their enemy, and despite the fact that they are a confederacy of three peoples, their numbers have declined. The weather is against them, various diseases imported by whites are killing them, the buffalo are declining in numbers. How can they face such odds? They face them by firmly believing that they are destined to triumph over all things around them. Therefore, they venture out into the Cree country to prove how invincible they are."

"Him that runs away lives t' fight another day," Frank quoted.

"True, and a part of the Blackfoot way of war for generations," Tom said, "or so I have been told. They only fought the Sioux and Cree when they had far superior numbers. Attack at night, at dawn, when the enemy was sick or otherwise hampered; they are famous for this. However, now that they have suffered so much, they seem to be changing many of the old ways simply for the sake of change."

"Ain't too bright," Frank observed.

"No, it probably isn't, but what group of people is not guilty of stupidity? Is it smart for the American North to deny the South the opportunity to sell their crops for the best possible price? Is it smart for the South to attack the North, who has all the industry, most of the transportation and international trade? Is it smart for brother to shoot at brother, and father at son?"

Frank did not respond for some time. They had finished preparing their weapons when he said, "Reckon ain't nobody got a corner on stupid. Folks do somethin' fer pride way over east an' it ain't long for families out this way just disappear."

Chapter 32

With the promise of dawn in the sky, the Cree came from both south and north. The lake was to the west, perhaps fifty yards behind Talking Sky's lodge, and a hill rose to the east. Tom was sure there would be a few Cree on that hill to stop any attempted escape.

The Cree approaching on the south side found no defenders. Someone was surely there and aware of their coming, for the Blackfoot horses milled about within the circle of lodges, only a few of them tied. Something was keeping them within that circle, but all that could be seen was silent lodges. A few robes lay scattered before those lodges. In the dim light of dawn even the lodges appeared flat, as if they were line drawings on a large hide.

The attackers had been watching the village for several days and expected to meet a third of the Blackfoot warriors on this south side. One of the attackers near the center of the approaching line was a white man. The Cree next to him pointed to three other men and gestured toward the closest lodge. The three warriors approached the lodge without a sound. One approached the door to the east. One slid silently to the rear of the dwelling, exposing himself to the inner circle, while the third approached the outer side. The last two lifted knives, ready to cut entrance for themselves. They waited for several moments, then the first brave came out of the lodge and made it clear by his gestures that the lodge was empty. The small lodge to the west and two more were checked in a similar manner. All were empty.

When they saw the horses had been moved, the Cree had expected strong resistance to meet them at the edge of the Blackfoot village. They were not particularly concerned about this resistance, for they knew they outnumbered the dog-dung, Blackfoot, baby-killers two to one. However, here they were within the village and had yet to meet an enemy. It was puzzling.

The leader waved his men on into the camp.

Suddenly, the buffalo robes scattered about erupted. Near the first lodge checked, a white man in buckskin and a Blackfoot woman were exposed. The white man rolled up onto one knee as he swung his weapon in line and fired. Much of the hastily fired shotgun blast passed between the Cree leader and the white man, but several thirty-caliber balls cut into them. The white man died instantly from a ball in his brain and the Cree bled to death within minutes.

Tom drew back the hammer on his Colt shotgun, swung the muzzle, and fired again. There were few defenders on this side, and he knew the survival of the village depended on his efficiency. Concentrating on his task, he was only vaguely aware that there was firing all around him. He was not aware of the firing from the other side of the village, and probably could not have heard it anyway over the din he and his companions were making.

There were only four defenders—Tom, Frank, Bear Child, and Running Bull—on this side of the village. The decision had been made because all four had repeating weapons and would, for the most part, be facing muzzleloaders, knives, and hand axes. Looking Back would re-load for Tom and Laughing Brook for Bear Child.

Frank levered five shots through his Spencer before the attackers were too close for effective use of the rifle. He dropped it and drew his Colt. Everything was happening too fast. Of his five rifle shots he was only sure of two hits, a fact that made him angry. He tried to do better with his Colt, but his frustration and excitement didn't help his aim.

Bear Child ignored his rifle and started with his pistols. The two Colts spoke alternately, more often scoring a hit than a miss. Laughing Brook sat on her legs beside him, a fully loaded cylinder in each hand. She was ready to pass them to Bear Child when needed but had a hard time making herself concentrate on that task. She wanted to drop the cylinders and pick up the loaded rifle. She would have been ineffective with the weapon for she flinched each time Bear Child fired.

Running Bull had no pistol. He levered his Henry repeater until it was empty, the last few shots from the hip. He dropped the rifle and drew a war axe and a knife.

The attack broke. Five Cree warriors ran from the circle of lodges, running east but on an angle toward the hill. They left twelve of their number and one white man behind.

Tom stopped firing. He had just dropped his shotgun and held the Colt revolving rifle, three shots still in the cylinder. He stayed in that position, one knee on the ground while he leaned on the other, and watched the enemy disappear in the gloom. He became aware of the diminishing fire on the north side of camp.

Running Bull hung his hand weapons from his belt and began loading his Henry. Frank began reloading his pistol. Bear Child changed the cylinders in his two pistols and began walking among the bodies of their attackers. He made sure there were no wounded. With his pistols empty once again and three bodies remaining he returned for his rifle.

Cries of victory could be heard from the other side of camp. Tom turned his head to see Red Shirt approaching. Suddenly, the war chief stopped and the satisfied look left his face. Tom turned his gaze to see what had drawn Red Shirt's attention.

Looking Back lay on her back, the shotgun cylinder in one hand and the powder horn in the other. Blood stained the breast of her dress and more stained the ground beneath her. Her face was completely relaxed, mouth slightly open. Her eyes were also open, but they would not see the rising sun.

Chapter 33

The four men rode west and south across the grasslands. Although they were four, the two white men tended to travel as a pair as did the two Blackfoot, Running Bull and Bear Child. Each hour they put the horses to a lope for fifteen minutes, and then brought them back to a walk. Each pair herded a packhorse, a simple task since the animals tended to want to stay with the four saddle animals.

For much of those first hours, Tom's mind played pictures from his past. His wife, daughter, and son lying in their coffins; the bodies of hundreds of his men lying on Russian soil; his farmhouse burning fiercely; the body of a fellow officer lying in a Karachi street. But the strongest image was the one from that very morning, the body of Looking Back lying on a Buffalo robe.

He had found her interesting at first sight. As he had said to Frank, he had tried to avoid involvement with the woman because he wanted no unbreakable links with Red Shirt's people. It was also true that he did not want to drag the Blackfoot woman into a world for which she was not suited. But the strongest reason, the one he kept within his heart, was that he wanted no one to interfere with the memory of his wife of twelve years. In a few short days, however—only two of which they had actually been together—Tom had come to appreciate the woman and enjoy her company. She was intelligent, caring, and, despite a less than easy life, had managed to maintain a wondrous sense of humor. She had treated him well, both physically and mentally, and seemed to know when he wanted quiet or talk.

Perhaps that was his problem; he hadn't known her long enough. Everyone has phobias and faults, but during a brief relationship we often don't get to see them. Perhaps if he had known her longer, there may have been something about her character that would have upset or even angered him. However, what he did know about the woman was all good and that made her death all the more difficult.

They brought their horses down to a walk once more and Frank rode up beside him. Without greeting or any other preamble, the young man began relating his story. "Paw was gone 'bout a year when a feller name o'

Taylor Martin come by. Said he was in the same outfit as Paw an' standin' right 'side him when he got kilt." Frank slapped the pistol resting against his leg. "Had him Paw's Colt t' back up his story.

"Weren't long afore we had t' move out o' the post. Three months they give us. That was down t' Fort Kansas. Weren't the army's fault. Jus' couldn't have no woman an' her tadpole t' worry 'bout when they had 'nough t' do, what with the war an' all. Sioux all'ays makin' a fuss. Anyhow, Maw got her a job up t' Fort Union, washin' clothes, swampin' out bunkhouses, an' such like. Martin stayed on an' helped us t' move.

"I figured that Taylor Martin was a ring-tailed terror. He was a wounded so'jer who still had most o' his ol' uniform an' a bad limp. An' he'd bin a three stripe jus' like Paw. An' he was a gam'ler. Powerful stuff fer a young un."

Frank paused for a long time, perhaps thinking about those first few months in Fort Union.

Tom had waited for weeks to hear this story and didn't want to stop the flow, but finally couldn't wait any longer. "But after a short time, you didn't like him any more." It wasn't a question.

Frank nodded. "Paw used t' say cardplayers made money an' gam'lers lost it. Martin was a gam'ler an' a damn poor thief besides. Weren't long 'fore nobody'd play with him, 'sept the odd trader 'r trapper comin' through. He was eatin' offen our work—me an' Maw's. I had me a milch cow t' tend, no fences 'round an' other chores here an' yon, an' Maw was cleanin' everythin' in sight.

"Now I didn' think much o' Taylor Martin no more, but I got t' downright hatin' him when he started in t' beatin' Maw. Took a couple years fer him t' start in on that, but once he started it didn't take him long t' get real good at it. Beat her up fer most anythin', 'r maybe nothin' ifn he took a mind to."

Frank stopped speaking and rode in silence. Tom suspected that it wasn't so much that the younger man wanted to look at the pictures from the past; he just found it very hard to talk about.

"You were scared of him," Tom offered. "He was an adult, after all, a soldier, and from your father's old outfit. But after a while, you didn't care if he was bigger. You were getting older and bigger with each passing day."

Frank nodded. "Sort o'. I didn' figure t' ever get big 'nough t' tangle with Martin, but I made me a plan. When Martin came back from the war an' give Maw the pistol he got from Paw, she put it away." He slapped the holster again. "I took t' sneakin' the Colt 'long when I went t' herd them milch cows. Draw an' fire, draw an' fire, over an' over. No bullets, just clickin' 'er off. Then one day I go off from them cows a ways an' I try some real shootin'. Worked closer t' them cows ever' day. Weren't long 'fore I could run five shots through 'er 'bout fifty feet from 'em an' they'd just stan' there an' chew grass."

Tom didn't like where this was going. "You shot your stepfather?" he asked.

"Plan didn' exac'ly work," Frank confessed. "Got good 'nough with the Colt that I'm thinkin' I'm pretty tough, but I put 'er away ever' night so's Maw wouldn' know. When he went t' beatin' on Maw, it would o' taken too long t' get at 'er. Weren't loaded, anyway. Kept one o' the cylinders loaded, but never left it in the Colt."

Once again they rode in silence for several minutes and then Frank continued. "Don' know as I could o' shot 'im anyway. Leastwise, not without he had a chance. Seen yuh after yuh sliced Lame Dog. Looked like a prairie wolf after bein' in a snare fer most o' the day. 'Course, yuh looked a damn sight better'n Lame Dog.

"Differen' thing when it's a fight goin' on. Weren't men comin' at me this mornin', jus' somethin' had t' be stopped."

Suddenly Frank turned to look at Tom. He hadn't intended to bring up the battle. His intention had been to help Tom forget about it. He quickly returned to his story. "So, anyhow, Martin takes intu slappin' Maw ag'in. I'm lookin' over t' where the Colt's hid under a couple blankets an' tryin' t' figure how I can get 'er an' get them cylinders changed. Martin looks t' me, an' I guess he's seein' I ain't no kid no more. 'R maybe he don' like the way I'm starin'. Anyhow, he tells me t' git out 'r I'll git the same.

"Now I know there ain't nothin' I kin do, an' I'm mad an' shamed. So I drop my head an' shuffle off t' the door. But I'm goin' by the stove an' there's this big ol' skillet sittin' there. Maw'd been heatin' 'er up t' start supper an' that's what he was beatin' 'er fer, cause she didn' have no supper ready.

"While I'm doin this, he's takin' intu swingin' ag'in, so his back's t' me. I grab the han'le on that skillet with both hands an' I just swing 'er."

Frank stopped speaking long enough to make Tom anxious. "So, did you hit him? Did he go down?"

"Hell, yeah. Killt 'im."

Now it was Tom's turn to be quiet for several moments. Finally, he asked, "What makes you think you killed him?"

"Blood comin' out o his ears. Eyes kind o half open an' all red lookin'."

That didn't mean the man was dead, Tom thought. "What did your mother do then?" he asked.

"Well, that's the thing. Reckon I waited a bit long t' belt 'im. Last couple a belts he give 'er musta bin too much. She was a layin' there kind o half under 'im, 'er eyes open an' not breathin'." The tone of Frank's voice had not changed. He was still a young man telling a story. However, the thick dust on his face was being washed away by a flood of tears. He wiped them with the sleeve of his buckskin shirt, which only succeeded in covering his cheeks with mud. He drew in a long breath somewhat with a slight jerk, then continued.

"Ain' no bunch o' traders n' trappers gonna take kindly t' a young feller killin' a war hero. Least, that's how they seen 'im, an' a lot o them boys was so'jers one time 'er 'nother."

"Surely some of them knew how he mistreated your mother," Tom objected. "Besides, they knew he cheated at cards."

Frank shook his head. "They was all pretty sure he'd cheat if'n he had a chance, but nobody caught 'im. They'd a caught 'im they'd a hung 'im. Far as Maw goes, she was jus' 'nother woman cleanin' stuff. Livin' with a man weren't 'er husban', an' I was 'er get."

Tom understood. Many men considered woman nothing more than property. Consideration for a woman living out of wedlock would amount to little more than jeers from some quarters. Her son would be an inconvenience, particularly when one considered the possible inheritance of goods, which included the Spencer rifle and Colt.

"So I taken up what I could lay muh hands tu an' lit out o there. Whole camp was use t' hearin' a beatin' over t' our place an' it endin' sudden, so that weren't nothin' new. Made me a pack out o' some blankets an' some ol' harness strappin' an' filled 'er full o' what was 't hand. Picked up Martin's Spencer an' Paw's Colt an' jus' slipped out intu the night."

"What happened to the pack?" Tom asked.

Frank shrugged. "Some o' them rivers I had t cross was a little bigger'n me. Reckon she's half way down the Mississip' by now. Weren't much in 'er anyhow."

"Why would you go northwest?" Tom wondered.

Frank looked at him with a sheepish grin. "Didn' think I was. I was figurin' on the Oregon country. Heard folks talk of it. 'R maybe the gold country out t' Californy. But time t' time I had t' move off from folks looked like they was huntin' me. An' what with the lay o' the land an' all, well I reckon I wound up in Rupert's Land."

"And saved a young Peigan boy's life," Tom added.

"Didn' reckon t' do that," Frank said. "Heard tell o' Blackfoot all my life. Best kill 'em where yuh find 'em, folks say. Turns out they's pretty fair folks. Leastwise, far as Injuns go."

"They've earned a reputation," Tom agreed, "and there are probably some good reasons for it. They are a very fierce and very proud people. But they've treated us well."

After they had ridden a mile or more, Tom said, "You didn't plan to save the boy because you didn't know he was there, but you did plan to save the woman."

"Didn' know she was Blackfoot," Frank responded. "All I seen was 'nother woman gettin' beat up, an' a feller dead what had 'im the same chance as a snowball in hell."

The four riders put their horses to a lope for several moments, and then brought them back to a walk. Perhaps a half hour later, Tom spoke. "Thanks, Frank."

Frank looked puzzled. "Fer what?"

"For taking my mind off Looking Back, however briefly."

Chapter 34

Standing by his horse, Tom turned and scanned the country. The flat he stood on was perhaps five acres in size and no more than two feet higher than the river. It had probably flooded several times in the past, and would have a great deal of gravel hidden under the blanket of grass. The gravel would be a problem. The encircling hills were high enough that, with the help of some careful planning and placement, details of figures on the crest would be difficult to see. Best of all, the river flat was easily seen and approachable from the south side of the river.

Tom dropped the reins and walked back to the packhorse. He untied an axe from the pack and extended the handle to Bear Child. "We will need six trees," he said as Bear Child took the axe. He held his hands to form a circle of five inches. "They should be about this big at the base, and we'll need all the branches that are the size of your fingers." He paused for a moment, and then added. "Are there any pine or spruce trees close by?"

Bear Child shrugged then swung his hand to indicate the barren slopes. "Maybe. Pretty hard to find trees."

"Well, never mind, we'll use blankets. We will also need one tree about the same size that is as straight as you can find. Full length for that one. Take it right down to perhaps two or three . . ." He formed his fingers into a circle. "About this size."

Bear Child nodded said something in his own tongue to Running Bull and walked to his horse. The two warriors swung aboard their mounts and rode west.

Tom unlashed a shovel and began walking toward the river.

"Suppose' t' stan' here an' twiddle muh thumbs?" Frank asked.

Tom stopped and drove the shovel into the earth. "You can unload the pack right here," he said, then retrieved the shovel, walked on another ten feet and began to dig.

When Bear Child and Running Bull returned, there was a trench in the earth about ten feet long by six wide. Twenty feet to the east of this hole, Frank was digging another round one while Tom sat in the grass.

There wasn't as much gravel as Tom had suspected, but it was still there, mixed with sand and river silt. Any holes they attempted to dig only caved in, so they dug larger ones than would have been otherwise necessary. Once they had the poles in the ground they would fill around them and pack it down as much as possible.

"Another two feet," Tom instructed and rose to meet the approaching Blackfoot. He examined the two bundles of trees as the riders dropped the drag ropes and dismounted.

"Any good?" Bear Child asked.

"They're perfect," Tom replied. He nodded at Running Bull. "Since he was the Corporal of the Guard, I expect he's a pretty good scout."

"Me better," Bear Child responded.

"I'm sure you are," Tom conceded, "but we will need some help here, and I have difficulty talking to Running Bull since I don't speak your language."

Bear Child shrugged and grunted.

"Could you ask him to go and see how far away the Long Knives are?" Tom asked. "We need to know how long we have to complete our work here." Since it was Bear Child who brought the initial news, and had also insisted the Americans would take this route, Tom didn't add that he wanted some confirmation that a column of soldiers actually had crossed into British territory and were approaching.

Bear Child grunted then turned to speak to Running Bull as Tom began removing the drag ropes from the bundled trees.

Tom stared into the fire, but did not see flames. He saw the body of a woman who had been happy. She had believed she was half as useful as she actually was, but still comfortable with the contribution she made.

He realized that someone had been speaking to him. "I'm sorry?" he asked.

"Look into fire, not good," Bear Child repeated.

Tom was embarrassed by the observation. It was something he had learned a long time ago. "Yes, you're right," he conceded.

"Why not?" Frank asked.

"One's eyes become used to the bright flames and it becomes impossible to see out into the dark," Tom explained.

Frank grinned. "We under attack?" he asked.

"Maybe," Bear Child put in. "Many enemy this land. Cree, Long Knife. Maybe even Nez Perce or Crow. Only know after you see body. Body maybe yours."

The high-pitched coo of the burrowing owl dominated the other night sounds. Feeling some embarrassment from having been caught looking into the fire, Tom attempted to turn the conversation. "I believe that is the burrowing owl," he commented, "sometimes called the prairie owl."

Bear Child grunted. "Maybe, sometime," he said. He tilted his head back, yipped like a coyote, and then added, "I call him Running Bull."

When the Blackfoot brave, now returned from his scouting mission walked into their camp, Tom found that, despite his best efforts, his embarrassment had increased.

While Running Bull reported his findings to Bear Child, Tom put the last fresh buffalo steak on the small fire to cook. Until the rest of the tribe caught up to them they would be eating jerky. When it was finished cooking, Running Bull ate while Bear Child translated his findings.

"So'jer chief have five men to scout," Bear Child related. "More than thirty so'jer with him. Counting traders, maybe forty five." He pointed straight up into the dark sky. "Sun is there two time, they find this place."

"The scouts or the whole column?" Tom asked.

"Scouts."

Tom pointed to where the sun would be in mid-afternoon. "When the sun is there, the column will be upon us?" he asked.

Bear Child shrugged, and then nodded.

Tom considered for a moment before he said more. "Ask Running Bull to return to his people. He should wait until the American scouts have looked all around. When they have seen us they will check the area, and then report to their comman. . . to their chief. Only when this has happened should his people move into place."

Bear Child nodded his understanding, and then turned to deliver the request.

Frank cursed, then asked, "We gonna sit on'r asses in the hot sun?"

Tom smiled. "After the amount of digging you did today I thought you would like a day to just relax."

"Ain't no damn shade."

"We don't have to stay here," Tom said. He pointed at the few trees on the east edge of the river flat. "We will erect a lean-to with saddle blankets in those few trees. It will offer some shade. Besides, we could go for a swim."

"Guess yuh ain't had a feel o' that there Milk River," Frank responded. "Colder'n a banker's heart."

"My, you're a hard one to please."

Chapter 35

On the sixth day of a very hot and very dry patrol, Captain McDougal saw one of his scouting party riding to meet the column. He drew his hunter, popped the cover, and read the time. This was no more than a ceremony and a reflex action for the watch told him it was three o'clock while the sun told him it was approaching noon. His hand still holding the watch he held it up to halt the column.

Two sergeants repeated the gesture. One of them rode immediately behind the Captain while the other was near the end of the column with the half dozen pack animals. Of course neither of the sergeants held a watch in his hand. They had no interest in knowing the time in Boston. They had little interest at the time in any location, including where they sat, except for meal times and bed times. If the Captain said it was time to stop, they were happy to comply, although they would have preferred to stop in shade.

The scout was a private in his late twenties. His faded shirt sleeve showed the marks of three chevrons that had once hung there. It could mean the man was a troublemaker who had been busted, but McDougal doubted that. Corporal Leeman, the man in charge of the scouting party, wouldn't put up with anyone he couldn't depend on. It could also mean that the man had only recently signed up, receiving this hand-me-down uniform from a financially devastated Army, although he was several years older than the ideal recruit. It was more likely that following the drastic cuts to the military that followed the Rebel War the man had hung onto a steady job by taking a demotion, a circumstance with which McDougal was all too familiar.

The Private brought his horse to a walk, then to a halt, and saluted. "Corp'al's comp'ments, Cap'n."

McDougal snapped off a return salute but held silent waiting for the scout to continue. Finally, he said, "Private, you came in here loping your horse in the hot sun. Treating your mount like that will get you two days walkin', so if you have something to say, now would be a good time to start. Did you find the Blackfoot?"

"Well, no sir, an' that there's the thing," the private responded. "See, there's this feller sittin' in a chair on the bank o' the river."

"In a chair? There's some sort of village then. A Blackfoot village, I presume."

"No, sir ain't no village. Ain't no Blackfoot neither. White man just sittin' there all by his lonesome. Well, 'sept there's this young feller standin' back o' him, kind o like at parade rest? Older feller just sits there an' drinks tea. Younger feller just standin' there back o' him."

"Tea, private? You went up to the man and tasted his beverage?"

"Well, no sir, I ain't seen what's in his cup. What I mean is, he just looks like a feller sittin' in some swell's parlor drinkin' tea."

McDougal stared at the man for several minutes. What had just been reported made absolutely no sense. "And these two are alone on the river-bank?"

"Well, ain't nobody fer maybe three, four miles in any direction," the private reported. "Corporal was sendin' out a couple boys t' have them another look-see when I left."

"Well, I have to see this for myself," the Captain announced. "How long before we can be there?"

"Maybe three hours, sir."

"Fine. Stay with the column, private, and give that horse a chance to recover."

The private started to lift his reins, and then dropped them. "One more thing, Cap'n. There's this pole stickin' out o the groun' with a limey flag flyin'."

"A Union Jack?" McDougal asked.

The private shrugged. If it wasn't his own "Stars and Stripes" he had no idea what it would be called, and didn't much care. "I reckon. English."

The pounding of hooves caused everyone to look back along the column. Everyone that is except the Captain; he knew who it would be.

"What's the holdup, Captain?" the newcomer asked, bringing his mount to a halt in a cloud of dust.

"Scouts have made contact, Coleman," McDougal responded. He cringed every time someone used the title of colonel when addressing this man and avoided the use of it himself. "Two white men on the river-bank."

"Pshah. Gold hunters or trappers," Coleman declared. "We don't have time for this. We're here to see that justice is done."

McDougal, who was sure Coleman's motives had more to do with commerce than justice, just looked at the man. The civilian appeared to have some history with his commanding officers, but there were some things the Captain would not do. He would take a drastic demotion because he had no place to go. He would lead a cavalry troop because he did not have the academic background to justify a posting to engineering, although his abilities in that area were well established. But he would not take orders from a pompous, opportunistic civilian. "That's correct, Mr. Coleman." McDougal loved it when the civilian reacted to his obvious refusal to use the military title. "Like any good justice, we will make every effort to collect all available evidence before pronouncing judgment."

It dawned on McDougal that a short march for the day would go a long way to maintaining their mounts in the heat. As an added bonus, a halt in the middle of the afternoon would help to show Coleman who was in command. "Private, these men you saw, they are on the north side of the river?"

"Yes, sir." The private had been around long enough to know that he didn't want to be between these two men. One was the troop commander and a good one, and the other seemed to be a friend of Colonel Gillard's. The best place for a lowly horse soldier was some anonymous spot back in the ranks.

"And is there a good spot for us on the south side?"

The private nodded. "Reckon so, Cap'n."

"Fine, that's where we'll be spending the night. Move 'em out, Sergeant."

Coleman's expression was one of disgust as he turned his mount to join his own men on the windward side of the column.

While a few men set up his tent, McDougal scanned the north side of the river with his binoculars. As the private had described, there were two men, although both of them seemed to be sitting on sturdy chairs with a table between them. On the table there appeared to be a pot and cups. Off to one side was a fire with an eight quart kettle suspended over it from a cross bar hanging on tripods. Behind the men was a pole from which the British flag flew.

"Let's get this foolishness over with," a voice said.

McDougal pulled the glasses from his eyes and turned to see Coleman sitting beside him. He couldn't think of any arguments to keep Coleman away, so he simply nodded and put his horse in motion.

As they crossed the river, McDougal thought he heard the sound of too many hooves splashing. He turned to see Sergeant Morin several yards behind. The man had been following him, or if the truth were really admitted, leading him for years.

"Suspect I can't handle these two, Sergeant?" he asked.

"Just curious, Captain," Morin replied.

McDougal smiled. The man had been protecting him since they had defeated General Garnett at Rich Mountain.

On the north bank, the two men rose. The younger man, dressed in buckskins, a fine grey hat, and a low-slung sidearm turned and walked to the flagpole where he turned back to face them, his hands clasped behind his back. The older man walked down to meet them as they emerged from the water. He was dressed in old but serviceable, high-top military riding boots, and grey breaches. Most out of place, however, was a very white shirt, stiff open collar, and ascot showing above a brocaded vest. The man's coat appeared to be hanging over the back of the chair he had just vacated. McDougal expected the breaches were hot enough for anyone under the merciless sun. The man appeared to be unarmed.

"Welcome, Colonel McDougal," the stranger greeted. "Or perhaps I should say, Captain McDougal, although you certainly deserve your earlier title. Step down and partake of a little tea. I know it's a hot day, but the residents of the area have convinced me of its benefits in escaping the heat."

The Captain suddenly found himself without his usual focus. "Do I know you?" he asked.

"We've met," Tom Brash replied, "although I would be greatly surprised if your exploits during the past few years had not driven our meeting from your mind. And of course, I have you at a disadvantage. I've been able to follow a few of your actions as reported in various American newspapers."

"What the hell are you men doin' here?" Coleman interjected.

Brash looked at the man and smiled. McDougal noted that the smile looked genuine and warm but the eyes, which had been full of pleasure a moment ago, were now completely void of expression. "And you would be the man who calls himself Colonel Coleman," Brash said. It was not a question.

"I am, and I asked..." Coleman blinked. "It's what others call me as well."

Brash nodded. "I'm sure they do." He turned his attention back to McDougal. "Care to join us for tea, Captain?"

McDougal was enjoying the treatment Coleman was getting, and was more than curious about the two strangers. "Sure, don't mind if I do," he responded.

"Damn it, we've got things..." Coleman began, then stopped and focused his attention on Brash. "I asked you a question."

Brash's smile quickly disappeared and he interrupted before Coleman could repeat his question. "Yes, you did, and quite rudely, I might add. A question that propriety only prompts me to address, since you have no official status giving you the right to ask the question, and, therefore there is no real need for a response."

It was Coleman's turn to interrupt. "What the hell are you talkin' about. I'm the man that'll be running this whole damn area." He swung his hand toward the north.

"No, you won't," Brash said, his smile back in place. "In answer to your question, I am here to represent Queen Victoria." He turned to indicate the table, chairs, and the flag. "I am in this specific spot to meet the leader of your party which, quite obviously, is Captain McDougal."

Coleman smiled. "What appears to be obvious may not always be true," he said. "I'm the leader of this group."

"Oh, you are?" McDougal said with more than a little surprise. He turned to ask the Sergeant a question, but Brash interrupted before an argument started.

"It doesn't really matter what you think, Mr. Coleman," Tom said. He wanted these men to focus their attention on him and not on each other. "You are a citizen of a foreign power who has now entered the bounds of those lands under the stewardship of the British Crown. I wish only to converse with the legal representative of your government, a position that can only be filled, in this instance, by a commissioned officer, which you are not."

"And what if I don't plan to abide by the rules of your British Crown?" Coleman asked. "Even without the good Captain's help, I've got enough of my own men to handle an English fool and a damn kid." He reached for his pistol. "Hell, I can probably handle this my..."

Quickly Tom said, "Don't shoot unless he clears leather, Frank." He never took his eyes from Coleman.

Very carefully, Coleman took his hand from his pistol and slowly placed that hand back on the cantle of his saddle. The boy back by the flagpole already had his pistol out, cocked, and pointed at him.

"Mighty handy," Coleman conceded. "But he can't handle all of us."

"Oh, he won't have to, Mr. Coleman," Brash said. He turned slightly. "Dip the colors, Frank."

The young man holstered his weapon, and then untied the rope at the flagpole. Having dropped the Union Jack a few feet, he returned it to its original position, and tied it off.

McDougal wasn't long in discovering the reason for the signal. The half circle of hills to the east, north, and west were suddenly lined with Indians, all of them holding weapons. "About sixty, Sergeant?" he asked.

"I was figurin' more like sixty-five, Cap'ain," Morin replied, then sent a stream of tobacco juice into the dust. "Ain't no never mind; sixty 'r sixty-five, they still kick our ass."

McDougal nodded, and then swung down from his mount. "I think I'd like to try that tea," he announced.

"You are more than welcome," Brash said, gesturing toward the table and chairs.

McDougal turned to face Morin. "Sergeant, escort Mr. Coleman back to camp and ensure the men are not neglecting their duties." He swung his gaze to the hills where the Indians had begun to disappear. Because they were no longer visible did not mean they were not there. "You might ask Corporal Leeman what he was doing all day."

The appearance of the Indians had taken some of the bluster from Coleman, but he was not about to be lead back to camp like a whipped dog. He turned and pushed his horse hard back across the river. Morin shrugged, directed another stream of tobacco juice at the dust, and moved his massive chaw to one cheek. "Reckon he don' like my company," he observed, then turned his horse and walked it away.

"I suspect Corporal Leeman is the man leading your scouts?" Brash asked as they walked toward the table.

"Yes," McDougal responded, then gestured with a gloved hand toward the hills. "He seems to have missed a thing or two."

Brash stopped in front of the table and gestured for Frank to approach as he responded. "Don't forget, Captain, my companions are Blackfoot. They have had a lifetime of avoiding detection, while your scout leader has had a few years. I was told your scouts were all soldiers; no Indians."

Frank took the reins of the Captain's horse and led it over to where three other horses were tied in the scant shade offered by a few scrubby bushes.

The Captain began to pull his gauntlets off. "Yes, that's a policy that my commanding officer has instituted. Claims the Indians aren't to be trusted." He waved a hand toward the horses and the shade. "Seems that would be the place to set up your table and tea."

"True, but it wouldn't attract nearly as much attention," Brash responded, then cast his glance to the surrounding hills. "And it would be harder for my companions to see what is going on." He held his open hand toward the chair on the right. "Would you care for that tea? We just made a fresh pot."

McDougal nodded. "Believe I would, but I'd like to meet my host."

"Dreadfully sorry," Brash said extending his hand. "Introductions were never completed due to the boorish interruptions. Thomas Brash, at your service."

McDougal took the hand and began the handshake, then stopped. "From whence do you come?" he asked.

"From the east," Brash responded.

"Why do you go from the east toward the west?"

Brash smiled. "To search for that which was lost." He released the Captain's hand and gestured once more toward the chair.

The Captain sat, glancing over at Frank who had returned to his station by the flagpole. McDougal would have been surprised to learn that what he perceived as the parade rest stance of a young, well-trained soldier was something that the young man had learned from Tom that very morning.

Tom poured tea then took the other chair.

"Brash, Brash," McDougal intoned. "Can't say as I recall the name, and I must apologize. Only excuse I have is that our recent difficulties have managed to erase some earlier memories."

"No apology necessary. Sometimes I look back on my own experience and wonder if death isn't the kindest thing that war offers a man."

McDougal sipped his tea, which he was enjoying immensely. It had been more than a year since he had drunk anything but water, coffee, or barracks whiskey. "We didn't meet in battle," McDougal observed. He grinned and jerked his thumb at the hills. "If you had set up a southern army the way you set this up, I'd not be here."

Tom smiled pleasantly, knowing that the compliment to his tactical abilities was merely a sop, an attempt to make him drop his guard. There had been many commanders in the Confederate Army with tactical abilities far greater than his. "But it was a battle of a sort," Tom insisted. "Williams College, 1846. I was fifteen and you were a couple of years older."

McDougal looked puzzled, then his expression cleared and his eyes glinted with pleasure. "Fencing match. A few of you boys came down from Nova Scotia to take us on, an' we thought it was a joke. You were one of the younger fellows playing with the big boys. As I recall, you whipped my ass."

"No, not exactly," Tom objected. "We were almost evenly matched with the foil, but you defeated me soundly with the saber."

"Well, sure, but I had at least a two-inch reach on you, and I outweighed you by forty pounds," McDougal objected. "Yes, I was declared the victor, but when all is taken into account, I was beaten. Our instructor used that weekend as an example to us all. Don't take your opponent or your own ability for granted."

"Exactly why the meet was set up, I'm sure," Tom said. "I know our own instructor used it to teach us we were not near as good as we had thought."

McDougal took another sip of tea. He thought again how much he enjoyed it. When he returned to post he would write and have someone send tea. And perhaps some of those light little cups. Perhaps if he asked for a half dozen, well wrapped, one of them would make the journey unbroken. He set the mug down and turned his gaze to his host. "So, speaking of a setup, why have you arranged this?"

Brash smiled. "Well, to the point. An experimental thrust with the rapier, as it were, to see what properties one's opponent has in reply."

The Captain nodded. "True, for I believe you are less well equipped at present than you were those many years ago at Williamsburg. It appears that you have fifty or sixty of the most fearsome warriors, capable of mounted or foot charges, or the most silent guerilla attacks. However, even if the higher number is true, your force only outnumbers mine by fifty percent. My men are veterans of several battles, better mounted and better armed. Not really as uneven a match as it might at first appear."

Tom smiled, poured tea in both cups, and then called over his shoulder. "Frank, would you make another pot and warm up some of that bannock we made this morning? Much superior to the tea biscuits served in jolly old England."

He turned his attention back to the U.S. Army officer. "Gill, please don't make the same mistake of underestimating your opponent. Perhaps your men are better suited for a repeat of the battles of Gettysburg or Chancellorsville, but that is not our present location. This is Blackfoot country, and they have the high ground. As for your horses, perhaps they would run over the Indian ponies in an initial charge—always supposing the Indians would let you set one up—but in the long term, those little Indian ponies will run your mounts into the ground. Regarding arms, I see you are equipped with the Spencer falling block carbine, and the officers and Sergeants have Colt pistols. A few of the civilians have repeating rifles, as well as their Colts. I'm not sure how many Indians have repeaters, but I do know there are at least four Henry rifles and perhaps two dozen revolvers." He didn't mention that the pistols were of a variety of calibers and makes with, in some cases, no more than one cylinder of ammunition available. This was true of some of the rifles as well. At first glance, the Blackfoot appeared to be remarkably well armed, but any extended fighting would rapidly turn those weapons into well-engineered clubs.

Frank set the replenished pot on the table and stepped back to the fire as the Captain nodded. Frank checked the bannock for warmth with the back of his fingers then slid it on to a buffalo-hide plate. The Captain continued to watch the young man as he returned to the table and served the prairie biscuits.

"Help yourself," Tom invited, gesturing toward the warm bannock.

McDonald tore off a piece, tasted it, and nodded his approval. "All you say is true, Tom," he responded, "but it still doesn't answer my original question. Why have you set up this very pleasant meeting?"

Brash finished his own mouthful before responding. "I don't really know where to begin. I want to avoid an international incident between my country, which is not particularly interested, or financially able, to send a strong force into this vast land to protect its holdings, and your country, which has just had a belly full of war, has decimated its army, and does not have the financial resources to expand its control of the continent, despite repeated assurances by some fools that it is the country's destiny."

McDougal's chuckle was short and bitter. "There's many that still claim it's our manifest destiny, but none of them were out in the fighting. I take it you haven't heard about the Fenians."

"The Irish?" Tom responded. "They made a raid in New Brunswick back in April. It was a disaster for them."

"They made another one in June," McDougal said. "Somewhere around Niagara. Place called Ridgeway? Never heard of it myself. Apparently it was much more successful, for your Canadian militia suffered some fifty casualties, ten or twelve of them mortal. The Fenians came away with a few wounded."

"Has anything further come of it?" Tom asked.

McDougal shook his head. "As you rightly noted, those in favor of making this country part of America have some significant power, but have little support in the way of numbers. Besides, we have a new law that prohibits foreign intervention. Of course, the Fenians have proved their worth as fighters, but they don't have the numbers either." He tore off another piece of the campfire bread. "By the way, this bannock is excellent."

"Thank you," Tom responded, relieved that the Irish had been turned back. Attack from the south was a constant worry of his friends in the Kingston area. Tom did not agree that it was likely, but it was still a concern.

"I'm happy to hear news of the political foolishness that constantly plagues the seats of power," Tom said. "The non-intervention law you spoke of, and the Fenian raid should make it clear that we must avoid an incident here. However, your companion and his men are making that difficult. They have been inciting the natives to violence against the crown, a crime in itself that is punishable upon conviction, by hanging. He and his followers have also been trading a particularly poisonous brew that they claim to be whiskey. Defaming the name of a good drink in such a manner should in itself be a capitol offence. Those who partake of this brew may die, but more often kill each other in a drunken frenzy."

Having taken another drink of tea, McDonald set his cup down, smiling. "You want me to turn Coleman over to you so you can hang him?"

Tom smiled in return. "I'd like nothing better," he acknowledged. "However, I do not have the required number of British citizens for a proper hearing, not to mention that such an action would create the international incident I wish to avoid. No, I would much prefer that you arrest him, try him, and hang him, on your own soil."

Chapter 36

For a moment McDougal thought that Brash was serious, then he noted the twinkle in the other man's eye.

"A few moments ago you made note of my present rank and that I am no longer a Colonel. The reason I'm a Captain is that I don't have any other immediate job prospects. Coleman is a friend of my commanding officer; acquainted with several of them in fact. Even if I had solid proof that he is guilty of what you claim, which I don't, I can't think of a quicker way of terminating my present employment than arresting the man. Trading rotgut whiskey to the Blackfoot is looked at quite favorably by my superiors, particularly if it kills the drinker. Mind you, seeing Coleman under guard would make it difficult for me to keep the smile off my face, but I'm afraid it would be a short-term thing.

"Not that I doubt your word," he added, "particularly since you're a brother and he isn't. I didn't like Coleman when I met him, and the last few days on the trail have done nothing to improve my original assessment. At the same time, he claims that the Blackfoot captured two of his men, hauled them north into British territory, tortured, and killed them. That's what he told Colonel Gillard."

"A good story," Tom conceded. "It has some small elements of truth, and conveniently supports his actions. I suppose he claims he is only a fur trader?"

McDougal nodded. "So there's some truth to his story?"

"Very little," Tom responded, and then told McDougal the whole story. "So, the truth of Coleman's story is that the Blackfoot did torture and kill one man. It's also true that he trades for fur, but he pays for it with a version of whiskey that kills far more people than it entertains."

"So what is it you really want?" McDougal asked.

Instead of answering directly, Tom said, "The Hudson Bay Company has a Royal Charter entitling them to all the trade in this land. The Treaty of Paris, the Treaty of Ghent, and several other treaties for that matter, confirm the British Crown's right to issue such a charter. The Company men are more than a little tight-fisted. Even though they find trading in this area to be more trouble than it's worth, they still get very upset when someone else does. Therefore, Coleman and his traders have no legal standing here, even though the Company hasn't made any great effort to run them out.

"Take your troop back across the border before there's an incident that can't be forgotten. If you go, Coleman will follow. He'll surely return to trade, may kill some more of those who oppose him, and may even gain a foothold. Without the assistance of the United States Army, however, he will have difficulty establishing an empire."

"Well, I have the story of events from the local British representative," McDougal conceded. "By the way, do you really have any official status?"

Tom smiled. "Colonel Thomas Brash, Her Majesty's Colonial Forces, retired." He didn't think it necessary to mention that the colony in question had been in the Far East or that his advancement had been a temporary battlefield commission.

McDougal smiled in return as he rose from his chair. "Retired. So, can I get one of my Sergeants over here and get you to sign a deposition?"

"Concerning the story I just related?" Tom asked. "Sure. And there's something else you might relate to your commanders, although I won't be putting it on paper for Coleman to find. It might lead to your experiencing a sudden accident on the return journey."

The Captain's smile slipped slightly on hearing the serious tone in Tom's voice. "And that would be?"

"In '62 my father died," Tom said. "I went back to England to clear up the estate. When that was finished I returned to the Canadas on a British merchant ship that carried clothing, weapons, and ammunition. In Jamaica that cargo was transferred to a black, three-masted schooner in exchange for a cargo of cotton. The name on her stern was "Cloud" and she flew the flag of the Confederate States of America. Her master called himself Captain Jack Cole, and it was either your Colonel Coleman with a full beard, or his twin brother."

McDougal was silent for moment, simply staring at Brash, and then he said, "I have no reason to disbelieve a brother of the craft, but he served with people I know and wore Union blue."

"Perhaps it would be a good idea to try and find out when he first appeared in that uniform," Tom suggested. "I think you will find it was after it became apparent that the Union would win."

McDougal picked up his gauntlets from the table, then said, "And also a good idea to be careful asking such questions. I expect Mr. Coleman would be more than a little anxious to ensure his past isn't exposed."

Tom nodded, and then stood. "Shooting a Cavalry Captain in the back wouldn't be too terribly rough on his conscience."

McDougal smiled. "From our first meeting I felt that Mr. Coleman wasn't the type to be overly hindered by conscience," he observed. "It makes it fairly easy to believe your information that he was a blockade runner and profiteer. Or perhaps I simply want to believe it."

Tom nodded again as he extended his hand, which McDougal grasped.

"Perhaps we could interest you and your junior officers in an evening meal?" Tom asked. He dearly hoped McDougal would refuse for they had little to offer save stew made from buffalo jerky. However, he thought it important to keep up the front he had established.

"It would be my pleasure," McDougal responded. "However, I have no lieutenants, and after what you have just told me, I would prefer to leave my two sergeants in camp to keep an eye on Coleman and his men." He stopped for a moment and looked across the river at his camp, his lips pursed in contemplation.

Silently, Tom cursed. Perhaps he could have Frank ride over the hill and get a meal from the Blackfoot.

Tom looked at Frank, pointed to the horses, and nodded. Frank stepped out to retrieve the Captain's mount.

"On second thought, I believe I will decline your offer," McDougal said. "I'll mount the troop and head south across the line as fast as possible. Hopefully, we'll be across the border before Coleman's objections become too much to handle." He turned and took his mount's reins offered by Frank, who then moved back to his position by the flagpole. The Captain watched him intently.

"By the way," McDougal said, turning his attention to Tom, "your young assistant reminds me of a boy I saw at Fort Union. I only saw the boy once, so I could be wrong, but he was the son of Sergeant Alex Clement."

Tom held his smile in place, hoping it didn't look as forced as it was. Perhaps the U.S. Army was looking for a young boy who had murdered his stepfather. Would this destroy his attempt to achieve a diplomatic solution for his Blackfoot friends?

"Is that so?" Tom reasoned. "Of course, when one passes thirty and his belt starts to expand, I suppose many of those young, slim fellows start to look the same."

McDougal nodded more an acknowledgement of what was said than an agreement.

"Did you know this Sergeant?" Tom asked, hoping to draw the Captain's attention from Frank.

"Served under me," McDougal responded, and then turned to tighten his cinch. "He was captured by the Rebs in Virginia. Spring of '63 at a little place called Chancellorsville."

Tom couldn't resist an interruption at this point. "Your General Hooker was somewhat over confident, as I recall."

McDougal paused and a small smile touched his lips. "You made your point," he said, then continued with his narrative. "At the time, we thought Clement was dead. A soldier by the name of Martin claimed he was ten feet from Alex when they were hit by an exploding shell. Martin was wounded by the fragments from the same shell and sent to the rear.

"Martin came west and moved in with Clement's widow at Fort Kansas; it's a post a few days' ride east of here. I guess this Martin was lazy, a drunk, and a woman beater. Recently I heard he was found with a knife in his back and Mrs. Clement's hand near that knife. She was dead too. He'd beaten her to a pulp."

McDougal lifted his reins and swung into the saddle.

"That's not my idea of a cheerful, parting story," Tom observed. The obvious thing would be to ask what happened to the boy, but he didn't want to bring McDougal back to that subject. Quickly, however, he decided it would be a mistake not to ask the question. "What became of the boy?"

"Nobody knows. They'd moved off the post, so it wasn't like there were a lot of soldiers around to keep an eye on the comings and goings of folks. They'd moved northeast to Fort Union; it's a traders' place, not military. After they found the bodies they went looking for the boy and there wasn't a trace."

Tom nodded. "Probably beat by this Martin and died out on the prairie. Perhaps that was the final act for the mother and she struck back. A sad end."

McDougal nodded. "No sadder than many other stories that came out of that damn war, but it isn't the end. A couple of days after they buried his wife, Alex showed up."

"He's alive?"

Again McDougal nodded. "They had him down in Fort Lauderdale. They'd moved him around a bit, but that's where he ended up. By war's end he was a mighty sick man, what with the swamp fever, and all, but when he was well enough, he headed back to his family, only to find it wasn't there any more. Most folks, including Alex, figure the same as you; the boy's buried in some pit out on the prairie."

"And the father?" Tom asked. "What has happened to him?"

"Headed west," McDougal advised. "Said he wanted to be alone." He lifted his reins, and then nodded his head toward Frank. "When you tell the young fellow, you might suggest the Columbia gold fields, or even farther north."

Tom's smile was genuine as he watched the soldier ride away. "Captain McDougal," he called. McDougal turned in the saddle to look back. "It's been a pleasure to speak with a gentleman," Tom said, then snapped to attention and offered a very proper, British officer's salute. McDougal returned the more casual salute of an old, tired U.S. Cavalry officer, and rode his horse into the Milk River.

Chapter 37

"They gonna leave?" Frank asked.

Tom turned and looked at the boy. He wondered how the boy would handle the news of his father. "Yes. The Captain intends to break camp immediately and push hard for the south. He might even make the border before they camp." He decided he would just come out and tell him. "He told . . ."

"Damn good," Frank interrupted. "Them boys'd do a lot o damage t' 'r friends up there on the hill."

"Friends?" Tom asked as he walked over to the fire and began emptying the pot on the coals. "I thought you were upset about having to put up with the damn savages." He would slip McDougal's news in somewhere.

"Well, I guess they ain't so bad." Frank conceded as he began kicking dirt on the wet charcoal.

Tom turned to look across at the American camp. He could see a group of men not in uniform gathered around McDougal who still sat his horse. Undoubtedly a heated argument was going on, but the men in uniform appeared to be breaking camp.

Tom began stirring the ashes with a stick. "The Captain had some news from south of the border,"

"So, what'd ya hear?" Frank asked again.

"You didn't kill Martin," Tom advised.

Frank looked off across the river. "Reckon I did. Seen 'im go down."

"Check his pulse? Put a mirror under his nose to see if he was breathing?" Tom asked.

"No, but I didn't see his chest movin'. Didn' wanta get up close t' 'im."

"He was found with a knife in his back, and your mother's hand on the knife," Tom said.

"She weren't dead neither?"

"She was when they found her," Tom said, "but it's obvious neither were quite finished when you left."

Tears began to run down Frank's cheeks. "So I might o' helped 'er, I'd stayed."

Tom shook his head, and put his hand on the boy's shoulder. "If you were a doctor you might have been able to make her pain last a little longer. She died from the beating she had already received, so there wasn't a thing you could have done."

He looked over to see Red Shirt riding down the hill. "Chin up, boy. Nothing has changed, except that you are not wanted for murder. We'll talk more when we're alone." He squeezed the boy's shoulder again, and then turned to meet the approaching war chief.

"Bonjour, my brother," Red Shirt said, then nodded his head toward the dust cloud off to the south. "Long knives will not fight?"

Frank turned away and wiped his face with his buckskin sleeve.

"No, their officer is taking them back across the border . . . medicine line," Tom replied.

"Too many Blackfoot?" Red Shirt asked, his expression somewhat puzzled.

Tom shrugged. "I think the numbers we showed them only made them stop and think. They know this is not their land, they should not be here, and this is not their fight. There are many men south of the medicine line who think all this land should be a part of their country, but the soldiers have had many battles and are weary. The one who calls himself Coleman has many friends among the white chiefs. He pushed them to this. The soldiers have no wish to be here, and without their numbers, the traders must leave."

Red Shirt nodded, and then inclined his head toward Frank whose back was still toward them. "Shoots Quick is sad to see them go?"

Tom glanced toward the younger man, knowing that he was gaining an ever-increasing knowledge of the French language. He saw the boy's back straighten. "No, it is another thing. The soldier chief had news of his mother."

Red Shirt nodded. "It is not good to be apart. It is many winters since my mother's spirit went on the long journey. Even after all this time her memory makes me want to laugh or cry, or be a child again."

He swung his hand toward the crest of the ridge. "We have made camp. It is not a good place to camp, but it is late. Tomorrow we will have a good camp."

The white men swung into their saddles as Red Shirt said, "That was a good trick. The long knives thought there were many of our people."

"Remember that it only worked because I kept their leader busy," Tom advised. "Had they sent out their scouts, or had time to look at you through their telescopes they would have known the numbers were in their favor."

"Blackfoot bad enemy," Red Shirt responded.

"Yes, you and your people are very good fighters," Tom agreed, "and had you joined battle with the Cavalry many of them would have died. However, Captain McDougal and his men, including the traders, outnumber your fighting men three to one. For the most part they are also better armed. True, you have a few repeating rifles, but, in the end, it would be arrows against bullets. Besides, they can always come back with even more men."

Red Shirt nodded. "It was a good trick you played."

Chapter 38

That night they sat outside the lodge while Tom smoked. The sun had just dropped behind the mountains, setting their peaks and the sky on fire. It had been a hard day for the Blackfoot and, except for the guards, most had taken to their beds.

"You had somethin' t' tell me?" Frank asked.

With the extra time that circumstances had forced on him, Tom had tried to calculate the best way to tell Frank his news. He had been unable to come up with anything that met with his satisfaction, so he decided to be blunt. "Approximately three weeks ago your father was alive," he said.

"Yuh mean Miller?" Frank finally asked.

"No, I told you this afternoon he had been found with a knife in his back. I mean Alex Clement. He came back looking for his family and arrived shortly after they found your mother and Miller."

"I got t' go back," Frank said.

"Now, just wait a minute," Tom said, turning to look at the younger man. "He's not back there." He explained all that McDougal had told him. "So, as you can see, we're already headed in the right direction. He may be well on his way to the very land we had decided to find."

"Maybe Californy 'r Or'gon Territory," Frank objected.

Tom nodded agreement. "Or the island settlements, or perhaps north to the Russian colonies. However, if we go where most of the gold seekers are to be found, and ask a few questions, we will hear word of him. Or he will hear word of us."

"Yeah," Frank said, drawing the word out. "Yeah, he hears o' me he'll come lookin'." He looked off to the west where mountain peaks were becoming black shadows on a sea of fire. "So when d' we chuck these folks an' make tracks?"

"Well, that depends," Tom responded. "Do you want to meet your father while you're still alive, or would you prefer to meet him in the hereafter?"

"Huh?"

"These people have saved us from slaughter and starvation. They are still saving us from the latter as we have little food of our own. They are also saving us from the former, since this is their country. Should we strike off west on our own we will undoubtedly encounter some other tribe of Blackfoot who have not heard of our greatness or having heard are less than impressed with such foolishness. They would find our horses a welcome addition to their herd."

"So we're stuck," Frank said.

"No, we are moving along quite nicely," Tom countered. "Should make several miles tomorrow."

"North ain't same as west," Frank observed, "'r didn' they teach yuh that in 'em fancy schools?"

"Whatever the direction, we need water." Tom pointed north. "The closest water is that way, and it's a river that runs from the mountains in the west."

"You sure 'nough figure that war chief's gonna show us a way?" Frank asked.

"I'll bet you the first ounce of gold you take from a stream over those mountains that he'll not only show us the way, but one of the best."

They sat in silence for several moments before Frank responded. "I'll take yuh up on that bet, but she'll be tough fer me t' collect when I win."

"And why is that?"

"'Cause we'll most like be dead."

It was a long day for the men and the Blackfoot as they pushed north over land made of powder and barely held in place by tinder dry grass. It had been more than a week since they had seen rain and that only enough to wet the ground. The country they were now crossing had been dry for a very long time.

A very warm but slight breeze from the southwest blew the high clouds of dust off to their right so the village stretched out in a single file. Such a line of women, children, and loaded horses was a weak and tempting target for any enemy, but the dust was a choking, killing thing. The warriors were interspersed along the line, two of them riding with the boys who brought the horse herd along in the rear.

Near midmorning, when they had already been on the trail several hours, Frank rode forward from the horse herd to ride near Tom. "Damn early start, an' pushin' mighty hard," he commented by way of greeting.

Tom batted his dust caked lashes and nodded toward the head of the column. "No water. River up ahead, but it's a long march."

They listened to the sounds of the village as they rode. Hoof fall in the sand, the creak and drag of travois poles, the squall of children. Frank looked off at the majestic mountains that raised the horizon line on their left. "We gonna get through 'fore winter?" he asked.

"Red Shirt says he has seen snow in all seasons, but that there is a way that is often passable. It lies almost due west.

"We will reach this water to the north, Etzi-com Coulee, then follow it west and slightly north" Tom continued. "Perhaps five days' ride will put us at a meeting place where they intend to come up with others of their people. There is a bend in the stream at that point, and it is a regular meeting place. We will rest and trade with them, then Red Shirt and a few of his men will lead us south and west to this mountain pass."

"What's t' trade?" Frank asked.

"I'm hoping to trade a few extra horses," Tom advised.

"Fer what? Pemmican?"

"Yes, that and dried meat. We will be meeting two other groups who have been trading with the white men. I'm hoping to get coffee, salt, flour, and whatever else is available."

Frank grunted. "So when's that put us into the mountains?"

"Mid-September, perhaps. I'm told we must be well past the summit by the middle of October."

Frank's eye's sparkled. "Well, we don' make 'er I reckon meat of a packhorse'll last us t' spring."

Tom returned his smile. "Only if we butcher the animal before it becomes too skinny."

Chapter 39

It was difficult for the two white men to leave the village under the shoulder of the mountains. They had traveled with the Blackfoot for more than four weeks, worked with them, been cared for by them, and ate at their fire. Even Frank who claimed, at the slightest provocation, his need to be away from the "damn savages," and who was anxious to begin looking for his father found himself reluctant to ride out.

Lead by Red Shirt, Bear Child, and Running Bull, they rode south and west for three days. The two packhorses were well loaded with supplies, much of it pemmican and jerked buffalo meat, and they lead two extra mounts. They were rich and happy men.

"We travel late," Tom said as they rode downslope toward a wide river.

"We stop here," Red Shirt advised. He pointed with his chin at the river. "White men call this the Flathead River. It is their country and they are our enemies."

"And there are only five of us," Tom observed.

"Tomorrow you must ride on, but the trail is as I have told you," Red Shirt continued. "You must hurry to cross through the mountains before the snow, but there is time."

It was usual to cross a river before camping, but if they did that the three warriors would only have to cross back again in the morning for their return journey. The sight Red Shirt chose was exceptional, and as with all good spots, showed signs of having been used many times in the past. There were several logs of six or more inches in diameter that had been blown down in a crisscross fashion by some long ago wind to form a natural corral for their horses, protection from wind and attack, and firewood. The camp was in a small clearing almost completely surrounded by this deadfall, and over the years new growth had risen to provide a screen that increased the efficiency of the windbreak. It probably saved their lives.

There was a chill in the air and heavy mist when they rose just at daybreak. To east and west they could see the hills rise on each side of the river, but from head level to the ground, all was obscured. Frank went to gather the horses as Tom started the fire and coffee. The three Blackfoot rose, stretched, and disappeared into the mist and brush between the camp and the river.

By the time Frank returned with the horses the heat from the fire had made a hole in the mist perhaps twenty feet across. He tied their lead ropes to a log with the color and feel of old bone.

The sound of someone hitting a dead tree with an axe was followed immediately by the sound of a shot. Frank dropped to the ground. On the steep slope to the southeast he saw the tell-tale cloud of smoke rising from a small grove of pine trees. He looked around quickly to see if there was any other movement, and even though he expected no attack from the river, scanned that area as well.

"Tom, you all right?" he asked.

"Sounded like it hit over near you," Tom replied.

"Hit one o' these here logs," Frank said. "That there's more 'n three hun'rd yards. Long damn way t' make a shot into a camp that's covered in mist."

"You think the shooter is just trying to draw our attention while the real attack comes out of the mist toward the river," Tom said, completing the thought behind Frank's observation.

"Seems likely."

"Well, you do appear to be learning, and, once again, I'm proud of my student," Tom said. "However, if such is indeed the case, and I would not be at all surprised, they will be in for a rude and probably final shock. That's the way our three traveling companions went to relieve themselves."

Perhaps a dozen shots were fired from the hill that rose to the east. The range was slightly more than a hundred yards and the bullets thunked, cracked, and whistled through the brush and trees. They could see no attackers for the screen of new growth cut off their view in that direction. However, they could see the tops of another grove of pine similar to that from where the first shot had originated. Through the tops of the young trees they could see the rise of powder smoke.

"Coffee ready yet?" Frank called loud enough to be heard by the attackers. Still laying flat on the ground he hauled his Spencer from the scabbard and checked the loads.

Tom reached out and pulled the boiling brew back from the fire. "Yes. Give it a minute to settle."

Still speaking loud and clear, Frank said, "Sure glad they had some back t' the village. Mornin' ain't rightly started without coffee." In a soft voice just loud enough for Tom he added, "Keep an eye up an' down river. On'y be a minute." Still on his belly he slid around the horses, into the brush, and under the deadfall.

When he reached the east edge of the deadfall and the base of the hill, the first shooter was just leaving his grove of pines and making a dash to join his companions in the grove almost straight upslope. Frank rested the Spencer on a dead log and took a sight on the running man. Shooting uphill he suspected his bullet would land short, so he put the bobbing head just above his front sight, and then lead it by several inches. He took a deep breath and let it out slowly, all the while tightening his finger on the trigger. Just at that moment when he was out of air, the hammer fell.

The bullet was still in flight when Frank dropped flat and moved to a new spot. He looked up to see his target drop his rifle, fall, and role several feet down hill. The man crawled upslope toward his rifle, dragging one leg.

The group directly above him was firing at his old location. He watched the smoke rise from their firing, then sent five shots at those spots as fast as he could lever and squeeze. Again he dropped to his stomach, but this time slithered back toward the clearing.

When Frank scurried up to the fire, Tom had a cup of coffee in his left hand, and his Colt revolving rifle lying across his lap, hand on the action. He sat with his back against a log and his eyes on the man trying to crawl along the hill.

Tom gestured with his cup toward the crawling man. "Very good shooting," he said. "You seem to be learning how to deal with the tension of battle."

Frank only nodded his acknowledgement as he poured a coffee, propped up on one elbow, and set the cup on the ground. "Mus' be a mighty big man. Thought it was 'bout two hun'red yard, but I come up short. On'y hit 'im in a leg."

"Very deceiving, shooting up hill," Tom remarked, then, noting the look from Frank added, "or so I've been told."

Frank grinned. "Ah, hell, yuh ain't that bad a shot." He nodded his head toward Tom's lap. "Don' know as I could hit a man at much more'n a hun'red yard with that revolvin' rifle."

"It's a Colt," Tom said.

Frank wrinkled his nose and slapped the pistol strapped to his waist. "Colt makes pistols, an' good un's."

Tom swung his coffee cup and nodded over his shoulder to indicate the area toward the Flathead River. "I do believe I heard something off toward the west. However, you were making so much noise with that Spencer I can't be sure."

At that moment the three Blackfoot warriors entered the clearing. They were bent almost double and moved swiftly and silently to the fire. Tom reached out and filled three more cups, then asked, quietly in French, "How many?"

"Kill four," Red Shirt replied. "Three more run."

A voice called from the grove of pines upslope to the east, a voice Tom immediately recognized. "We have you surrounded, Mr. Brash. You and your partner can ride away on one horse apiece, but leave those damn killers and everything else."

Tom smiled. "And what killers would that be, Mr. Coleman? Or is it Cole? What name are you using today?"

There was a short pause before the whiskey trader called back. "Those damn Blackfoot you've been protecting. They stay, and so do all your goods."

Frank looked at the two fresh scalps on Bear Child's belt. Running Bull and Red Shirt each had a blood-dripping trophy. "Who's protectin' who?" he asked.

"We should talk," Tom called back. He dropped his voice, switched to French, and said, "Red Shirt, it's very open downriver, but perhaps you could go upriver a short distance, then work your way up hill and get behind them."

"We could meet down at the base of the slope," Coleman called back, "east of your camp. But out in the open, and no weapons."

"Bear Child can go up that slope and the white men will never see him," Red Shirt said.

Tom looked at the slope to the southeast. It looked to him like the only cover was grass and that was not very tall. He shrugged. "They are your men, and if we could get around them from both sides, it would be much better."

"You will make a trade with this Coleman?" Red Shirt asked.

Tom shook his head. "I've embarrassed him in front of his men and in front of the U.S. Army," he said. "He may even know that I know he is a turncoat and a traitor. He has great dreams of being the ruler of this land, and I stand in his way." He shook his head again and looked up through the treetops at the grove of pines. "His only plan is to split us up, weaken us, and kill us all."

Switching back to English, Tom raised his voice and called to Coleman. "I'll be right out. No weapons." He unthreaded his belt, slid his large fighting knife to the back where it would hang under the tail of his coat, then re-tightened the belt. "Would you care for a cup of coffee, Mr. Coleman?"

Tom gestured to the southeast and northeast, and said in French. "You and your men try to go around and come in behind. I'll keep him busy with talk while Frank watches our back."

Red Shirt turned and began issuing instructions to the two warriors while Tom poured his own and Frank's cup full of the remaining coffee.

"Did you understand what I just said?" Tom asked.

Frank nodded. "I'll bring that there revolvin' rifle 'long in case we need t' shoot 'r way back."

Tom stepped up on a log and began working his way through the brush. The three Indians were already in position and silently working their way through the grass. Frank followed Tom but stayed beneath the logs, crawling on his stomach, the two rifles resting in his crooked elbows.

Chapter 40

Tom passed Coleman the cup in his left hand. They both sipped the hot coffee.

"Very good coffee, Mr. Brash," Coleman said.

As he nodded acknowledgement, Tom casually transferred his cup to his left hand. Sweeping back his coattail he put his right hand on his hip. He could feel the handle of the knife with his thumb.

"What was it you claimed your name was?" Coleman asked.

"I make no claims to any name," Tom responded. "My mother wished me to be called Thomas after a favorite uncle, and my father's family name was Brash."

"Which is what you have been," Coleman observed. "But it appears your brashness is about to cause your death."

Tom smiled. "I make no apologies for being either brash or my father's son, particularly in circumstances such as these."

Coleman took a drink of coffee, as he intently studied Tom. "Maybe that's it," he said. "Maybe you want to die. You sure act like it."

Tom smiled. "And whatever would make you say that, Mr. Cole?" He took a drink of coffee and allowed his eyes to wander along the hill to his right. By the faintest of movements he managed to make out the form of Bear Child working his way uphill and through the grass.

"It's Coleman. Colonel Coleman and you've been pushing against something that's far bigger than you. You interfered with two of my men out on the plains, and then you interfered with my expeditionary force, and the U.S. Army. I can't have that sort of thing. It might give people the idea that anyone can interfere with my plans."

He sipped his coffee, and then added, "You must have known that you had no force that could defeat me. Hell, there is nothing in all of what you call the Territories that can stop me."

Tom could see that Bear Child was almost level with the grove of trees where Coleman's men hid. The Blackfoot was beginning to angle his approach toward them as he climbed ever higher. He could see no movement in the other direction where Red Shirt and Running Bull would also be moving in.

"Mr. Cole, I have met many men, and a few women, like you," Tom said. "I've had them in my units, and I've had them as commanders. I've had them as students and neighbors. As with many of your ilk, you have something missing from making you a man. You are silly, lazy, and too stupid to see that you have nothing . . ."

Coleman reached for what would probably be a hideout gun. Tom slipped his knife out and put the point against Coleman's neck, then continued. "You have nothing and will always be nothing. Then you will die. And it might be today."

"I have you surrounded!"

"No you don't, and you never did. It's just like all the rest of your plans. It's a scheme with nothing to back it up. Four of the men who came up the river are dead. The others have run away."

"Cowards!" Coleman proclaimed.

Tom nodded. "As is their leader. A man too cowardly to face the fact that he has no honor and is respected by no one."

Carefully, so as to not press against the sharp point of the knife, Coleman attempted to show his courage. He lifted the cup and drank, his face showing no expression. "I'm a hero of the Civil War," he protested.

"You don't know, do you?" Tom said in more of a statement than a question.

Coleman raised his eyebrows. "Don't know?"

"I recognized you. You're not a hero; you're a traitor and an opportunist. I saw you in Jamaica when you were Captain of the *Cloud*."

There was a scream from behind Coleman. Tom jumped clear of him, but still kept the knife up and pointed. Coleman turned and looked up at the grove of trees, but nothing could be seen. He turned back and faced Tom.

"You told McDougal, didn't you?" Coleman asked.

"He's an honorable man and deserves to know what he's getting into," Tom replied. "Certainly I told him."

In what seemed like one motion Coleman threw the coffee in Tom's face, dropped the cup, and drew a small pistol from behind his wide belt.

Frank couldn't fire. Coleman had stepped slightly to one side, which put Tom in the way.

Tom blinked the coffee from his eyes as Coleman began to pull the hammer back. They were about four feet apart, too close to throw the knife. Reaching out, Tom brought the razor sharp edge down in a flashing arc. The pistol fired into the ground as it fell along with Coleman's thumb and index finger.

In the grove of trees uphill, several shots were fired.

Coleman squeezed the stumps on his hand as Tom said, "Your position has been overrun by Blackfoot warriors, Mr. Cole. The same savages you wanted me to leave for you to slaughter." He gestured to the hand dripping blood on the ground, despite the pressure Coleman was applying. "If you don't bleed to death, and if you can sneak away, and if you can get to a horse, you might live."

Blinking, already beginning to feel dizzy, Coleman turned and headed south at a stumbling lope.

"You have about as much chance as a snowball in hell, Mr. Coleman," Tom called after him. "But then, you may be familiar with hell." He leaned over and picked up the pistol. It was a short barrel, Colt, Navy Pocket model.

Up on the hillside, four men walked out of the grove of trees. They formed a square with their rifles facing out, one man walking backward. Crab like, they moved south along the slope, angling toward the top of the hill.

Frank stepped up beside Tom and passed him the Colt rifle.

"'But the transgressors shall be destroyed together: The end of the wicked shall be cut off,'" Tom quoted.

"What?"

"It's a line from the Old Testament, and should provide comfort. Book of Psalms, I believe. Somehow I don't feel comforted."

"Be the last we see o' Coleman," Frank said.

Tom shook his head. "With luck perhaps, but I suspect he will show up again."

"Bleed t' death 'r the army'll hang 'im."

"No, the Army won't hang him. It will be difficult to prove that he supported the south during the early years of the war. If there is a chance of such proof being made available, Mr. Coleman will be unavailable for prosecution. As for his bleeding to death, he will soon build a fire and stick his hand in it. In some ways he's a coward, and he is certainly a fool, but he is a tough man."

Frank studied Tom for a moment to see how much of what he had just said he truly believed. "Yuh should o killed 'im then."

Nodding his head, Tom let his breath out in a long sigh. "That is probably true, but there are many deaths on my head. I've had enough."

Chapter 41

As Jack Lawson rode toward the single rider trailing two extra horses he tried to notice every detail, just as he had been taught. He failed, however to note the small detail of his own position. He was on the rough-looking stranger's left front, putting himself in the very spot a fast gun handler would prefer.

Jack Lawson was not a stupid man, just inexperienced. He had tried to learn all he could about being a peace officer and, up to that point, had done very well. However, he had no experience with gunhandlers. Personally he believed that most of the fantastic stories about quick draws and gunfights were just that, fantastic stories. True, young Clement was very fast, but he was an oddity. Jack would have been surprised to learn that three of the men he talked to every day had been noted gunfighters or that there were others in town that had been in gun battles. He also suffered slightly from a malady that often affects the young, a conviction of invincibility.

Lawson drew his horse to a halt. With pressure from his legs he made it appear that his horse had a mind of its own as it turned slightly to the left, effectively blocking the trail. Once he had his mount in the position he wanted, he dropped his left hand, still gripping the reins, to the saddle horn. His right hand came to rest nonchalantly on his thigh near his holstered Colt.

"Afternoon," Jack said as the stranger halted. "Like to ask you a few questions."

The scarred faced turned as the stranger's eyes scanned the trees. His long, greasy hair swung slightly to reveal that the scar ended where the left ear was missing. Hunched forward, he rested both hands on the saddle horn, right on top of the left, before responding, "Free country."

"I was wondering if you could tell me where you got those horses," Jack asked.

"Pro'ly could if I thought it was any yer business."

"Well, that's exactly what it is," Jack responded. "I'm Constable Jack Lawson with the British Columbia Colonial Police, and I notice the brand on your mount and the last horse . . ." his eyes swung to the two animals roped together behind the strangers mount, the second animal carrying a small pack.

As Lawson's gaze shifted to the horses, the stranger reached for the front of his open jacket. With his hand already in position, Jack drew and cocked his Colt.

"You just sit quiet," Jack instructed. The stranger slowly placed his right hand back on his left atop the saddle horn.

"As I was about t' say, those horses appear to be wearing a V H connected. That happens to be the brand I've been looking for and, I'm sure, the very horses. I expect you'll be real surprised to know they belong to a couple of brothers waitin' up in the trees. Just like I'm surprised that One Ear Charlie Brown would steal horses." Jack smiled.

The long scar and missing ear made Brown easily recognizable. For five years One Ear had been a small but persistent thorn in the side of law-abiding citizens on both sides of the British Columbia/United States border.

Jack turned his gaze to the tree-covered slope on his left. "Peter? Henry? Come on down here and identify these horses."

The .36 caliber ball from One Ear's Manhattan Revolver entered behind Constable Jack Lawson's right ear and exited the left side of his forehead near the hairline. It may very well be that he did not hear the shot.

Up on the ridge, the Vanderhorst brothers did not see the actual shooting. They had just turned to mount their horses when the sound of the shot rang through the timber and bounced back to them from high mountain walls. They both turned quickly to see Jack fall loosely from his rearing mount.

As Jack Lawson's body came to rest his horse hit a full gallop on its way north to Wild Horse Creek. One Ear Brown dismounted with pistol drawn. The brothers swung to their saddles and did their best to catch up with Jack's horse.

Back on the trail, One Ear cautiously approached the downed lawman, his revolver cocked and ready. He had no idea where his shot had struck—was actually somewhat surprised that the black powder charge had ignited—and did not intend to be caught by someone playing possum, a trick he had used himself. As he circled the young man he saw the hole in his forehead and knew no one with that kind of damage would be getting up.

One Ear dropped the hammer between unfired nipples and put the revolver back under his coat. Then he knelt beside the body and began a quick search for whatever loot the lawman might have brought him.

There was not a great deal to find. The first thing he tried was the lawman's fine hat, which sat on his matted, greasy hair like an acorn on an egg. He sailed it into the brush and replaced it with his own beat-up headpiece. A pipe and sack of tobacco was welcome, as were three British sovereigns, three American silver dollars, and a twenty-dollar gold piece. The only other things on the body were a few scraps of paper and a small notebook that he threw down in disgust.

There was, however, a fine big pistol. It was an Army Colt .44 with an eight-inch barrel. Five of the six chambers were loaded while the five-chambered weapon he had carried up until now only held three loads. He stripped the belt from the corpse, strapped it on, and holstered the pistol.

"Mighty fine lookin' gun," he said aloud, hitching the belt into a comfortable position. "Got a real barrel on it, an' it's a Colt. Bet I could kill me a deer with this."

Reaching inside his coat he removed the Manhattan with its four-inch barrel that had been stolen from a farmhouse down in the Territories on the south side of the line. "Here yuh go, Mr. Lawman." He dropped the pocket model beside Jack's body. "'Fraid I can't rightly 'member where I got that so you might as well have it. Sorry I can't leave yuh extry balls. Ain't got a whole bunch to spare." He giggled at his own wit and turned to his mount.

It was Saturday, April 6, 1867.

On that same morning, in the community of Wild Horse Creek, four miners were taking their leisure in front of the mercantile. Frank Clement leaned against the hitch rail and Sam Moren stood on the boardwalk leaning against an awning post. Tom Brash, and Sam's partner, Clyde Phillips, sat on the bench, their backs against the store.

"Gettin' altogether too rough around here," Clyde Phillips proclaimed.

Sam shrugged the one shoulder that wasn't up against the post. "Seen worse."

"Well, I expect we all have," Tom agreed, "but that still doesn't mean it isn't too rough around here." Through the winter he had regretted leaving Coleman alive. He knew the man was out there looking for him.

Frank didn't offer an opinion. He thought it was a lawless area, but hadn't seen enough to compare it to anything else. As he walked and rode across the plains, by himself, with Tom, and later with the Blackfoot, he had needed to keep his eyes on everything, and that wasn't quite necessary here. It was however, a mining town, full of rough men with rough ideas that were nothing like he had dealt with at Fort Union. Wild Horse Creek was his first attempt at being a gold miner and the combined experience of the other three would add up to far more than his age.

"I'm not sayin' it ain't rough," Sam conceded. "An' I ain't denyin' there's been one or two boys lost their polks to one form o' crook or another. I'm just sayin' we got the law in this camp, an' they ain't doin' a bad job."

"It's too wild for just three policemen," Clyde objected. "That's what I'm saying. Oh, they're good boys, an' I like all three of them, but they just can't catch all the thieves when there's so many of them."

"Don't have any right now," Frank said in his low, slow way. This was a subject where he did know something the other three didn't.

There was a short pause, the three older men looking at Frank before Clyde asked, "Don't have any what? Fire a shot in the air and it's likely to land on a crook."

"Lawmen," Frank responded.

"We're talkin' about Carrington, Normansell, and young Lawson," Sam said, his tone quiet and patient. Sometimes he wondered if young Frank was all there. The boy hardly said anything, and when he did talk to you he was always looking off into the distance.

Frank nodded. "Yup, I know. John an' Jimmy ain't aroun'. Carrington's been gone four or five days. Seems t' me it might o' been a trial he had to attend, or some such. Normansell left day 'fore yesterday to check out some doin's to the north. Lawson left this mornin' with them two Dutch fellas rode in yesterday."

"Well, there you go," Clyde observed. "That's exactly what I been talking about. Too much crime, and too big an area to cover. Now what happens, do you suppose, if some drunk decides to cause a ruckus? Or what do we do if we get back to our claims and find somebody squattin' on them?"

"If somebody causes trouble 'cross the street," Sam observed, tipping his head toward the Wild Horse Saloon, "I 'spect Brian'll talk to 'em by hand for awhile an' heave 'im out into the mud. Anybody's on our claim I'll read to 'im from the book just before I bury 'im. 'Course, that might take awhile since we'll have to wash the gold out o' all the dirt 'fore we throw it back in the hole."

The other three men smiled as Tom responded. "Mighty nice of you to make sure the scoundrel has a clean place to rest."

At that moment two men rode into the south end of the street, one of them leading a horse with an empty saddle. Frank Clement dropped his smile. He was the only one of the four who recognized the riders as the ranchers from south of the U.S. border who had left town that morning in the company of Jack Lawson.

As soon as he saw the empty saddle Frank knew that he would no longer be exchanging jokes with Jack Lawson. His single quiet word was a mild curse.

"What's wrong with you all of a sudden?" Clyde asked.

"Them's the two Dutch fellers left town with Jack this mornin'," Frank responded, and then paused before confirming something he didn't really want to think about. "An' that's Jack's horse."

An uneasy feeling fell over the town, just as if the whole area could hear what Frank had said. The bartender, Brian Sullivan, accompanied by one of his customers, stepped out of the saloon, ducked under the low edge of the porch roof and stopped in the street to watch the Vanderhorst brothers pull up in front of the mercantile. Two men walking down that side of the street stopped their conversation and movement, eyeing the six men across the street. A woman carrying a shopping basket, who had just started across the street to avoid passing in front of the saloon, also stopped.

John Semple, owner of the mercantile, stepped through his own front door, a troubled look on his face. "What's the problem here?" he asked. His gaze traveled around the group of loafers then settled on the two mounted men.

The only sound was the creak of saddle leather, the heavy breathing of the horses, and the shuffle of those joining the group in front of the store.

The older brother, Henry Vanderhorst, tried to speak, but his mouth only opened and his lips shook. With his free hand he rubbed his face, shook his head, and then swung from the saddle.

Peter Vanderhorst shifted in the saddle, cleared his throat, and said, "Dat young policeman huz bin shot."

In the silence, Henry wrapped the reins of his and Lawson's horse around the hitch rail. He leaned against the cross piece, looking at the dust. "Suj a happy boy," he said a quaver in his voice. It appeared that it would take very little for him to start crying.

Clyde Phillips stood and stepped forward to stand beside Sam Moren. "I think we'll need a little more information," he suggested.

Peter nodded. "My bruder und I have ranch just sout' ov da border. Sunday morning, while we eat, uh man steals two horses. We follow dis man und find his camp yesterday. Then we come here und find da policeman. Dis morning we leave here und go back down da trail to get our horses, but we see dis thief come toward us. Jack tells us to wait in da trees und he will get our horses. He goes to talk to dis man und da man shoots him."

"Yuh sure he's dead?" Sam asked.

Peter put his right index finger behind his right ear. "I tink da bullet go in somewhere here." He moved his finger around to his forehead. "We see very big hole here."

Sam and Clyde both nodded, then Clyde asked, "What did this horse thief look like?" Even though logic told him that the thief was now a murderer, something stopped him from confirming the young lawman's death by using the title.

"He huz long black hair and beard," Peter replied. "Da hat is old wid a hole in the top part und a rip in . . ." He paused and touched the brim of his Stetson, "dah peak?"

"The brim's torn," Clyde offered.

"Dah, und Jack call him 'One Ear'."

Few of those in the crowd needed any further description. Most knew then who the killer was.

The four friends had just been talking about the rougher element and the need to look after their community. With no policemen available, the circumstances demanded an immediate response from someone. Clyde and

Sam looked at each other and nodded. Turning to Tom and young Frank they received similar nods. They would handle this problem themselves. Without a word three of them moved out at a brisk walk toward the livery stable. Frank quickly inspected the contents of Jack Lawson's saddlebags before he followed.

"I'd like to have that pistol," Frank said.

Holding the Manhattan revolver and Lawson's grey Stetson, John Semple turned from watching Brian Sullivan tie the Constable's body across his own saddle.

"I expect Jimmie Normansell will need it as evidence," Sullivan responded.

"'Spect he will," Frank agreed, "but when they're done, I'd like to have it. Jack was the best friend I ever had."

"So you want his gun?" Semple asked.

"Ain't his gun," Frank replied. "Jack's was new, a .44, and cared for. That thing's rusty." Leaning forward in the saddle he reached out and John passed him the gun. He pulled the caps from their seats, inspected them, and then peered into the chambers from either end. "Powder's been wet and then dried. Hasn't been oiled in a fair spell. The caps are even corroded. Don' make no sense it fired."

Frank passed the gun back to Semple, and then added, "That's the gun that killed Jack."

"So it's likely that One Ear has Jack's," Tom Brash concluded.

"Yup, an' I want it, too," Frank said, turning his horse toward the trail.

Chapter 42

Jack Lawson was one of the first people Frank and Tom met when they arrived in Wild Horse Creek. They had gone to the police lock-up to start inquiries about Frank's father. When they entered the building the young policeman's eyes locked on the pistol tied to Frank's leg.

"We like to discourage people from wearing firearms here," were the first words spoken.

Looking off toward the potbelly stove, Frank said, "Put 'er in muh saddlebag right now."

"When you leave is soon enough," the young lawman responded. "Just so you know it won't be needed here."

"We get us a claim staked, yuh gonna keep claim jumpers off?" Frank asked.

"Frank?" Tom said.

"Jess like t' know," Frank said.

"If you can prove your claim, the Colonial Police will see you keep it," the lawman said.

"Well, if'n I'm dead, ain't no way fer me t' prove muh claim," Frank noted. "So, long as you're about, you c'n look after me. You ain't about, I'll pack the Colt."

"I understand the British Columbia Police cover a very wide area," Tom interjected, hoping to change the subject.

"We're responsible for the whole colony and it's a big one."

"My name is Tom Brash, and my young friend is Frank Clement."

"Jack Lawson," the lawman responded, and extended his hand.

When everyone had shaken hands, Tom continued. "Frank thought his father had been killed in the American Civil War and left his home. Perhaps two months ago we met a man on the road who said that Frank's father had returned, and finding no one home, assumed that Frank was dead. There was some talk of the father going to the gold fields, so we would like to put the word out that Frank is here, and would like to get together with his father."

"Well, 'gold fields' covers a lot o' country," Jack responded. "Sometimes I get the feelin' the whole colony is a gold field. But I'll sure pass the word on to New Westminster. They'll let the other officers know. What's the name?"

"Alexander Clement. He was a Sergeant in the Union Army, and may still wear some of his old uniform."

Jack nodded as he wrote the name. "Country's full o' old soldiers from both sides. Don't have as much trouble between 'em as you might expect, though."

Tom had wanted to mention Coleman, but he really had nothing more than a feeling that the man was out there. He had just convinced the law to help Frank. It wouldn't help to have both the policeman and Frank laughing at his fears.

Though their first meeting appeared to put them at odds, Frank and Jack became good friends. Jack introduced Frank to the few young ladies in the area. Their fathers would have never tolerated a buckskin-clad miner around their daughters, but when he was with the young peace officer, it was a different matter entirely. Frank taught Jack how to draw his Colt, how to shoot, and some tricks of proper care for the weapon.

As they followed the trail of the killer, Frank felt a big hole where his stomach should be. He was beginning to have some understanding of how Tom must have felt when Looking Back was killed. He knew he would miss the policeman for a long time.

The self-appointed posse was armed with a variety of weapons. Frank carried his Colt .44 similar to the one taken from Lawson's body, and the stock of his Spencer carbine protruded from the saddle scabbard. Sam Moren carried a Colt Dragoon .44 in a Confederate Army holster with the CS letters still visible on the cover, and an Ethan Allen double-barrel, eight-gauge in the saddle boot. Clyde had a .32 rimfire Smith & Wesson behind his belt, and a ten-gauge, double-barreled, Lefever shotgun on the saddle. Tom carried his ten-gauge Colt revolving shotgun in his arms, and the revolving rifle was in the saddle scabbard under his leg. Brash also had the .36 Navy Colt he had taken from Coleman, but it was back at their cabin. He didn't even think Frank knew he had that pistol, and he wanted to keep it that way. In their pursuit of One Ear, each man also carried a small amount of fear and a great deal of respect for the man who had shot Jack Lawson.

"How'd he get the name 'One Ear'?" Frank asked of no one in particular. They were strung out on the trail with Clyde and Sam in front of Frank. Tom brought up the rear.

"Man's on'y got one ear," Sam replied, happy for an opportunity to supply Frank with one of his own uninformative replies.

"Well! Ain't that a shock an' a reveelation," Frank responded, mimicking poorly a tone of excitement.

Sam smiled his satisfaction.

"Had his ear shot off," Clyde responded from the rear. "Few years back he was in jail over in Victoria. The gentleman's real name is Charlie Brown. They wanted t' move Mr. Brown to another cell, and he decided he didn't want to go. After a bit of a go-round he wound up with the guard in a headlock.

"I guess the screw was fed up with foolin' around. He drew his pistol and shoved it up by Charlie's head and says, 'Let go, or I'll blow your head off'. Well, Charlie didn't believe him, and squeezed a little harder.

"The screw pulled the trigger, but he missed. It blew Charlie's ear off and left some powder burns alongside his face. And that's how Charlie Brown became 'One Ear Charlie'."

They rode on in silence for several moments, listening to a faint breeze in the trees, birdcalls, and the chatter of squirrels.

"Any idea what the jailer's name was?" Sam asked.

"His name was Charlie, too," Clyde replied. "Give me a minute I'll think of the rest of it. Why?"

"Well, I reckon, this is all over, we best hunt 'im up and teach 'im how t' shoot," Sam replied. "Man knew what he was doin' we wouldn't be out here, an' Jack Lawson would still be alive."

Chapter 43

The shooting had taken place on the main trail east of Wild Horse Creek. Sam Moren studied the tracks and discovered that One Ear had continued north, then east on well-traveled trails.

Clyde Phillips had once stated that Sam Moren could read tracks better than his partner could read English. This was meant to be a high compliment since Clyde had studied law before he was drawn into the Civil War.

"Are you sure we're on the right trail?" Clyde asked.

"Sure I'm sure," Sam responded. He pointed at the trail in front of his mount. "There's his track right there, plain as day. Horse he's ridin' has shoes on the back an' barefoot up front. One o' the one's he's leadin' is barefoot with a big crack in the off hind foot. Easier 'n seein' where your big clodhoppers been goin' 'round camp."

"Well, I just want t' make sure. There's a lot of tracks here."

"An' all of 'em from yesterday."

Tom and Frank hung back while Clyde and Sam studied the confusion of tracks on the trail. "Thought I was your best friend," Tom said.

Frank's face flushed under the deep tan. "You're my partner, and the best there is. But Jack was a lot closer t' my age, an' we had things we could kid each other 'bout."

Frank paused and studied Tom's face. He could tell by the stoic expression that he hadn't really comforted his partner.

"Ain't seen my pappy since he went off t' war when I was twelve. An' Miller sure weren't nothin' t' copy. You've learned me how to read, how to speak proper, an' how to box, and you've made me a partner. I got half a claim, an' we're pannin' some flakes out o' it. Got me somethin' o' my own, an' mostly on account o' you.

"Jack Lawson was only a few years older 'n me an' he was my best friend. You've been a mighty good friend too, but your sixteen years older 'n me."

They rode on for a few moments before Frank added, "Ain't right t' go talkin' up the gals with yer pappy along, an' you're the closest thing to a pappy I've had in a long time."

Tom Brash cleared his throat, and then stretched his neck. "Well, thank you very much, Frank." He tilted his head toward the other two men. "Looks like they've found something," he said and poked his horse into motion.

They had only gone a few steps when Tom stopped his horse again and turned in the saddle to face Frank. "I'd be proud to have a son like you, Frank, and thank you. And I enjoy teaching you things. In turn, you have taught me how to shoot, and how to find gold in a stream."

They moved out again and Tom said over his shoulder, "By the way, I don't learn you things, I teach you things."

When they came up to the other two, Clyde said, "Sam thinks he may have headed out on this track to the south."

"Don' think nothin' o' the sort," Sam responded. "Know damn well he did. There's a crossin' o' the St. Mary downstream a ways from the ferry that he might be headed for. Thing is, this time o' year, spring runoff an' all, she'll be a bear to cross down there. Don' see why he'd go that way, an' I 'spect he'll come back upriver to cross. That would put him on this trail, which also turns south a might further on and comes out at Galbraith's Ferry."

"Perhaps he expects us to believe he's headed west to the Kootney," Tom suggested. "If he can cross without someone spotting him, as they surely would at Galbraith's, maybe he expects to escape south."

Sam nodded. "Maybe. He's been makin' a try at hidin' his trail. If he didn' have a tracker behind him, an' if he wasn't so lazy, he might a done it."

"We think it's a good idea to split up," Clyde interjected, halting their speculation. "Since we think he may turn back to the ferry, someone should be there to meet him. At the same time, someone should be behind him."

Tom nodded agreement. "May I suggest that I go with Sam as his back-up? He can track and shoot, and I have a shotgun to help overcome my failing in the latter department. Although Frank can't track as easily as Sam, he is by far the best shootist among us and can help Clyde with his shortcomings in those areas. In turn, they will be more inclined to pay attention to Clyde at Galbraith's than they would be to either Frank or I."

Sam looked at Frank and was not quite successful in suppressing a smile. Tom had bragged about his young partner's shooting before, but

Sam suspected it was because Tom hadn't seen many men shoot. However, he also thought it didn't really matter at this point. "Makes sense to me," Sam responded, turning his horse toward the eastern fork of the trail. "Wait for us at Galbraith's."

"I can shoot," Clyde said with some indignation.

"Yup, yer not bad fer a Connecticut Yankee," Sam responded, trying to get off the subject and onto the trail. "But if yuh had shooters like young Frank on yer side it wouldn't a taken yuh so damn long t' beat us. Good thing yuh brought yer shotgun."

"And I notice you're carrying a shotgun as well, you loud-mouth Arkansas Rebel."

As the two partners traded insults each group drifted apart on their respective trails.

A half-hour later, just to break the silence, Frank said, "Somebody tol' me once yuh studied law, but I didn't know you was from Connecticut." Frank had been taught not to ask a direct question about a person's past, but he was curious. True, both he and Tom had liked Sam and Clyde from their first meeting, but they didn't know a great deal about either man, except that they presently held the claim next to Frank and Tom's, and had been in the area since the previous spring of '66.

"I'm not," Clyde responded, "I was born and raised in New York. That's just Sam's way of trying to get under my skin. I do the same to him. He's from Kentucky."

"Did you run up against each other in the war?"

Clyde shrugged. "No way of knowing. It's probable. I know we were in the same battles, but we never talk about it. It was gray shooting at blue and family members wearing both colors. Stupid damn thing, war."

"Then why're yuh out here chasin' this Brown?" Frank asked.

Clyde turned to look at Frank's face, and then replied, "Because this is a rough land full of violent, lawless people. If we allow this sort of thing to go unchecked for even an instant they will be all over the rest of us and none of us will have a life."

They rode on for a few moments, and then Clyde asked, "Why are you here?"

"T' kill the man that killed my best friend," Frank said, much the same as he might have said he was going out to shovel some gravel into the rocker.

For the remainder of the ride to the ferry crossing Clyde Phillips was very uncomfortable.

Chapter 44

At the crossing of the St. Mary's River, Clyde asked the ferryman if he had seen a man with three horses and one ear.

"No, One Ear Charlie Brown has not crossed my threshold," the ferryman replied in a proper British accent, "and if he should, I will be sure to greet him with a load of heavy shot."

Frank and Clyde bought a ride on the ferry, and once on the south side, began to set up a camp. As Frank was mixing bannock, Sam and Tom appeared, riding upriver on the north bank. They were leading a third horse.

Having made their own ferry crossing, Sam and Tom stripped the gear from their horses, hobbled them, and then approached the fire.

"We ain't far behind 'im," Sam announced.

Clyde moved the boiling coffee back from the coals and looked up.

"When he seen the river was high he took time t' build him a raft," Sam continued. "The raft broke up an' he lost his food stuffs, but him an' two o' the horses made it across." He gestured with his thumb at the strange horse. "This one here ain't wearin' the V H connected; it's a Lazy T. Must be the horse he had afore he stole the two from the Dutchmen."

Clyde nodded as he sliced bacon. "So now where?"

"Well, a man named Joe Davis has a camp on a wash that runs into the St. Mary's," Tom advised. "The trail from that lower ford should lead right to him. I understand he is a man who keeps his eyes open and rifle within reach. He'll know of any traveler, and point us in the right direction."

"Now how in hell d' yuh know that?" Sam asked.

"He's all'ays askin' questions an' drawin' maps," Frank advised.

"That's correct," Tom said. He gestured down the trail that ran by their camp. "According to my latest map, there is another trail intersecting this one a few hundred yards to the south. It should lead east to Davis' camp."

"Well, as it happens, you're right," Sam said. "I ain't been on this trail, but I bin over t' Joe's by the lower ford. It was August, mind, an' she was a mighty easy crossin'. Can't see anybody tryin' 'er when she's runnin' high like she is, raft 'r no raft. Man has t' be crazy."

"Ain't no doubt o' that," Frank said. "He shot a policeman."

During the several moments of silence that followed, the four men held their own thoughts. Frank watched the flames dance around the frying pan and reach for the bannock while the other three watched the setting sun.

"Well, we'll let the horses rest, get some ourselves, then take the trail before daylight," Clyde said, breaking the silence. "We may run these horses to a frazzle, but we should have him by tomorrow night. His horse won't be as rested as ours."

Sam and Tom looked at each other and smiled. "I think you're weighin' yer gold 'fore you've shoveled any gravel," Sam observed, "but we'll give 'er a try."

After they'd eaten, Sam and Frank settled into their bedrolls. Tom loaded a pipe, lit it, and walked off toward the horses. After a few moments, Clyde rose and followed him.

"Nice night," Tom said as Clyde came up behind him.

They each stood for a moment looking at the stars before Clyde said, "You'll need to have a talk with your partner."

Tom turned and looked at him, still puffing on the pipe, and raised his eyebrows. When he realized that Clyde couldn't see his expression, he asked, "How so?"

"He told me today the only reason he's here is to kill a man," Clyde informed him.

"One Ear Charlie Brown," Tom responded.

"That's the one."

"And why are you here, Clyde?"

"Oh, I expect we'll either wind up shooting him or hanging him, but that isn't really our purpose," Clyde responded. "It isn't mine, anyway. I'm here as a responsible citizen who wants an end to terror."

"A fine sentiment and a noble ideal," Tom observed. "Tell me Clyde, are they more important than a quality life, or does the good life lead to ideals?" He paused, drew on his pipe, and looked up at the stars as if to find an answer to his own question.

"As far as being a citizen," Tom continued, "none of us are. They've been talking about a thing called confederation, and that may have already taken place. If it has, I may be a citizen of this country, since I was born in Upper Canada. If it hasn't, I'm a British visitor to the British Colony of British Columbia. You three are Americans."

There was a long pause before Clyde responded. "I may need some time to answer your question about ideals."

"I wasn't really expecting an answer," Tom said. "I'm with you on this, but I don't think we have any right to be too sure of ourselves."

Tom began tapping out his pipe, and then added, "As for Frank, don't worry about him. I've known him for about a year, a very eventful year, and he's one of the brightest young men I've ever met." He put his pipe in his vest pocket, and then shrugged. "There may come a time when Frank Clement becomes a gunfighter, for he's altogether too good with that pistol he wears, but I think he's too smart to go in that direction. I think you'll find, when he finds himself up against a wall, he'll do the right thing. Or, at the very least, learn the right lessons from the mistakes he makes.

"Let me tell you what happened out on the plains. I saw Frank shoot the whip out of a man's hand without hitting the hand. A few weeks later our camp was overrun by a band of Blackfoot, and I expected him to fire on them. It took very little effort on my part to stop him from shooting, for he knew in the instant that we would have been killed. We lived with that band for several weeks, and although he had been taught to hate them, it was never apparent while we were among them. No, when it comes down to it, Frank can be depended on to do the right thing."

They stood together in the dark for a moment. Tom expected Clyde was thinking about Frank, but when he spoke, he said, "You lived with the Blackfoot?"

Chapter 45

"Yup, come in here yestiday," Joe Davis advised. "Seen 'im comin' an' didn't take to 'im. Time he could see me he could also see muh Sharps an' that she was cocked. On'y had 'im the one horse, though, a sorrel."

"Must have lost the other in the river," Clyde said.

Joe pointed to a tripod of poles where some pieces of meat were hung. "Tol' 'im t' take a front quarter o' Elk an' t' git. Wasn't 'till he was cuttin' the meat down that I noticed he had one ear. Didn' know who he was 'till then."

The four mounted men nodded their understanding, then Clyde said, "He shot young Jack Lawson yesterday morning."

Davis' expression didn't change but there was concern in his voice. "How's the boy doin'?"

Clyde and Tom shook their heads while Sam and Frank looked off to the mountains. "Through the head," Clyde said.

Davis cursed. "Should a shot 'im in the back when he was cuttin' that meat down."

"We'll get him," Frank advised.

"Well, he took the main trail, but you can gain a bit on 'im by goin' over the shoulder o' the mountain," Davis advised. "It's a little shorter. An' when yuh come back t' this trail you'll find a Chineman washin' gravel. He'll tell you where he went."

"Thank you, Mr. Davis," Tom said as Frank lead off, heading toward the bottom of the mountain trail.

As the four riders disappeared, Joe Davis stood watching them with a grin on his toothless face. "Reckon that's the first time anybody every called me mister. Right nice gentleman, that fella."

The posse made good time on the mountain trail. However, it was not a trail for the faint of heart, or for anyone mounted on horses raised on the flatlands. It wasn't as high as some of the country Tom and Frank had ridden through to reach the west side of the Rockies, but it was very rugged and steep. There were times when a rider could look down past his right foot and see absolutely nothing for several hundred yards. Though Frank and Tom's French Canadian horses showed the whites of rolling eyes on more than one occasion, they followed the Montana mounts of the other two men without hesitation. The horse they had found followed with no show of fear.

Tom believed they saved five miles while traveling twelve over the mountain. Shortly after gaining the main trail it veered to the west, crossed a small stream, then turned south again and paralleled it for some distance. A few hundred yards farther and they could see where a sand trap had been dug into the east bank of the brook directly in front of a small, ramshackle cabin. In front of the trap out near the edge of the water sat a sluice box beside which stood an Oriental man wearing a conical hat. He leaned on a shovel as he watched the approach of the four riders.

The posse members pulled up on the south bank of the stream and halted.

"Have you seen a lone rider on a red horse?" Clyde asked.

The Chinese man nodded vigorously, his long pigtail bobbing and snapping. Still leaning on the shovel with his left hand he pointed south with his right. "Monster devil man." He pointed across his face at the left side of his head. "No ear. Want bullets. I tell him no got. He go." Once again he pointed to the trail south.

"Much obliged," Sam said, turning his mount back to the trail. The three others nodded and turned to follow. Just before they disappeared from sight, Tom looked back to see a second man with a pigtail and holding a rifle step out of the brush near the cabin. He smiled with some degree of satisfaction then hurried to catch up with Frank.

"That doesn't appear to be the type of place one would look for ammunition," Tom observed.

"He must know someone is after him," Clyde observed. "May have even seen us. He's probably getting desperate."

"How many bullets do you suppose he has?" Tom asked.

"No more 'n five," Frank offered.

Clyde pulled his horse to a stop and looked at Frank. "What makes you say that?"

Though he was too far ahead to hear what had been said, Sam noticed the others had stopped and halted his own horse. Without the sound of the horse hooves to interfere, he also heard Frank's reply.

"Took a look in Jack's saddle bags. He had two extra cylinders that he kept loaded, an' they were wrapped up in the saddle bag. In the other bag were a few caps. He always carried five rounds in his pistol, an' I never knew him to carry bullets in his pockets."

"Brown might have had some .44s before he ran into Jack," Clyde observed.

Frank nodded. "Maybe, but not likely. The pistol he threw away was a .36, an' the Dutchmen said they didn't see no rifle."

Clyde nodded, and then urged his mount down the trail.

Before Sam continued he made one further observation. "He maybe has five shots, but yesterday he did alright with one, seems t' me. It might a' bin dumb luck, but I don' know any time my luck was that good. Five shots an' four o' us."

Chapter 46

Well past noon they approached the small logging community of Yahk. On the edge of town stood a few corrals clustered around a small barn. In front of this barn lay a circle of fire within which lay a steel wagon tire, being heated in preparation for installation on a wheel. Holding a smoldering branch of green willow that he had been using to heap the coals against the tire, the blacksmith straightened, drew on his pipe, and watched them approach.

"Afternoon, boys," the blacksmith greeted, taking in the sweat, dust, and tired mounts.

Each of the posse members returned the greeting before Clyde came to the point. "We're looking for a fellow riding a red horse, probably in worse shape than these. Long black hair and missing an ear."

The blacksmith grinned around the pipe stem, removed it and asked, "The man 'r the horse?"

Only Tom Brash returned the smile. The other three faces remained hard. The blacksmith decided that perhaps a long ride had narrowed their sense of humor.

"Either one," Tom responded. "If you've seen him, perhaps you could tell us."

"Yeah, I seen 'im," the blacksmith responded before replacing his pipe and returning to banking the coals. "Come in here 'fore noon," he continued through clenched teeth and around the pipe stem. "I was shooin' a horse at the time, an' he started off 'bout how the B.C. police were gettin' awful pushy. Said they wouldn't be pushin' him since he shot one yesterday. Went on 'bout how the next t' get it would be a couple o' Dutchmen."

He pointed with his willow toward the barn. "Headed over t' the customer's wagon, sittin' there by the fence. When he started into braggin', I wasn't real comfor'ble, so I set the horse's foot down real casual like, an' kinda wandered over t' the barn like I needed to get somethin'.

"Back o' the wagon was some supplies. He started pawin' 'round in there an' come up with a sack o' flour, some salt, bakin' powder, an' such like. But when he come up with it I was inside the barn an' he was lookin' at the muzzle o' my rifle.

"Well, he outs with that fancy pistol he was carryin' an' down behind the wagon. He hollers over, 'I got five shots an' you got one. I'm gonna take some o' this stuff an' light out. Ain't nobody needs to get shot.'"

The blacksmith removed his pipe, and then spit into the dust. "Now, I never found where a gun fight was a lot o' laughs, 'specially when I'm outgunned. So I stayed in the barn an' left 'im to it.

"John Nobel come back fer his rig," he continued, "an' found some o' his supplies missin'. He was down right peeved when I tol' him what happened. I tol' him if a few supplies was so important to 'im he should go get 'em back. Noticed he didn't."

"And which way would that be that he headed?" Clyde asked.

"One Ear? Well, he headed south. Reckon he's into the territories by now."

The four horsemen turned their mounts and headed toward the small stream where the loose horse and Sam's regular mount were already drinking. "Thank you for the information," Tom said as he turned to follow the others.

As they allowed the horses to drink, Clyde looked to his partner. "Well, what do you think? Should we cross the line?"

"We ain't lawmen," Sam observed as he began loosening his saddle. "Don't think it matters to us where the border is. 'Sides, Tom's the only one ain't American, an' it was 'merican horses that was stole." He turned to Frank, sitting on his right. "Any idea where them Dutchmen got their place?"

"Some place north o' Bonners Ferry."

"Jack ever carry any money?"Sam asked as he carried his blanket and saddle to the spare horse.

Frank nodded. "Usually all he had, which was never much."

"I 'spect this killer will be about ready t' spend whatever he has," Sam observed. "If he figures on hangin' around 'till he can get at them Dutchmen, that means he'll go to Bonners. Pro'ly figures we won't foller him there, an' he can get him some whiskey."

There was a pause while each of them considered this possibility. Sam tightened the saddle on his new mount.

"Will these horses make it to Bonners Ferry?" Tom asked.

Sam nodded once, and then patted the neck of the horse he would be riding. It was the Lazy T horse they had found at the crossing of the St. Mary's River. "They'll make it. It's helped we've had this one t' change off on. Be done when we get there, but they'll make it."

"Sitting up on that one after we get south of the border might not be healthy," Clyde observed. "We don't know who actually owns it. Someone's likely t' get shot out of the saddle."

Clyde nodded. "Best leave this un here fer them Dutchmen t' pick up."

Shortly after they left the blacksmith, the trail they followed became wider. There had been more traffic in this area, some of it wagons. The partners rode abreast, Sam and Clyde leading.

"When did this fella lose his ear?" Frank asked.

"That was in '62, I think," Clyde replied. "Either '61 or '62. You'll know I wasn't there an' just goin' by hear tell."

"So where's he bin fer the last five years?"

"As I heard it, he hung around Vancouver Island for awhile after that. I think he spent some time in the Bastion Jail, even after he lost his ear. At least once."

"What for?" Frank interrupted.

"Selling whiskey to the Indians, usually. Sometimes for stealing this and that. His so-called whiskey might be made of anything. I heard he once sold a barrel of seawater as whiskey.

"He's been doing the same thing along the border for the last three or four years. Stealing horses in the Territories and selling them in B.C. That's probably what he intended with the Dutchmen's horses. Or he might rob an isolated miner of his dust. At least once he bought some wood alcohol in Rossland, put some tobacco, red pepper, and who knows what else in it and sold it to some Indians. No way to know how many people have died from drinking his whiskey."

"An' folks just let this go on fer four years?" Frank asked.

Clyde shrugged and Tom held his hands palm up in a gesture of resignation. "People just want to get on with their lives," Tom said. "They're busy raising cows, or panning gold, or cutting timber. If they can stop someone from taking something from them, they will, but once it's over they mark it down as part of the cost of living out here, and go on with their lives. With a long winter staring you in the face, for example, you had best look to your own survival, and forget about some no-account thief that you'll probably never see again."

Frank shook his head in disgust. "An' after you've let it go on fer awhile he comes back and steals from you agin'. Or shoots one o' yer friends."

"That's why we're here," Clyde observed. "We have to let men like One Ear know that we won't put up with their shenanigans. Otherwise, if they don't have a reason not to, those who might be just on the edge of the law will step over the line. They'll take everything we've worked for."

"Ain't the same fer us," Sam observed.

"The same as what?" Clyde asked.

"Well, we ain't bin tryin' t' build much all these years. We don' got no family t' worry over. I don' know 'bout Frank an' Tom, but you an' me bin doin' our job an' shootin' at other folks doin' their job. Seems t' me it's a fair step up t' go after a thief an' a killer."

"Frank and Tom have been livin' high on the hog," Clyde said. "Livin' with the Blackfoot, don't you know. Eatin' buffalo meat and fightin' the Cree."

Sam looked from Clyde to Tom, then back to Clyde. When he again swung his eyes to Tom, he received a nod of acknowledgement.

"The hell you say. The Blackfoot. That'll make the hair stand up on your neck."

"Did mine," Frank admitted. "Fer a while, anyway. Turned out t' be fine folks. Saved our hides' more 'n once."

"And didn't raise that hair that you said was standin' up," Clyde added. "That's another time they saved your hide."

Tom still thought of Looking Back on occasion and wanted a change of subject. He also expected this was as good a time as any to explain what he wanted to happen. Perhaps it would make Frank think about his vendetta.

"This Brown we're following," he said. "It's important that we take him back to Judge Haynes. If we do, the story will go around all the camps, and people will know that most of us won't stand for this sort of thing. Since we have witnesses to the shooting of a policeman, One Ear will hang."

For several seconds, Frank looked at his partner, and then asked, "If most of us won't stand far it, how come we're the only ones here?"

"As Sam said, we don't have families," Tom said, then shrugged. "Perhaps we see the importance more than others."

Chapter 47

To their right the setting sun had turned the sky several shades of red as the four riders came in sight of Bonners Ferry. For some moments they had been overtaking a small party who now pulled to the side of the trail to let them pass.

They were Kootney Indians, a young man and his woman. The young man rode while his pregnant wife walked. Clyde was upset by what he saw as an impropriety until he noticed the dark stain on the young man's shirt on the left side under the arm. He also noticed that the young Indian held the saddle horn with that left hand, the barrel of his rifle resting on his forearm. The right hand was on the rifle action, thumb on the hammer.

"Looks like you've had some trouble," Clyde observed.

The young man nodded. The young woman shifted nervously, her wide eyes scanning the white men.

"Crazy white man," the young brave said, nodding his head back up the trail toward the north. "Try to take woman and bullets. We go away quick."

"What'd this crazy white man look like?" Sam asked.

"One ear and scar," the young brave replied.

Sam's teeth showed through his dust-covered face in what might pass for a smile. "We're ahead of him, boys."

"When did this happen?" Tom asked the young Indian.

The young man pointed his rifle muzzle straight up. "The sun was here."

"About noon," Clyde observed. "So he's probably not too far behind you."

The young Indian shook his head. "He look for us maybe long time. Maybe try to get bullets from others."

Clyde nodded and urged his tired horse on down the trail. "We'll have time to get some fresh horses, boys."

Once again, Tom thanked the young couple before he followed the rest of the posse.

At the livery stable they had no difficulty trading their horses for fresh mounts. When they explained who they were following, the livery operator was happy to help them.

It was well after dark when they again hit the trail, this time headed north.

"Up here a ways there's a ridge runs along the east side o' the trail," Sam explained. "I don' know as I can find it in the dark, but if we can, it'll be a good spot to wait."

Frank looked up at the sky studded with stars. "Should be some moonlight later."

"I'm not sure I like that," Tom observed. "He won't know we're ahead of him, so we have the element of surprise. However, if he sees us in the moonlight, some of us may wind up getting shot."

Sam smiled in the dark. "No more 'n four of us, unless he found some bullets."

"There are only four of us," Tom observed.

Sam chuckled. "Well, I don' figure we'll run into 'im tonight. Reason animals like One Ear do what they do is they figure they're too smart to work for anything. That's why we got ahead o' him; he ain't pushin' hard as us, an' he took that other trail loops west 'fore it comes back on this un. He won't go anywhere in the dark unless he figures we're right on his tail, an' I 'spect he figures we give up at the border."

As the moon peaked over the mountains on the east, they were just nearing the section of trail that Sam had mentioned earlier. He led the way up slope on the right, over the top and into a small glen surrounded by sandy hills topped with pine trees.

"We'll go up and watch for him on the ridge," Clyde announced, as he swung to the ground. "We'll set up a picket line here for the horses. Frank, you stay here and keep an eye on them."

"Why?" Frank asked, also dismounting.

"Because they're strange horses, and I don't want them getting away," Clyde responded. "Walking back to Bonners isn't my idea of a good time." He reached into his saddlebags and removed a set of moccasins and a leather thong, then dropped to the ground to remove his boots.

"Why not one o' you with the horses?" Frank asked.

"Because we have the shotguns," Clyde responded. "You have your Spencer. Your handgun won't be much good for this." With his moccasins on, Clyde tied his boots together, then stood and hung them over the saddle horn. Then he drew his ten-gauge from the scabbard.

"You've never seen me shoot," Frank objected.

"No, I haven't," Clyde responded, then turned and started up toward the top of the ridge. Tom and Sam followed, shotguns in hand.

As they reached the top of the ridge, the three men turned back to see Frank in the moonlight. He was stringing a rope between two trees to which he would tie the horses.

"Thanks, Clyde," Tom said. "I was wondering how we would keep him out of this."

"Why keep 'im out 'o it?" Sam asked. "Young fella has t' learn sometime."

"Because I wouldn't like to see him make his living with a gun," Tom informed him. "He intends to shoot One Ear for killing Jack."

"Well, we ain't taken him yet, alive or dead," Sam observed and lead the way over the top and down the other side.

Tom had the last watch. As the promise of dawn lit the east his tired mind went back to another ambush. Was this how it was for the Cree as they waited for enough light to hit the people of Talking Sky? Did Coleman's men wonder about what was to happen before they fired on the camp on the Flathead? He liked to think some of them were human enough to worry about what they had been about to do. However, they were a different breed, many of them. Some of them might not give it a second thought.

The sun was well into the sky when a lone, long-haired rider on a red horse appeared. Tom woke the other two and they sat up, rubbing tired eyes and peering through the trees at the oncoming rider.

"Looks like him," Clyde observed, picking his shotgun up from where it leaned against a tree and wiping sand from the butt. The entire ridge was covered with fine golden sand and pine needles.

Below the three men a relatively clear area ran down to the trail. When One Ear was closer, they planned to go down the hill, step into the trail, and confront him with the scatter guns. No one, they reasoned, would try to beat an eight-gauge and two ten-gauges, one of them a five-shot revolver.

"That young Indian last night," Tom said in a low voice, "appeared to be fairly capable. And Jack Lawson was no slouch with a pistol."

Sam spat tobacco juice into the sand before responding. "This One Ear ain't no pilgrim, an' that's a fact."

"Time to shut up, boys," Clyde ordered in a hoarse whisper.

One Ear bounced in the saddle of the fast walking horse; his back hunched, hands on the horn, eyes scanning the trees.

Sam opened the trapdoor breech of his eight-gauge and checked the loads, though he knew it was loaded, the powder dry.

Clyde put the butt of his weapon against his thigh and let out his breath in a long sigh.

Tom blew imaginary dust from around the percussion caps and the cylinder of his ten-gauge.

One Ear was still more than a hundred yards north of them when Frank Clement stepped into the trail.

"Damn," Tom said and took off running along the ridge toward One Ear and Frank.

Sam and Clyde looked at each other and gave chase. They're moccasins in the sand made less noise than their breathing.

Down on the trail, One Ear jerked his mount to a halt. He could see that the man who had suddenly appeared from the trees was not much more than a kid and, from his buckskin clothing, a hick kid at that. The belt and pistol, however, were all grown up.

Frank's voice was clear and steady when he said, "That pistol you're wearin' belongs to a friend o' mine. I want it back." He stood straight, trying to will his bunched muscles to relax.

There was a pause while One Ear scanned the ridge to the east. Had he heard something up there? Was this dumb kid alone?

"Yer friend don' need it no more," One Ear observed. "I don' kilt 'im."

Frank nodded slowly. "An after I git that pistol we'll take yuh back an' hang yuh fer it."

Before the kid finished speaking, One Ear reached for his .44. It wasn't even clear of the holster, however, when he knew he was dead. The kid already had his out, cocked and coming into line.

Frank never fired. From behind him and to his right, a shotgun bellowed, followed almost at the same instant by two more. One Ear Charlie Brown flew from the saddle and bounced on the ground. The VH horse trotted down the trail a few hundred yards, stepped on a rein, and came to a halt.

Still holding his cocked pistol, Frank walked slowly across the trail toward the body of the bad man. What was left looked small and insignificant, like a pile of old rags. Having just absorbed most of three shotgun loads it also looked like ground meat. Frank swallowed hard several times to keep from heaving.

Sam Moren crossed the trail to the body. The other two stopped beside Frank. They all stood and looked at One Ear as Frank holstered his pistol. Bending down, Sam unbuckled the gun belt, pulled it from beneath the limp body, then picked up the pistol from where it lay near an outstretched hand. Turning, he slid the pistol into the holster and passed the assembly to Frank.

Frank took the offered belt, nodded, then turned and walked back across the trail, over the ridge and to their horses.

They buried One Ear Charlie Brown where he fell, forty miles south of the British Columbia border. Having accomplished that, no easy task in the loose sand, they lead the VH horse to Bonners Ferry and turned it over to the liveryman who promised to keep the animal until the Dutchmen returned for it. The next day, mounted again on their own horses, they rode north and back to Wild Horse Creek.

After the shooting, Frank did not speak. Though there was no noticeable change in the younger man's expression or carriage, Tom rode beside him, worried about his partner's silence.

It was late that next day when they were near the border that Frank finally spoke.

"Were you the first one to fire?" Frank asked.

Tom nodded. "Yes." He paused then explained, "I didn't want you to shoot him." He thought for a few minutes and then added. "The others were ready and just pulled their triggers."

There were several minutes of silence before Frank spoke again. "Thanks," he said.

Chapter 48

Frank was shoveling muck into the rocker far more violently than necessary. "Damn it, it's June already. We bin here ten months an' we ain't heard nothin'."

Tom began shaking the rocker, and then opened the sluice gate to allow water to run through the muck. He raised his voice to be heard over the rattle of stones and the creak of wood. "We have almost forty men looking for your father. Once he comes into the colony the police will find him."

"Maybe he's in Californy," Frank suggested.

Frank's impatience to find his father had been building for weeks. The chase for Charlie Brown had interrupted the growth of that impatience, but the sight of the riddled body on the side of the trail had increased it. Tom suspected the young man needed to do something. Perhaps it would not speed up the discovery of Alex Clement, but it would make Frank feel better.

Tom had to admit that he would also feel better about moving on. There wasn't a day during which he didn't think about Coleman. It hadn't helped that he had recently heard that the new country of Canada would soon be a reality. Would this change in government end Coleman's dreams of controlling his own empire? It was more likely that he would become meaner and push harder for Tom's death.

"Well, perhaps you should go to town and ask Jim Carrington to send a telegram to the states," Tom suggested.

"Already done that," Frank responded. "Jack sent wires out 'fore he got shot."

"To what areas? Remember that communication and cooperation between the states is not always what it should be. Why don't you try and have messages sent to the capitol? They do have federal marshals. That would put the search in a larger area."

Frank nodded his eyes on the gravel and water in the rocker, but not really seeing them. "Tomorrow I'll do that."

"The day is young," Tom said. "Go now. As a matter of fact, I'll go with you. We'll send messages to the U.S. Marshal, and to the states and territories in the west."

"Cost a lot o' money," Frank objected.

Tom smiled. He opened the sluice gate again for a little more water. "Frank, we're averaging twenty dollars a day from this stream. There are hard working men that do not make that much in a month."

Tom shook his head in wonder, and then added, "When I was your age I spent my pay like it was water. You have to be the tightest man I ever met."

Frank shrugged. "Might wanta eat tomorra."

"Well, our financial situation is quite good. We'll finish washing this load of muck, then we'll head to town. We'll send some telegrams, have a few drinks, and perhaps dance with the Hurdy-Gurdy girls."

Frank shook his head. "Them gals is chargin' a dollar a dance, way too much fer a spin 'round the floor. They ain't there 'cause they like the comp'ny, they're job is sellin' booze."

Tom stopped rocking and moved down to inspect the fine sand in the riffles. "So buy a drink and have another dance. You're too serious."

Frank also focused his attention on the sand. "Don't get much out o' drinkin'. One drink I enjoy, then I start seein' Miller when he was drunk an' beatin' on Maw. Sorta cuts down on the pleasure."

As they rode away from their cabin that afternoon, Tom suddenly halted his mount, his eyes scanning the lay of the land across their claim.

"See the way that trench cuts along the base of the hill?" he asked, pointing it out to Frank. "It looks like the creek ran closer to the hill at one time."

Frank looked across the stream to the other bank. "Well, if it did, she was a mighty big stream."

"It could have been a roaring torrent," Tom agreed. "I think this trench is a very old river bed. I think we should buy a wheelbarrow while we're in town."

"Need a packhorse t' bring 'er back," Frank noted.

Tom nodded. "We should ride out and check on our horses. It's been a week since we looked at them, and if they eat up all the grass, there isn't much to stop them from drifting all the way to New Westminster."

"Hear tell there's desert off that way," Frank said.

Tom shook his head and started his mount down the trail. The boy was far too serious.

The next day, Tom explained his plan. "We need to start a tunnel. We'll start up here near the edge of the claim and work back down toward the center. We'll need to leave some space for the overburden so that it doesn't block us off from access to the rocker.

"Yuh keep sayin' we're doin' so good here, twenty bucks a day, an' all, so why're we doin' this?" Frank asked.

"Because what we've done so far doesn't seem to make you happy," Tom said. He didn't explain that he had no interest in their daily take, whether it was two dollars a day or two hundred. He still had a few English pounds and a Kingston farm he could sell if the need arose. What he wanted was for his young partner to be learning, busy, and content.

"An' what's bein' happy got t' do with anythin'?"

Tom started digging and pitching dirt off to his left. He nodded his head at the new wheelbarrow. "Fill her up and dump it on the other side of where I'm starting a pile."

Frank started to dig as Tom spoke. "Being happy is the whole point. We need to work so we can pay for clothes and food, and a roof over our head. Even if you have all the money in the world, you need to keep busy so you don't stiffen up, or get fat and die. I have noticed, over the years, that when I'm not busy doing, or learning, or even just trying to solve some problem, that's when I do something stupid that I'll regret.

"Take my time in the service, for example. As long as I was busy, I was fine. As soon as I had time to think about the horror of it all, that's when I couldn't do it anymore."

Frank finished filling the barrow, so Tom waited until he had dumped it and returned before continuing.

"Some of the men who died in those battles were no older than you. A few were even younger. Many of them die at my age, or perhaps forty-five or fifty. That's not very long to be learning, building, and generally making life better for the children that will come after us. But if you're not enjoying it, just trudging on from day to day, it can be a long old grind."

"Supposed t' be a grind," Frank said. "Pay fer the sins o' man now so that we c'n go on t' better things."

"That's a load of..." Tom stopped himself. "That doesn't make any sense. If we are indeed put here to grow and multiply, then why hinder that growth? We create and develop far better when we are happy; therefore it makes more sense to enjoy."

This was an idea completely counter to what Frank had been taught to expect from life. He decided he needed to give it some thought before they went any further.

"So what's that all got t' do with us diggin' a tunnel?" Frank asked. "If'n I ain't happy washin' muck, what makes yuh think I'm gonna be happy diggin' a tunnel?"

"I don't," Tom replied, "but I think we should move on to something else. Perhaps farming. Raising horses, perhaps. We have four good mares. We'll try something else and see if you're still impatient and restless."

Frank wheeled the barrow away, dumped it, and returned. "Maybe it's you bein' an officer," he said.

Tom stopped digging for a moment and looked at the younger man. "What does my having been an officer have to do with anything?"

Frank shrugged, and then began filling the barrow again. "Makes yuh dumb, I reckon. See this here, this shovelin' dirt ain't a whole sight different than what we bin doin'. An' maybe you bein' an officer yuh wouldn't know that this here ain't farmin', neither."

"Well it's about time." Tom said, once more throwing dirt to his left. "Do you realize that's the first time in weeks that you've made a joke? It's like living with Lame Dog."

"Yeah, sure. The tunnel?"

"When this stream was a river, there's a chance that more gold was washed down from wherever the source is than the volume of water presently running is capable of carrying. If this is the case, then the gravel under the old riverbed should contain a larger percentage of gold. If we angle out and tunnel down, we may even hit bedrock, which may contain actual veins of ore in the fissures, in the cracks."

"This all don' make a lot o' sense," Frank said. The barrow was full again, so he stopped digging and leaned on his shovel. "You already said we got a good bit o' gold, an' we should be doin' somethin' else. Now you're tellin' me we should do all this work t' find more gold."

Tom stopped digging and also leaned on his shovel. "We have about twelve hundred dollars in gold dust. We have four mares and two geldings, two pack saddles, one of them Blackfoot made, and not made for long-term use. We will use up a lot of money buying equipment and stock for a farm." He returned to digging.

Frank turned up his nose, then lifted the handles of the barrow and wheeled it away. When he had returned and was shoveling again, he asked, "So how long is this gonna take?"

"Oh, perhaps two weeks."

"We bin workin' this claim since water started runnin'. Must be four months now, an' we got twelve hun'red. Either yuh don' figure on needin' much more, 'r you figure there's a whole pile o' rich ore under this here dirt."

"Neither will matter," Tom said. "If there is rich ore under here, it will be a bonus, but all we need to do is show the possibilities. We'll spend a week digging, and then let it be known that we're ready to move on. Perhaps go to town and throw a little gold dust around like we have plenty, and let it be known that we're looking for greener pasture. There are many around that hold gold in higher esteem than we do and would be anxious to buy a proven claim. If there's color in the tunnel, and I think there will be, we'll get a higher price."

Chapter 49

They had spent three full days on the tunnel when Tom said, "Today we need to find timber." It was hot in the cabin, so they were out by the firepit. Tom was laying a fire for their breakfast.

"Shore up the hole," Frank said.

Tom nodded. "We'll take all three horses and skid back as much as we can."

"Wondered why yuh didn' take that mare back when we got the barrow hauled. Gettin' hard t' find grass."

"We'll see how much we can get in today. Perhaps skid a few more in tomorrow, then you can take the mare back out and turn her out with the others."

"How deep we makin' this tunnel, anyway?"

"Perhaps twice as deep as it is, but on at least one trip today we'll only have two horses dragging timber. Your mount will be carrying the meat you will shoot while I'm cutting trees."

"Be couple more days 'fore the meat we got goes bad," Frank noted.

"True, but we don't have enough for guests, and I'd like to invite Clyde and Sam over."

"Guess I must be some kind o' poor cousin," Frank said.

"How so?"

"Don't seem t' get told nothin'."

"That's because I'm making this up as we go along. I have the basis of an idea, but I keep adding to it."

"Well, while y're makin' up stuff, make us up a good meal. I'll bring in them nags an' get 'em saddled."

They were on their way back uphill for the second load of logs when Tom left Frank and rode over to the neighboring claim. Clyde and Sam were feeding and shaking their rocker when he rode up.

"Frank shot a nice, fat doe this morning," Tom said. "Would you be interested in some fresh venison tonight?"

"Why, sure," Clyde responded. "Fresh or otherwise, I'd come just so I don't have to cook."

"You done the cookin' last night," Sam said. "My turn t'night."

"Another reason not to eat at home," Clyde said.

Sam ignored the slight to his domestic abilities and asked Tom, "Yuh all not workin' yer claim t'day?"

"Well, in a way, I suppose," Tom responded, a small smile on his lips. "But we're not panning gold."

As he rode away he hoped his last remark would create some intrigue and interest.

From the moment the two men stepped onto the claim they scanned the small pile of logs and the scar in the hillside, but it was after supper before anything was said. The hosts and guests sat around the fire with their belts released when Sam said, "Cuttin' yerselves a tunnel."

"No, no, Sam," Clyde said. "They're hunting for gophers." He shook his head in resignation.

"Well, could be a sand trap fer when the wind blows," Sam noted. "Might big fer that, but . . ." He shrugged. "Yuh all can't be figurin' the mother lode's in there, so why the tunnel?"

Tom pointed up the hill with his pipe stem. "See that trench up there that runs over through your claim? I think it's an ancient riverbed. If it is, there should be gold under it, and perhaps a great deal down at bedrock."

Clyde and Sam sucked on their own pipes for a moment, creating clouds of smoke while they scanned the hillside in the fading light.

Clyde nodded. "You may be right. We should have noticed that."

"There was no need," Tom said. "You have a good claim and you're doing well."

"So what made you look?" Clyde asked. "I thought you boys were doing pretty well here, too."

Tom nodded. "We've done alright, but Frank wants to become more active in the search for his father. If we're going to be traveling, we'll need a pretty good stake to start."

Sam grinned. "An' it'll be a sight easier t' sell with a tunnel on 'er."

Tom's only response was to draw on his pipe and discover it was out. He leaned over to pull a burning twig from the fire.

Clyde was nodding his understanding and tapping the ash from his pipe against the heel of his hand. "Seems to me Barkerville would be a likely place." he said.

"Why?" Frank asked with more than a trace of surprise.

Clyde nodded. "I hear it's well on the way to being the biggest city north of San Francisco an' west of Chicago."

"More people comin' an' goin'," Sam added.

"Might be a good place t' look fer Paw," Frank said.

"Exactly what I was thinkin'," Clyde said.

"And there will be people who have interests other than mining," Tom added.

"Of course, I doubt there's any sense of us trying to settle in a town, particularly one that big," Clyde said. "We've been away from it too long."

"I understand the Colonial government is giving away land along the Caribou Road," Tom said. "They are trying to encourage settlers rather than just miners. Of course, there are requirements we would have to meet, but I think we could do just fine."

"Folks's ally's needin' horses," Sam said. "Hell, I'll bet that B.X. stage line runs over there could use up all the horses we could raise."

Clyde stood. "Come on, Sam. These boys already got a good start on us. If we're going to Barkerville we'd best decide where to put our tunnel."

"I take it you agree with us," Tom said. "You plan on pulling out?" He was only slightly disappointed. He had hoped the two neighbors would buy the claim, but he would enjoy having their company.

"Time t' move on t' other things," Sam replied. "I'm a feller likes t' farm, an' Clyde here'd like t' build things."

"If you boys can give us a little time to catch up on the tunnel, maybe we can sell both claims," Clyde suggested.

Tom shrugged. "Frank's a might impatient to be going, but we should be able to work out something."

"Four men travelin' t'gether ain't likely t' have as much trouble as two," Frank said. "Tom an' I c'n use the time t' let folks know we might be ready t' sell."

Chapter 50

It was the first week of August, 1867 when the four men rode into Barkerville. It had not been an easy trip from Wild Horse Creek, for most of it had been made in the rain. True, what had been the Caribou trail was now a well-engineered road, and they made good time along it, but it took them eighteen days just to reach it from Wild Horse Creek. The horses had developed saddle sores from the wet equipment strapped to their backs, which further slowed the journey. It was fortunate they had extra mounts.

When they reached the Caribou Road they encountered different problems. On one of the few dry nights, when they expected to finally enjoy a night's sleep, five men attempted to rob them. The five outlaws had escaped with their lives, but only after denying the four travelers well-needed rest.

They sat on the north edge of Barkerville, holding their horses off to the side, and surveyed the town. It was a mad house. No one could possibly know the numbers in that cyclone of activity, but it was obvious that tens of thousands of people were trying to move themselves, their animals, and freight through streets far too narrow for the task.

The four partners felt no attraction to join the madness. As Tom had hoped, they had found seams of gold filling the cracks in the bedrock, so all four men had done well on the sales of their claims. They could afford to take their time to build something that would last.

"Couple a' places back yonder'd make good pasture," Sam commented.

"And some places that could be easily irrigated," Tom added. "These men will need more than just beef."

"Pretty high up," Sam said. "Mus' be gettin' close t' four thousan' feet. Might get some early frost."

"Too late in the year to worry about raising crops or cattle," Clyde noted. "Better to spend the fall and winter getting the lay of the land."

"Ain't too late t' build fences an' cut hay," Frank said.

Clyde nodded his understanding. "That's true. And we'll need something to live in."

"Let's go in and find an eatery," Tom suggested. "Enjoy someone else's cooking, and get an idea of what the town is like. Maybe it won't last much longer, although that's pretty hard to believe from what we see right now."

A large tent advertised "MEALS." They rode up in front of it and swung down. It was the middle of the afternoon so the hitch rail was almost empty.

"Where'd you get that pistol?" a voice asked.

All four men turned to see a man standing in the street, his eyes firmly fixed on Frank. He was only a few inches over five feet, but appeared to weigh about a hundred and eighty pounds, his chest almost as deep as it was wide. He wore wool pants stuffed into riding boots that came almost to his knee. Above the heavy trousers was a flannel shirt under a leather vest. His face was covered with a full beard of grey that matched the hair visible under his battered black hat. Despite the heavy clothing and the afternoon heat, his attire was clean and cared for.

"Got it from my Paw," Frank responded.

"What's yer name?" the stranger asked.

Frank studied the man a moment, his eyes losing all expression. Finally, he said, "Frank Clement."

The stranger nodded, then moved forward. "Thought yuh was dead, boy."

Frank's eyes clicked back to life as he asked, "Paw?" He threw his arms around the older man and pulled him close.

Frank's three partners stood with wide grins plastered to their faces.

Alex Clement did not return the hug. Twice he made motions with his arms as if he might, but then the third time he put his hands on Frank's shoulders and pushed him back. Father and son were about the same height, though Frank was much lighter.

"Yuh growed up some," Alex Clement said.

"I reckon," Frank said.

Alex looked down at his son's hip. "I want you t' take that iron off."

Frank drew the Colt and passed it to his father, butt first. "Shouldn't have it on in town anyway," he said.

Alex shook his head. "Don't want to see yuh carryin' it ever ag'in." His attention turned to the three men standing behind Frank. "Which one o' you men got this boy packin' iron? Hangin' low like that, makes 'im look like a damn gunfighter. Gunfighters get shot. Aughta be 'shamed o' yerself."

Tom's grin disappeared immediately to be replaced by a stony, unreadable expression. The grins on the other two men faded slowly into uncertainty. Looking like a young boy who had been reprimanded, Frank unbuckled his gun belt and rolled it into a bundle.

"I've known Frank the longest," Tom said. "I met him well over a year ago. He was carrying that weapon when I met him, and has always treated it in the most respectful manner. His abilities with it have saved lives. On more than one occasion, mine."

"Lucky the boy ain't dead," Alex Clement said. He turned his attention to his son. "Get yer kit, boy. We need t' talk."

Frank blinked a few times, and then said, "The boys'll be in town a spell. We c'n have us a meal, an' do some talkin'. Be plenty o' time t' round up my riggin'."

"Better get 'em now, boy."

Frank turned to his mount and tied the rolled up gun belt behind his saddle with his bedroll. "Later, Paw." He turned and walked down the street.

Alex Clement glared at the three partners, then turned and followed his son.

There was silence among the three men for a moment, then Sam said, "Don't reckon that was quite the ree-union the young feller had in mind."

"Well, you don't say?" Clyde said, shaking his head. "The kid looks after himself for I don't know how long, watches his mother drawn into the pits of hell, works harder than most men, and acts like a gentleman, only to get a slap in the face from the man he's dreamed of for all that time. Now why would that upset him?"

Still watching the departing backs of the two Clement men, Tom said, "Many times the foolishness you two demonstrate has given me a lift. Right now, however, I do not find it humorous. Shall we have that meal?"

They turned and entered the tent. It contained two long, plank tables with benches along each side. Near the back was a large cook stove, benches holding pots and pans, a barrel full of water, and a large basin. A man and a woman stood near the stove and turned to watch them enter.

As they took a seat on one of the benches, Clyde said, "The kid was looking forward to a good feed as much as us."

"Be more 'n one eatery," Sam said. "He'll sit down with his ol' man an' try t' talk some sense into 'im."

Tom nodded. "All we can do is continue developing our plan as mentioned. I'm sure Frank will eventually rejoin us, perhaps with his father. It may not be soon, but someday."

It was two hours later that Frank returned. He found his three partners sitting in front of the Caribou House saloon. It was nearing the supper hour and traffic in the street had increased so that the three men didn't see Frank approach.

"I ain't gettin' no where's with Paw," Frank said.

Tom looked up at him and nodded. "May take some time."

Frank shook his head. "Mighty set in 'is ways."

"Have you told him about our travels?" Tom asked.

Frank shrugged. "Don' get much chance t' tell 'im nothin'. Ever time I try talkin' he cuts me off. Sez this business o' chasin' gold is a fool's game, an' it's time I settled down t' live like a man."

"Yuh didn' tell 'im what we got planned," Sam said. It was not a question.

"Didn' get no chance," Frank responded. He jerked his thumb over his shoulder. "Got 'im a contrac' t' build a hotel down the street a ways. Wants me t' work with 'im."

There was silence for a moment, then Frank said, "He's my paw, boys."

Tom nodded, and then rose from the bench. "Back out on the trail about a mile we passed a good spot to camp for the night. We'll ride out there and separate your goods from ours."

Frank put his hand on Tom's shoulder. "It ain't right. We've come a long way together."

"Yes, we have," Tom responded, "and we still have a long way to go." He reached around Frank's extended arm, put his hand on the younger man's shoulder and squeezed. "Someday we may be doing it together."

Two of the extra horses were Frank's, but he insisted on only taking one of them. "Get her bred an' raise me some good colts," he instructed. "Matter of fact, Paw may not like the idea of feedin' an extra horse," he added, gesturing to the mare who's pack held his goods. He thought for a moment, and then nodded. "I'll unload my riggin' an' then bring 'er back. That is, if you don't mind lookin' after her?"

Tom shook his head and smiled. Frank had insisted on leaving most of his gear with the three partners. He had taken only his clothing and a few tools. "Certainly not," Tom said. "And anytime you want anything, whether it's mine or yours, you come and get it."

"Or mine," Clyde said.

"Damn right," Sam said.

"As to bringing the mare back," Tom said, "it might not be a good idea to start your relationship by lying to your father."

"I wouldn't say Paw is a real big talker," Frank said. "I won't have to say nothin'. I'll just unload an' bring her back."

Tom nodded, then turned and looked west, hands in his pockets. "Back down the trail perhaps fifteen miles there are a couple of places that may suit our purposes. Perhaps we will see you here in town sometime and let you know where we've settled. Otherwise, you just keep looking and there we'll be."

Frank nodded, then went and shook the hands of Clyde and Sam. He lingered over the shaking of Tom's hand, and then clapped him on the shoulder, turned, and swung into the saddle.

"One more thing," Tom said, before Frank put his mount in motion. "Don't forget that Coleman is still alive. The man is full of hate, and he's dangerous."

Frank nodded, and then rode out of camp. Tom continued to stare toward the east long after the rider and horses were visible.

"Noticed somethin'." Sam said, breaking the long silence. Both men turned to look at him sitting on a log at the edge of the firelight. "You bin learnin' that boy t' talk fer a mighty long time, an' I ain't noticed he does any better'n me. Ever since he come back from talkin' t' his paw, seems t' me he talks mighty near as good as Clyde."

Clyde lifted the pot and poured three cups full of coffee. It had been simmering near the coals for some time and appeared to have achieved some considerable substance. He then retrieved a bottle from his gear, poured generous portions from it into the brew and passed the cups around.

"That boy has learned a great deal from you, Tom," Clyde said. "He may prove, one day, to be one of your more successful subjects."

Tom nodded, and then took a drink from his cup. "If he lives long enough to use it."

Chapter 51

Every two or three weeks the three men rode into Barkerville. They trailed a packhorse and bought supplies, but their main aim was to "partake of the fruits of civilization," as Clyde said sometime during each such excursion.

"She's a damn sad comment on civee-i-zation," Sam would always respond.

Sam and Tom seemed content to pay their dollar and dance with the girls of the halls. However, Clyde was harder to satisfy. He paid his money and made the steps along with his partners, but he spent much of his time walking about the town.

On one such occasion, Sam and Tom were catching their breath and a few drops of whiskey between dances. Sam meant to comment on Tom's dancing, which showed considerable experience when he reached over, touched him on the arm, and said, "Say..."

Tom spun, upsetting the chair he was sitting in. He stood, almost crouching, in the very spot where the chair had been.

"Damn, yur gettin' jumpier ev'ry day," Sam said.

Tom nodded, tipped the chair back on its legs, took a seat, and reached to the table for his drink.

"Clyde didn't stay long today," Tom noted, not wanting Sam to dwell on the state of his nerves. Each day he expected to see Coleman. No one had told him the man was on his trail, but he knew. And the man would not be alone, for he would need every advantage. He would be riding at the head of an army.

Sam shrugged. "Big town, lots t' see."

"They claim it's the biggest town west of Chicago, and I have no reason to doubt it. There are also more Chinese here than I have ever seen in one place." He took a drink of whiskey. "However, it's still just a town, and there are only so many things to see. This is our third visit to this den of iniquity, and Clyde seems to avail himself of very little of the wickedness. One or two drinks, as many dances, and he leaves to wander the dusty streets. That can't be good for his health."

Sam grinned. "I think he's met him a woman."

"That could be the case," Tom said. "The women are here, but most of them have no shortage of suitors."

"True, but Clyde knows how t' turn on the charm. Reckon he learned it talkin' t' juries."

Tom took another sip. His breath had almost returned meaning it was time for another dance.

"Has he mentioned seeing Frank in his travels?" Tom asked.

"Yup, talked t' him fer a minute our last trip in. Claims the lad's gettin' t' be a fair carpenter, though I don't know if that means anythin', judgin' by the work that Clyde does."

Tom smiled. "He is a wonder to behold with tools. He does so much want to build, but I do believe a grizzly bear would do him less damage than he does to himself with hammer and saw."

"Fine cook, though."

Tom nodded. "Everyone has their strength."

Chapter 52

They found the sod too sandy to use for a sod roof, and were placing split aspen logs in an overlap pattern that would shed most of the rain or snow melt. From the roof they could see the rider coming for a half hour, so when he pulled his horse to a stop, coffee and lunch was ready. The rider was a Colonial Policeman.

"Howdy," the stranger said to the two men on the roof and the one standing in the bunkhouse door who greeted him in turn.

"Step down and have a bite," Clyde said. "Got some cold venison, fresh bread, and coffee."

The stranger sat his saddle. "I'm Constable Griffin with the British Columbia Police," he said, his accent, though slight, betrayed his English origin. "I'm looking for a Mr. Brash, a Mr.Moren, and a Mr. Phillips."

Tom was the first to reach the bottom of the ladder. He turned and faced the mounted stranger. "It appears your search is concluded," he said.

"Who's in charge?" the policeman asked.

Tom gestured toward Clyde who still stood in the doorway, his left shoulder leaning against the frame. "If it's a legal matter, that would be Mr. Phillips."

Griffin swung his attention to Clyde. "I understand you gentlemen were part of the group that apprehended Charles Brown last spring."

Clyde stood straight and crossed his arms. "We are the group," he said, thinking perhaps that Frank might be better off if he wasn't mentioned.

"We appreciate that Mr. Brown murdered a policeman, which lead to your following him," Griffin said, "but we will not sanction vigilante action in the Colony of British Columbia."

"Seams t' me we done heard this speech already," Sam said, then turned and started down the ladder.

Clyde scowled at his partner's descending back, and then swung his gaze back to the officer. "Yes, from Corporal Normansell at Wild Horse Creek."

"I'm sure," Griffin agreed, and then looked around at their work. "You have done a considerable amount of work. It can't allow you much time to pan for gold."

"We don't plan to spend too much time at that," Clyde responded. "We've done our share."

"I know of no other single men in the area who are after anything but gold," Griffin said. "A few loggers, but this doesn't seem to be one of the claims best suited for that."

"Ah, speaking of claims," Clyde said, suddenly understanding where the policeman was headed. "We have filed claims along the river and on the stream, but our primary concern is what is on top of the ground, not under it."

"You'll have to work those claims to maintain them," Griffin said.

"True, and we have," Clyde said.

Griffin nodded. "Yes, I looked them over this morning. There is no doubt someone has been working them."

Sam grunted, leaned back against the ladder, and drew his pipe and tobacco. Tom looked at him, then at Clyde. It disturbed them that the officer had checked their claims without their knowledge.

"And you will be aware that land along the Caribou Road has been set aside for homesteads," Clyde said. "That would include this land up here on the flat."

The Constable nodded. "Homesteaders are usually families, not single men." He looked around the flat. "And I'm not sure this is suitable land."

"Judgin' by that trace o' Lancashire I hear its better'n most o' that pile o' rocks you hail from," Sam noted.

Tom stepped forward, his hands clasped behind his back. "Let me assure you, Constable," he said, "that our purpose is neither theft nor violence. We do not plan vigilante action, nor are we bounty hunters. We plan to be a source of supply for those in the area. Cattle and horses."

"I can believe that," Griffin said, nodding. "You've done good work that will last." He ran the reins through his fingers, and then added, "This has been an official visit, and I must return to Barkerville before dark. Perhaps on my next visit I can take time to accept your offer of food and drink." He turned his mount.

"Just a minute, Constable," Tom said, and when the officer halted, added, "The man who, shall we say, brought us to your attention is the father of the young man who works with him. Frank, the son, was my partner for some time."

Griffin's smile was fleeting. "I was not aware of that," he said.

"I didn't expect you would be," Tom said. "And I'm sure it's easier to do your job when you know the background."

"It can be in some cases," Griffin conceded. "In others it can get in the way."

As they watched the lawman ride away, Clyde stepped from the cabin to stand by Tom. "What made you think he'd heard about the shootin' from Clement?"

"Who else would have told him?" Tom responded.

"It'll be in the B.C. Police files."

"Sure, but why would he look?"

Clyde turned to his other partner. "And what's this about the rocks of Lancashire? I didn't know you'd been to jolly old England."

Sam grinned. "Ain't, but I heard tell."

Chapter 53

Every day there was traffic on the main road that ran along the base of the hills across the field north of their building site. Whether it was a train of packhorses; a heavy wagon; groups of miners, many of them afoot, or one of the stage line coaches, they all slowed to catch a glimpse through the trees of the progress the three partners had been making. The homestead became a marker telling the traveler he was near the end of a long journey.

It was late in the year, however, and most of the long distance travelers were bound for the outside. There were people coming in from places like Quesnel Forks, but most wanted to be out of the country before the heavy snows stopped all travel. There had been snow, but it had not lasted, and many mornings when there was more than an inch of ice on the water barrel outside the door.

Despite all this traffic, the partners seldom had visitors.

"Ol' man Clement's bin tellin' it that we're killers an' such," Sam said at the supper table when the subject of visitors came up. "Got folks scared to come callin'. Which don' upset me a whole bunch. Get more done when folks ain't pesterin' yuh."

"Probably doesn't have much to do with it," Tom objected. "There really is no reason to stop here. We don't know anyone very well, and they have either just been on the road for four or five hours, or they will soon be off the road."

"I don't know," Clyde said. "Sounded like the old man had been feeding that cop enough stories."

"Oh, I expect he has," Tom admitted. "I'm not suggesting that Alex Clement isn't taking every opportunity to let the world know what bad men we are. He's jealous of us for the time we spent with his son. Probably feels guilty about not being there for the boy when he needed a father. I just don't believe that has much to do with our not having company."

He paused for a moment, and then brought up a subject that Clyde had been able to avoid. "What about your lady friend? Has she heard any stories about us?"

"Why ask me?" Clyde objected, his face flushing. "What about your own lady friend?"

"We ain't got no gals," Sam objected. "'Septin' maybe the hurly-burly gals."

Clyde grinned, his flush retreating somewhat. He pointed at Tom. "I've seen you talking to that widow lady that works in the hotel. Twice." He pointed at Sam. "And everybody in the town, including half the Chinamen, know that you've been stoppin' by to have coffee with the liveryman's daughter."

Tom's grin didn't succeed in hiding his flush. "Shame on you, Sam. She's just a kid."

Sam shrugged. "Knows a lot about horses."

"Not to mention that she's as pretty as a new colt," Tom added.

"You should talk," Clyde put in. "Leading that poor, defenseless widow lady astray with your international charm."

"Defenseless?" Tom said. "She could rip the heart out of a mountain lion with her bare hands if it threatened one of her kids."

They ate in silence to the end of the meal, each of them unhappy that the others knew of their courting, but feeling guilty that they hadn't mentioned it to their partners.

Finally, Clyde pushed his empty plate back, cleared his throat, and said, "Elly hasn't heard any stories about us."

"I don't believe Susan has either," Tom said. "Working in the hotel as she does, I expect she would hear most rumors."

Sam shrugged. "Filly ain't heard nothin' neither."

Clyde and Tom looked at him for a moment, and then said in unison, "Filly?"

Sam's face flushed brighter than before. "What I call 'er. Real name's Felicity.

They looked at each other again, then back at Sam.

"Felicity?"

Chapter 54

On October 28 they woke to find an inch of white covering the ground.

"We've waited too long, men," Clyde said as he slid another platter of pancakes onto the table. "This trip in we'd best take two packhorses. We'll need a pile of supplies, and they may not have enough to do us."

Tom nodded. He was thinking it would be nice to have some sugar to sprinkle on the pancakes. "I'm sure it's been on all our minds."

"Yup," Sam agreed. "Jus' so damn much t' do."

"And it'll be there when we get back from town," Clyde pointed out.

"After breakfast I'll round us up some mounts," Sam said. "Two packhorses?" he asked.

"Let's hope we can get two loads," Clyde said. "They may be holding back on stuff until they get some idea how rough the winter will be."

Sam was still out after the horses when Tom and Clyde heard the wagon. They stepped out of the cabin to see a buckboard approaching with two men in the seat. The man driving was Alex Clement. They didn't recognize the passenger who was hunched over, his forearms held in his lap, but Tom thought he looked familiar.

"Well if it isn't the Queen's own, Mr. Thomas Brash," the stranger said, and Tom recognized his voice and southern accent.

The stranger sat up straight to reveal a revolver in his left hand, the barrel pointed at Clement's stomach, the hammer drawn back and under his thumb.

"Friend of yours, Tom?" Clyde said, although that was obviously not the case and he could guess who the man was.

"An acquaintance," Tom admitted. "A killer and a coward. He has used the names Cole and Coleman, but they were just convenient places for a coward to hide."

"We'll see who's a coward," Coleman said, then shoved Clement off the wagon with the three-fingered right hand. He jumped down behind the older man, put the claw-like hand around the older man's neck, and grabbed his throat. The pistol barrel he put back in his hostage's stomach and urged the man forward.

"I must admit I'm surprised to see you alone," Tom said. He had his hands in his coat pocket and began, gently to work his right hand through the slit that lead to the inside of the coat, giving him access to the Navy Colt. "I expected a disgusting piece of dung like you to be leading ten other equally disgusting individuals."

"Army started askin' questions, them big talkers suddenly found other places they had t' be," Coleman said. "I spent ten years settin' things up pretty good, an' then Mr. Thomas Brash come along and nigh got me killed. Had t' high tail it out of my own country."

"You made some bad choices and you got caught," Tom said.

"You meddlin' damn fool, don't you see?" Coleman said. "You're the one made some bad choices, stickin' your nose in my business. The damn country had nothin' in it but savages an' sand. I coulda made an empire out of it, but you stopped all that. I'm gonna gut shoot you and your partner there so you can watch him squeal in pain while you're doin' the same thing. Then I'm gonna take the old man here back t' town and do the same thing t' him an' his boy. Told the boy that before we left town. Got him tied up in their shack just waitin' for me an' his paw to come back.

"Few years from now," Coleman continued, "folks will forget all about the stories you told McDougal. I'll have me a new name, and I'll be back in the States and startin' all over again. You an' your partners will be dead and long forgotten."

Sam stepped around the corner of the bunkhouse, his pistol raised. Coleman shot him. The buckboard team reared, squealed, and broke away at a run. From the way Sam flew back and hit the ground, his partners knew he was badly hit. By the time they looked back at Coleman and his hostage, the barrel was once again in Alex stomach. Under his coat, Tom had his hand on the Colt, but he couldn't draw or fire without hitting Alex.

Frank Clement stepped around the opposite corner of the bunkhouse. His hands were empty and hung at his sides, but he had his Colt belted on.

Coleman swung his hostage around so they faced the younger Clement. Despite being much taller, Coleman was crouching slightly and well hidden behind Alex. Clyde and Tom had a view of his right side and arm, while Frank saw only the left arm, shoulder, and head. Tom knew he still didn't have a big enough target.

"You let your thumb off that hammer, and you'll die," Frank said.

Coleman smiled. The kid hadn't even drawn his pistol, and all he had to do was release the hold his thumb held on the hammer. "Well, in that case," he said, then started to swing the muzzle of his Colt, "I'll have to shoot you first."

No one, including Coleman or Alex who were looking right at him, saw Frank draw. Coleman didn't see the muzzle flash.

Tom and Clyde both saw the hole appear in the bridge of Coleman's nose. The bullet pushed the cartilage down and back and its upper edge caught the lower edge of the brow ridge. This changed the spin on the ball, which resulted in a two-inch hole appearing in the back of Coleman's head. His Colt discharged into the cabin wall as he fell back, already dead.

Alex Clement dropped to his knees, hands flat on the ground. He wasn't shaking, but it didn't appear that he could get his breath. Tom and Frank reached him at the same time. Clyde went to check on Sam.

"Lay down, Mr. Clement," Tom instructed.

Frank tried to catch his head. "You gotta be all right, Paw."

"Let his head down," Tom said. "Let him lay out flat. I'll get something to lift his legs." He turned and sprinted for the cabin.

It had taken some time, but Frank had learned to trust Tom, and to rely on his knowledge. He let his father's head down on the ground. "Lay quiet, Paw. Try t' take nice long breaths. Don't rush it. Just take your time."

By the time Tom returned with a bench and some bedding, Alex was beginning to take ragged breaths. He positioned the gear and propped the older man's legs up on them.

"You'll be fine, Mr. Clement," Tom said. "You just lie quiet and do what your son says. You'll be breathing fine in no time." He clapped Frank on the shoulder, rose, and rushed over to his fallen partner.

Sam was hit hard, but he was breathing, and there was no blood on his lips or nose. The bullet hole was high on the left side of his chest. With their battlefield experience, both Tom and Clyde had seen many similar wounds, some of them fatal.

"Bad spot," Clyde said, "but it doesn't seem to have hit a lung."

Tom nodded. "I don't know how, but it looks like it missed. Did it come out?"

Clyde shook his head. "Been afraid to move him. Don't know."

"I'll lift on his shirt just enough to take some pressure of the ground," Tom suggested. "You shove your hand under and see what you can find."

Clyde nodded agreement, and they tried it. When he pulled his hand out it was only covered with dirt. "No blood and I can't feel a hole or a lump."

"He has to be filling up with blood," Tom said. "We need a doctor. Now!"

Clyde nodded. "I sure don't know enough t' do it."

"He probably has our horses in the barn and saddled," Tom said. "Take all three of them. The one you ride in will be finished when you get there, and you and the doctor can use the other two to ride back."

"You go," Clyde pleaded, "I don't want to leave him."

Tom shook his head. "I've done more of this than you. Besides, if his heartbeat starts to slow, I'll cut him open to relieve the pressure, and I don't think you could do it.

"No, I don't suppose I could," Clyde admitted, then rose and sprinted for the barn.

Holding his watch in one hand, and resting the other on Sam's chest, Tom timed the heartbeat. Just as he flipped the watch closed, Clyde let out a yell and three horses thundered out of the yard. Out toward the main trail the buckboard team trotted after them for a few yards, then stopped and returned to cropping grass.

"How is your father doing?" Tom asked.

"I'm fine," Alex Clement responded. "Just a little trouble breathin', is all."

"The first time I saw that happen it was one of my senior officers," Tom began. "He was about the same age I am now. I don't think he was forty yet. The battle had been going on for several days, but it had been two days of almost steady fighting. We had lost hundreds of men, and fallen back several times. The only way our men could fall back was for the cavalry to go in with a quick charge so the infantry could retreat. Suddenly Colonel Moreland-Reeves couldn't get his breath. He collapsed, just like you did, and we called for orderlies. They rushed him to the company surgeon where he was pronounced dead. His heart, they said."

With his father's urging, Frank righted the bench and placed it next to the bunkhouse wall. Returning to his father he helped him rise and take a seat on the bench.

Tom was timing Sam's heartbeat again. When he was finished, he rose and walked over to stand before Alex Clement. "Mr. Clement, you start to feel dizzy or light headed, I want you to get off that bench and lie down."

"You an officer?" Alex asked, not looking up at him but at the ground.

"A long time ago," Tom admitted.

"Figured as much," Alex said, nodding. "Officers al'ays givin' orders, but it was us Sergeants what run the show."

"And that's the truth," Tom said. "But they run the show by following orders. If they didn't, important parts of the campaign could be lost. Like you."

Alex nodded, and then looked at his son who stood to one side, thumbs hooked in his gun belt and a worried look on his face. "Thought I tol' yuh not t' wear that thing," he said.

Frank looked down at the Colt, looked away, then back at his father. "Not this one," he said. "The one you told me not to wear was yours. This one was left to me by a friend of mine who was murdered. Feller by the name of Jack Lawson."

"Well, I'm mighty glad yuh didn' listen t' me."

"Glad maybe, but also alive," Tom muttered as he picked up the blankets to cover Sam.

During the next few hours, Sam drifted in and out of consciousness. Whenever possible, Tom tried to make him take water, and even managed to get a few spoons of venison soup into him that Alex had insisted on making. Gradually he noticed a change in the heartbeat, and it certainly wasn't getting stronger.

"Frank, could I ask you to haul a couple of buckets of water up from the creek?" Tom asked. "I may have to cut him open, and I'd like to have some boiling water to keep things clean."

After Frank went off with the buckets, his father said, "Didn't see no sawbones doin' much washin' up in the war."

"Nor did I," Tom agreed, "and almost every man cut by the surgeon died."

"That's a fact," Alex said. "This here washin' things up, that somethin' new?"

Tom shook his head. "It's an idea that's been around for a long time. Boil the instruments, keep the bandages clean. There was a woman that looked after the wounded in the Crimean who insisted that everything be kept clean, and that was twelve, thirteen years ago. It seemed to help, although I don't think anyone has ever proved the theory."

Tom never had to cut Sam open. The doctor arrived, and though he was a man given to strong drink, the wild ride with Clyde, and several cups of strong coffee had put him in better condition for an operation than he had experienced in years. Sam was awake a few times the next day, and three days later for several hours. He missed having to answer all the questions from the Colonial Police, but a week after the shooting he was sitting up and complaining.

"Yuh ain't never had it so good," Alex said. "I do a fine job o' cookin', an' Clyde don' have t' cook so he can do your work, which yuh ain't doin' 'cause yer layin' aroun' all day."

"Well I wouldn' be layin' aroun' I didn' try t' save yer hide," Sam responded.

Tom, Frank, and Clyde looked at each other with glints in their eyes and smiles on their lips. They all knew better than to interfere. They busied themselves with the food.

"Savin' my hide," Alex said with derision. "Steps aroun' the buildin' with that big ol' cannon held out like its suppos't' mean somethin'. You get in a ruckus like that, you step in shooting'. On'y way."

"Yuh don' know what yer talkin' about' you cantankerous ol' cuss. I was tryin' not t' shoot you."

Alex turned from the stove, a wide grin on his face. "Yeah. I sure am glad the boy was doin' the shootin'."

There was silence for a moment and all five became serious as they relived the event in their minds.

"Well, this is a hell of a fix," Sam said.

"What now?" Clyde asked.

"All o' us bin loners all our lives. We have us a big t' do 'bout how t' build this here cabin so we can have an extra bunk fer the kid, should happen he takes a notion t' come aroun'. Now there's five that get along, an we gotta figure a way t' fit another bunk in. Keeps up like this, we'll have us a damn town."

They all grinned, and Clyde said, "We'll just get Frank to dust them up a bit with his Colt. That'll keep everybody in line."

The thought of the shooting made them silent again for several moments.

Tom's thoughts returned to the cemetery where he buried his family. He remembered the fever he had while alone on the plains. He saw Frank step out of the brush to defend the Indian and his wife, and the charge of Red Shirt and his warriors into the clearing in the Cypress Hills. He saw all the events of the past two years, and realized that the four men with him had become his brothers.

"There's no doubt about one thing," he said. "The time is gone for us to think of ourselves as loners."

Author's Note

Old Woman Lake

Located in what is now south-central Saskatchewan. Aboriginal legend claims that a group of Assiniboine (or Cree or Blackfoot or Crow, depending on the storyteller) were surrounded here by a group of Blackfoot (or Cree or Crow, again depending on the narrator). An old woman in the group volunteered to keep the fires burning while the rest slipped away in the night. The end of the legend, again depending on the narrator, has the old woman killed by the attackers, adopted, or the campsite vacant with no sign of the old woman.

Probably in an effort at political correctness it has been renamed and now appears on Saskatchewan maps as "Old Wives Lake."

Blackfoot

Actually a confederacy of three Algonquin nations, the Kainai, Sitsika, and Peigan, the name "Blackfoot" supposedly placed on them by the Lakota or Sioux. Outnumbered by everyone except the whites, they made up in ferocity what they lacked in population. The fear they engendered in other peoples was only equaled by the Kiowa and later the Apache far to the south.

Colonel Coleman

It is true that Colonel Coleman is a figment of my imagination. However, during the time period depicted and because there was nothing to stop them, there were several individuals who attempted to create their own kingdom in what is now Southern Alberta and Saskatchewan. According to the Hudson Bay Company's charter (and the British Crown) the entire area was part of that company's area of operation and thus under their protection until 1869. However, practically speaking, this area was buffalo country with a white population consisting of about 500 whiskey traders and few trappers. Thus the company held very little interest in the area and had no force capable of stopping or even slowing incursions.

The North West Mounted Police, formed to prevent incursions, eliminate whiskey, and protect the population, did not arrive in the area until 1874.

Captain McDougal

Like Colonel Coleman, Captain McDougal is a completely fictional character. However, the U.S. Army of the day was populated with officers (and troopers) who took demotions following the end of the Civil War in order that they might have a home. A few of these officers and their men were of less than stellar character, but many, such as the fictional Captain McDougal, completed almost impossible tasks despite being virtually ignored by Washington.

Bear Child

He was known by the white man as Jerry Potts, but his Kainai name was Bear Child. He was the son of a Scott, Andrew Potts, an American Fur Company clerk at Fort McKenzie and Namo-pisi (Crooked Back) a member of Black Elk's band.

Jerry Potts has been called the greatest scout and guide of the old west, which, considering the competition, may or may not be completely true. There is no doubt that the two people most responsible for the early survival of the North West Mounted Police, and thus the continuing longevity of the Royal Canadian Mounted Police are Colonel J.F. Macleod and Jerry Potts.

British Columbia

Actually, the "Colony of British Columbia" never existed. Instead, when it was a colony of the British Crown it was called "New Caledonia" and did not become British Columbia until it became a province of the Dominion of Canada upon joining confederation. I chose to use the British Columbia name in an attempt to avoid confusion.

Constable Jack Lawson

Constable Lawson, a rookie with the British Columbia Police force was probably the second police officer to be killed in the line of duty in what is now Western Canada. A few days before his death on July 18, 1867, Canadian Confederation had been achieved, but British Columbia had not joined at that point and was still a British colony. While investigating the theft of horses from Oregon Territory, Lawson was shot by "One Ear Charlie."

Charles H. (One Ear Charlie) Brown

One Ear Charlie was a totally despicable thug with a long criminal career that covered the Western United States and the Colony of British Columbia. During one of his many incarcerations he attempted to overpower a prison guard who shot off his ear.

Charlie's last crime was the killing of Constable Lawson who was widely liked by the miners of Wild Horse Creek. Since no other officers were immediately available, four miners trailed Brown south into Oregon where they shot him out of the saddle on July 20, 1867.

Despite diligent research, I could find no mention of the names of the four vigilantes and so I have given them names.

CPSIA information can be obtained
at www.ICGtesting.com
Printed in the USA
LVHW02s0414231018
594471LV00001B/5/P